Can I Trust Her?

Frances Lucas

About the Author

Frances Lucas discovered her passion for young adult novels through her students, establishing an after-school book club and free little library in her classroom. She taught animation, technology, and filmmaking in Anchorage Alaska for many years and cofounded the Black Bear Film Festival for middle and high school students in 2012. She now lives in Southern Colorado with her wife and dogs and spends her days writing, reading, and exploring Colorado's many small mountain towns.

Bella Books, Inc.
P.O. Box 10543
Tallahassee, FL 32302

Printed in the United States of America on acid-free paper.

First Edition - 2022

Cover Designer: Heather Honeywell

ISBN: 978-1-64247-396-4

PUBLISHER'S NOTE

Can I Trust Her?

Frances Lucas

BELLA
B O O K S
2022

CHAPTER ONE

VIRGINIA

Thursday, December 12, 11:30 a.m.

It wasn't melting snow that caused Marisol Cowsill to fall and break her neck on the film club stairs. Her shoes were dry, and she hadn't been outside all day, according to the local media. Anchorage police interviewed North High School's administrative staff, our journalism teacher, Mr. Cooper, the freshman girls who found her, and David Teal, the last person seen with Marisol Tuesday after school. An APD spokesperson has called it a tragic accident, further recommending Principal Foster install better lighting in the stairwell as soon as possible. "The poor girl was in a hurry to get to a meeting. She obviously slipped," Mrs. Foster was quoted as saying in the *Anchorage Daily News*.

All this is public information.

But did she really slip? I'm not so sure. It's true that as editor-in-chief of our school newspaper, senior class valedictorian, NHS president, and varsity volleyball co-captain, Marisol had a lot on her plate. She was always on her way somewhere, but she wasn't clumsy. Marisol Cowsill was a *force*.

"I can think of other words to describe her. Petty, vicious, spiteful. Should I keep going?" Matty mutters out of the side of his mouth at lunch a couple of days later.

"Shh." I press a finger to my lips.

"It was horrible! I still can't believe it. You should have seen her lying at the bottom of the stairs like a broken doll," says a blonde with red lowlights, one of the girls who discovered Marisol's body apparently minutes after she died. She's sitting at a nearby table.

"You mean a mannequin," says her friend.

"What? Oh, right. Right." The first girl tilts her chin as if giving that some thought. "We were discussing her latest list of story ideas for the *Gazette* so we couldn't start without her. Mr. Cooper told us to look for her. Naturally, we checked the bathroom first."

The others at the table lean in, inviting her to go on. Like me, they've heard it before, but can't get enough. No one can. Only my best friend, Matty Brown, is brave enough to say what others are undoubtedly thinking. *Good riddance, Marisol Cowsill.*

"Don't look now, isn't that Katie McRanes?" He gestures to the doorway connecting the cafeteria to the main hall as the freshman conversation lulls.

I twist around, my eyes widening and my heart beating faster, as Katie strolls in with Rocky Dare. She looks twice as stunning as she did in eighth grade. Rocky whispers something in her ear, and she laughs. I inhale a shallow breath, seeking to ignore a familiar ache in my chest.

"Hi, Katie," I call out as they walk by.

Katie glances in my general direction, looking slightly startled. "Oh. Hey. How's it going?" And then they're gone, having moved on to another table.

"Forget about her, girl. She's not good enough for you." Matty taps my hand, giving me a sympathetic look. Yoon-hi adds an encouraging nod.

But that isn't it. Everything's changed. And I've got to figure out a way to change it back.

CHAPTER TWO

KATIE

Three and a half years earlier.

Mom and Dad are fighting again.

Dad: "Fish again? Give me a break."

Mom: "You want something different, fix it yourself."

My father hates Alaska's cold weather and the winter dark. My mother loves it. Cross-country skiing, quilting, baking god-awful carob brownies with our neighbor Mrs. Taylor, all of it. When we first moved from Portland a year and a half ago, it was Dad who embraced life in the frigid north. He's a chiropractor and tends to be a bit too gleeful when a cyclist takes a spill along the Coastal Trail, or downhill skiers twist their ankles at the Alyeska Resort in nearby Girdwood. I don't think he expected Mom to like it here so much. He works all the time, and then sulks when he comes home and dinner isn't hot and ready to eat the second he walks through the door.

I'm sick of listening to them argue. I go outside and immediately wish I hadn't. Marisol is in the corner of her yard, tossing dog shit into ours.

"Hey, lesbo," she calls out. "You need to clean up your backyard."

I flinch, glancing back at the house. You'd think a ninth grader would be more mature. She's already like some big deal at her school. Virginia says she's on the JV volleyball team and freshman class president.

"Where's your dyke girlfriend?" she shouts, when I turn away. I hope Dad can't hear her. Mom has set salmon bones on the back steps to be tossed in the trashcan after dinner. I know— bad idea, right? I have half a mind to throw them at Marisol, but then what? A fish war?

"Go away," I tell her, which only makes her laugh.

"Is that the best you can do?"

"Maribel Clarabelle," Virginia sings out as she opens our back gate. "Please tell me your folks haven't stopped feeding you?"

With a last name like Cowsill, Marisol is used to being the butt of cow jokes, but she takes one look at the dog turd poised to catapult from the end of her trowel and drops it. Her face turns bright red. Still, she manages, "Oh, burn."

"Now she gets it." Virginia laughs, a sound as beautiful as the summer wind chimes on our back porch. Then she picks me up and plants a big kiss on my lips.

Marisol grumbles something under her breath that ends with, "You guys make me sick."

"Mission accomplished," Virginia can't help yelling back. Then, "Wait, don't you want this?" She reaches for a turd.

"Don't," I say. But it's too late. She wraps a leaf around it and lobs it across the chain-link fence. It doesn't come anywhere close to Marisol, but I'm appalled. Virginia is tall, strong, and stringy. The most badass girl I've ever met, but she also worries me. The girl won't back down from a challenge. Everyone should have limits, right? You dare her to pull a fire alarm at school, or skate across Westchester Lagoon near the end of May, she'll do it without any hesitation. She says her older brother Pete is the same. He dated Marisol's sister, Camila, all through high school. Last spring, when he went into the military and Camila went to college in Seattle, they broke up. Pete says Marisol was always weird, hanging around them when they wanted to be alone.

"Gross." I let out a breath when Virginia lets the leaf flutter to the ground, which is the dumbest thing I could say because she sticks her tongue out and pretends to lick her hand. "You're not kissing me after that," I tell her.

"I'm not?" She assumes a look of innocence and spins me in a circle before laying another smacker on me.

I can't help myself. I squeal with delight and drag her behind the shed, out of view from the house, and kiss her with everything I've got. My heart flutters. These are the moments I most look forward to.

"We're not lesbians because we only love each other," I say, drawing back a minute later. I have to admit Marisol's insults bother me, and if my parents knew we kissed, my father would probably kill me. Mom…I'm not so sure about. We've never been close. She'd probably say I need more vegetables. Everything is about healthy eating since she gave up red meat. Like that will solve all her problems with Dad.

A shadow crosses Virginia's face. "Being gay isn't a bad thing, you know."

"I know. I'm just trying to say I love you."

"Well, I love you. A little."

"Just a little?"

"This much." She holds her thumb and forefinger an inch apart, a wicked expression on her face. So, of course I take her by the arms and stick my tongue in her mouth. Her breath tastes like blueberries and honey. I could kiss her all day long.

She draws back breathlessly a minute later. "You're getting really good at that. Here, I brought you something." She pulls a packet of OFF mosquito wipes from the pocket of her shorts—a half-second *after* a mosquito bites my neck.

"Thanks." I slap my neck and tear the pack open, swabbing my face, neck, hands, every inch of bare skin. Nobody tells you how bad the bugs are here in summer. Mom won't let me use any repellant with DEET. "You'll thank me later when you don't have cancer," she says. Usually I'm a mass of itchy welts, but lately Virginia's been supplying me with the good stuff. Soon I'll have beautiful, clear skin like hers.

"Want to come to my house?" Virginia asks, as I stuff the rest of the packet in the back pocket of my shorts.

"Sure. Why not?" I definitely don't want to go back inside and listen to my parents snipe at one another. We set off for the mile-long walk through the park at the end of the block for her house. I can't wait to find out what Virginia's mom has fixed for dinner.

CHAPTER THREE

VIRGINIA

Thursday, December 12, 11:45 a.m.

Peanut butter with strawberry jelly, I hate it. I ball my hand into a fist and dig a thumb into my sandwich in frustration. Then wrap it back in plastic and toss it in the trash.

"Some of us might still be hungry," Matty protests mildly.

I can't even muster an apology. If I weren't so lazy, I'd fix my own lunch. Katie's mother used to do amazing things with halibut and salmon. In eighth grade, we traded lunches almost every day. I'd get her smoked salmon on saltines. She'd get my meatloaf and mayo crammed between two slices of white bread. I guess you always want what you can't have. To be fair, Mom works, Mrs. McRanes didn't. And I didn't *love* her gluten-free carob brownies. Katie despised them. I used to make her kiss me before I'd give her one of Mom's Duncan Hines Double Chocolate Delights.

"You didn't say what you thought of my new wig," Matty says in a clear attempt to distract me from staring across the cafeteria like a lost puppy.

"Diana Ross, the early years?" I ask.

"Please. My idol, Whitney Houston."

"Oh, I see," I say, even though I don't. "It really brings out the blue in your eyes." Matty is the only Black guy I know with blue eyes. He says he's a freak of nature. "A freak in many ways," he told me proudly last year.

We had some classes together freshman year, but I didn't really know him. He was quiet. Out, but not in your face about it. I mean, he carried a purse, but he didn't shout from the rooftops that he favored women's clothes. That's changed the last few months. He gave up heels after the first day (who wouldn't?), but lately he's been sporting a tight red leather jacket and rhinestone pocket jeans. "Designer," he told me, naming some fashion guy I can't remember.

He taught me how to apply lipstick, but I draw the line at eye shadow and say a firm no thanks to press-on lashes like his.

Back to his purse. One day I came barreling down the hall to sophomore English when I noticed Zach Pratt and Rocky Dare had Matty backed into a corner by his locker. Matty's a big guy, but he isn't physically aggressive, and he looked scared. Zach called him a tranny, and I lost it. I shoved Zach into Rocky, and they stumbled over each other and fell flat on their backs. It's not like I'm all that tough, but if my Dad's taught me one thing, it's to stand up for myself and those who can't. And with an older brother like Pete, I've had plenty of opportunities to wrestle. Also, I don't think Zach and Rocky saw me coming. Matty finished them both off by clobbering them with his purse, and we've been best friends ever since.

Yoon-hi's harder to explain. I think she likes us because we're different. North has its share of Asian students, but Yoon-hi seems to enjoy our company. Or maybe it's Matty's makeup tips. He writes a blog with paid sponsors.

The bell rings, and we get up. As we pass Katie's table, Matty moves protectively to my side. I notice Katie looking up, then Matty blocks my view. He knows the story. She broke my heart. She's been back in Anchorage since the start of the fall semester and at North for several weeks, but the most we do is say hi to each other. And barely that.

"Are you guys going to Marisol's service?" Yoon-hi pauses to deposit her empty lunch tray on the rack by the door.

"Do we have a choice?" Matty grumbles. Actually, we do. School is being dismissed early. The memorial service will be held in the auditorium. No one has to go, but most of us probably will.

I can picture it all in my head. Marisol's parents sobbing. Her sister, Camila, acting stoic. Principal Foster had a light mounted on the stairwell ceiling and locks installed on both the upper and lower floor doors, for all the good locks will do. Mr. Ivy, the film club sponsor, gives his students the key. With its ambient lighting, the stairwell is a perfect place to shoot horror movies, and kids still use the staircase as a shortcut to the first floor and the northeast parking lot.

Marisol falling doesn't make sense, and I know others have their doubts as well. As we start down the main hall, a freshman behind me says, "If she was pushed, it's got to be that Native David. He makes my skin crawl."

"I know. Doing his sister," says another. "How disgusting is that?"

I'd like to turn around and punch them. I don't know David Teal very well. Okay, that's not true. I don't know him at all. But just because he keeps to himself doesn't mean he had anything to do with Marisol's death. My mother was an undercover cop before she became a store detective, so she still has contacts. Last night, she said, "He told the police Marisol asked him if she could interview him for the school paper."

"About what?" North High School has an excellent journalism program, and in fact, NBC's Dan Daily is supposed to come up and do a segment before Christmas break. Part of his *Ten Noteworthy Public High Schools You May Never Have Heard Of* series.

"I don't know. Itinerant Natives?"

"Itinerant?"

Mom purses her lips. "I gather he's homeless. I'm sorry, honey. I wish I could tell you more. Do you want me to see what I can find out?"

"No, that's okay." Mom thinks I care because Marisol was my friend, which isn't true at all. She's a year ahead of me, and we had Spanish together. I didn't exactly hate her, but I couldn't stand the way she treated Katie when they were neighbors. The truth is, I'm simply curious. Okay, nosey. Not much happens in Anchorage. We have our occasional ground-shuddering earthquakes and moose walking up on downtown rooftops during snowstorms. But the juicy stuff usually happens in the bush where survivalists and fugitives from the law go to chop down trees and kill each other.

Yoon-hi veers off to her locker, and Matty and I follow. "See you guys at the service. First one there saves the others seats?" I suggest.

Yoon-hi spins the locker dial and pops it open. Her locker is as neat as Matty's is messy. His is full of drag clothes vendors send him to review. He posts photos of himself on his blog with comments like, "This one isn't right for dark skin," or, "No self-respecting queen under thirty would be caught dead in floral." That's my Matty, a budding social influencer. He says his followers are mostly high school guys trying to find the best way to come out.

Yoon-hi's locker contains a stack of textbooks with bindings all facing the same way. A pencil pocket hangs from a magnet just inside the door. Her blue wool coat looks freshly dry-cleaned, and an old camera rests inside a pair of fleece-lined rubber snow boots on the bottom shelf. "I'm not going to the service," she tells us. "I've got a meeting with my advisor about my missing math credits."

Technically, Yoon-hi should be a senior even though she's our age because she's just that smart, but the school's been having trouble getting a copy of her official transcript from her old school in Busan. I'm surprised Marisol never did an article on it for the paper. "Life in Busan, South Korea's Ghetto." Or, "Asians Who Can't Make the Cut." Definitely a stereotype, but not outside Marisol's story realm.

"I'm not going either," Matty says, sounding nonchalant.

"Why not?" I feel my eyebrows pull together.

"Don't want to."

I wait a couple of seconds, but he doesn't elaborate. Even Yoon-hi gives him a funny look. Matty loves drama, which there is sure to be. "Okay," I say at last.

He shrugs his Hermès Birkin handbag high up on his shoulder and says, "You can tell me about it later. See ya, gargoyles." He takes off down the crowded hallway. What's with him? He hasn't been himself of late, even missing film club, which meets every afternoon after school.

My thoughts are distracted by Katie and Rocky walking down the hall in front of me. He's got four fingers down the back of her pants, his thumb hooked on her belt. A flush hits my face, and I want to tear his arm right out of his socket and break his fingers. Rocky isn't the dick he was last year though. Mostly, I suppose, because he's a big-time hockey player now and has an image to maintain.

"Katie," I call out as a sudden inspiration hits me. "Wait up."

Yoon-hi excuses herself and heads off in the other direction as Katie stops. I know she recognizes my voice because her shoulders tense even before she does a slow one-eighty. My heart skips a beat every time I look at her. She has plump cheeks with dimples and soft, dark curly hair. Her body has filled out very nicely, but it's her eyes I like best. They're gray with flecks of gold that always seem to have a smile that's just for me. Or at least they used to. She gives me a look now like I'm an annoying waitress who's forgotten to bring the Sweet'N Low she's asked for umpteen times.

Rocky kisses her cheek and says, "See you, babe. Gotta go." Then he offers me a friendly wave. Like I said, I want to rip his arm off.

"Virginia," Katie says as I catch up. For a second it feels like we're the only people in the hall. This is the moment when I sweep her in my arms and we perform a classic ballroom dance à la *Beauty and the Beast*.

Cue the music.

"Can we talk?" I try to sound casual.

She glances over her shoulder like she's got someone waiting for her. "I can't be late for class. It's chemistry with Mr. Henderson."

As lies go, this one's pretty good because everyone knows Henderson is a stickler for promptness. Three tardies and you earn yourself a detention. But I can't help thinking of all the times we skipped classes in middle school. We'd slip out back by the gym and head across the street to a grassy ravine hidden from the classroom windows. We'd eat the orange sections Katie's mom would put in her lunch sack. Katie sucking one end of the slice, me the other, like *Lady and the Tramp*. Oops, my second Disney reference. I didn't get into crime shows until Katie introduced me to *The Equalizer*.

"I don't mean now," I stammer. "After school. After the service. You could..." I stop just in time from inviting her to my house. I can tell from her alarmed expression that isn't going to fly. "We could meet in the south parking lot." Full view of the front office and school security guards so I can't molest her or whatever it is she's worried about happening. "It won't take long, and it's important," I add, noting indecision warring with good manners on her face.

"Okay. But just for a minute," she says. "I need to get home and..." Her words drift off.

And what? Sex text Rocky? Acid churns in my stomach. "Great. See you then."

She heads off toward the chem lab, and I turn around to find Zach Pratt standing behind me. How long has he been there?

"Can we spell awkward?" he says in his usual snarky voice. Zach and Rocky aren't that close anymore as far as I can tell. Maybe Rocky's grown up some, but Zach is still the obnoxious guy I remember from elementary school. He's taller now. Thinner, too, with the worst breath I've ever smelled on a human being. It's like an animal must have died inside his mouth. I try not to stare at his brownish teeth.

"Haven't you got some place you need to be, maybe a morgue or a dungeon?" I push past him. He's pale, like he doesn't get enough sun. Probably spends too much time in the video room of film club. To give him his due, his last horror movie for North's fall film festival was legendary. *The Dead Can't Talk.* I don't know how he convinced the drop-dead gorgeous Lilly Kahale to wear zombie makeup, but she looked like a character straight out of *The Walking Dead.*

"Now is that any way to be?" Zach calls to my back as I walk away. "I just wanted to let you know that Rocky says your former girlfriend is an uber kisser. I'm sure you taught her everything she knows. Have a nice day," he yells when I still don't turn around.

Asshole. I resist the urge to give him the finger. Look at me, taking the high road.

The fact is, Katie taught me a thing or two.

CHAPTER FOUR

KATIE

Three and a half years earlier.

"Moose ahead," a hiker coming from the other direction notifies us. Virginia takes my hand and leads me down a side path. It's such a "gentlemanly" thing to do, I almost laugh. But I know she means well and feels protective of me.

When we moved to Anchorage from Portland, I didn't know how dangerous female moose with calves could be, or that bears could be within a hundred yards of you, watching you, and you wouldn't even know it. Another thing to be aware of is the mudflats. Every couple of years runners get stuck between Fire Island and Kincaid Beach when the tide comes in. The glacial silt can suck you down like quicksand. One of Virginia's father's friends nearly lost his life there.

We reach her house safely enough, and her mom greets us in the kitchen. "Katie, how nice to see you. Have you eaten? I just put a Texas casserole in the fridge if you're hungry. It should still be warm."

In case you're wondering, the Eatons are not from Texas. Virginia has lived here her whole life. But her mom is an excellent host and favors quick and easy dinners that usually involve some sort of packaged pasta because she works all day as a store detective at Pinella's Department Store in the Fifth Avenue Mall.

"No, ma'am, I'm fine. Thank you," I say, my mouth watering at the scent of leftover ground beef in a skillet on the stove. My mother would turn her nose up at anything made with hamburger, but I'm not telling Mrs. Eaton that. I wouldn't want to hurt her feelings.

It's like I haven't declined anyway as she folds me in an affectionate side hug and leads me to the table. A first helping for me, a second or maybe even third for Virginia. I have no idea how she stays so skinny.

"Tell Katie about your shoplifter today," Virginia says to her mom, noisily slurping a spaghetti noodle.

"Yeah, tell us all." Pete, Virginia's older brother, clomps into the kitchen in his clip-in cycling shoes. He dumps his helmet on a chair and kicks the shoes into the living room, but not before wrapping a muscled arm around Virginia's neck and giving her a noogie. She responds by punching him hard in the stomach. He doubles over with a good-natured grunt, then sits and waits for their mother to fix him a plate.

It's a typical summer evening at the Eaton house. Rowdy, and I love it. Much different from mine. Pete is handsome in a chiseled jock sort of way with an easy, self-confident manner. He and Marisol's older sister, Camila, must have made an attractive pair.

"It was two women. Early thirties, I'd say, and acting suspicious." Mrs. Eaton joins us at the table.

"How?" Pete asks.

"Twitchy. Eyes darting back and forth. Clearly avoiding other shoppers." I nod in understanding. She's taught us all about reading body language.

"Definitive," Virginia says, smacking her lips as if tasting the word.

"Close enough. So I waited as they carried way too many blouses and scarves into the fitting room. When they came out empty-handed, I confronted them."

"But first you looked inside the changing room," says Pete.

"And waited until they were outside of the store," says Virginia.

Mrs. Eaton rolls her eyes. "What am I, an amateur?"

"Did they break down and throw themselves on your mercy, or try to run?" I ask. I'm on the edge of my seat. Virginia and I are going to be detectives when we grow up. We've already solved one mystery. This girl named Lindsey is like a total attention hog at school. Mrs. Eaton says there's a name for it: Histrionic personality disorder. One day signs started showing up on Lindsey's locker. "Slut," one day. "Bitch," the next. The security camera in the hall wasn't working, and nobody could figure out who was doing it. In the meantime, everybody felt sorry for Lindsey, and she was eating up the attention.

Virginia and I talked to a couple of people, then decided to stake out her locker from the alcove across the hall and guess what we saw? Lindsey taped the signs up herself. We got pictures of it on my phone! Our first real case. Later, we also discovered who was going through people's lockers during PE. That one was easy. Just keep an eye out for the one who always goes to the bathroom in the middle of class. Boy, did that girl get in trouble.

"Neither," says Mrs. Eaton, reaching over to steal a hunk of ground beef from Virginia's plate. She pops it in her mouth. "They tried to bluster their way out of it."

"Typical," says Virginia, subtly shifting the plate out of her mother's reach.

"Right. Then they said they hadn't realized they'd put the goods in their purses. They were going to put everything back on the racks." Mrs. Eaton smirks. "I'm sure they meant to be helpful."

"Warning or the cuffs?" asks Pete. The Eatons speak in a sort of shorthand that I'm still getting used to.

"Warning," says Virginia's mother. "And they've been banned from the store."

At that moment, Virginia's little brother, Reggie, wanders in, holding an old-fashioned Game Boy held together with dirty duct tape. He looks up and sees us sitting at the table. "How come nobody told me we were having second dinner?"

Pete tips back in his chair, grabs him around the throat and gives him a noogie, too. A fuzzy warmth spreads through me as I take them all in. I feel like I'm in the middle of a 1980s sitcom. Pretty soon one of them is likely to drag out a Monopoly board.

I find Virginia's knee under the table and nudge it with my own. "We probably better get busy rehearsing."

She smiles broadly and gives me a wink. "Good idea."

CHAPTER FIVE

VIRGINIA

Thursday, December 12, 1:30 p.m.

The bell rings, dismissing us to Marisol's memorial service. Sixth hour classes and all after-school activities have been canceled, which suits me fine since I haven't finished my first draft on major causes of the Civil War for civics due tomorrow. We have three causes to choose from: slavery, economic interests, or cultural values. "Pick the second," Pete advised me. It's what Mrs. Hicks is pushing, so I'll probably go for it. Pete took her class five years ago. He says not everyone who wrote their paper on it got an A. On the other hand, no one who chose slavery or cultural values earned anything above a B, until Marisol explored all three in a kind of compare-and-contrast type thing last year. Mrs. Hicks told us all about it. I'm shocked Marisol didn't write her paper in iambic pentameter, or as a sonnet. She was such an overachiever.

The syllabus says our next big assignment will be about how Indigenous children in Alaska used to be sent to boarding schools and weren't allowed to speak their own languages. A natural progression, I suppose, from how slaves were treated in the lower forty-eight. It makes me think of David Teal and his shabby clothes that look like thrift store rejects. He's in my math class, but he hardly ever comes to class.

Homeless. I guess it shouldn't surprise me. I've often seen him walking down the hall with the Indian Ed counselor who frequently supplies Alaska Natives with free lunches. I'm pretty sure the rumor about David's relationship with his sister came about because she doesn't attend our school anymore. The police showed up one day along with an officer from Children's Services and the next day, no more Ahna. Pretty flimsy evidence that David hurt her, in my opinion. I'm beginning to wish I'd accepted my mother's offer to find out more about him. If freshmen are dissing him, upperclassmen will be worse.

My English teacher, Mrs. Pugh, remains at her desk when I pass by on my way out. She's one of the sourest-looking people I've ever met, with her bitchy resting face. I don't think that's really her because she's upbeat when she teaches. I usually try to speak to her when I leave, even if it's just something like, "Don't work too hard," or "See you tomorrow."

"Are you going to the service, Mrs. Pugh?" I ask just before I reach the door.

"I have to. I'm supposed to speak." She sighs and gazes out the window toward the sun, already beginning its descent above the line of snow-flocked spruce trees along the edge of the parking lot. Then she gives herself a shake. "I don't mean it like that. I want to. It's just, it's all so unfortunate, a girl so young and full of life."

I don't think that's what she means at all. "You didn't like Marisol?"

My interrogation skills have obviously gotten rusty since eighth grade because I can see at once it's the wrong thing to say. Too direct. She pushes back from her desk and starts toward me like she's going to grab me by the arm and march me straight to Principal Foster's office. "Of course I liked her. Please go, Virginia. I'll be along in a minute."

I scoot on out the door. *Bad play, Virginia.* I should know better after listening to Mom's old cop stories and practicing suspect/witness interview techniques with Katie. "Rehearsing," we called it, which was also our code word for kissing.

* * *

The auditorium is only about half full. Seniors are supposed to sit in front, juniors behind them, and underclassmen in the back. I head down to the junior section, leaving an aisle seat for Matty in case he changes his mind. Half a dozen members of the jazz band are on stage, playing an instrumental version of "Wind Beneath My Wings," and Mrs. Foster stands nearby with Marisol's parents. Camila is with them. I haven't seen her since she and Pete graduated. She manages to look both distraught and cool in an elegant black dress, with pearls around her neck, and tastefully matching studs at each ear. Two men in black uniforms who definitely aren't school security flank the stairs leading to the back of the stage. My antenna shoots up because I know that cops frequently attend services when circumstances surrounding a death look suspicious. I glance around and spot Katie, Rocky, and Zach a couple of rows behind me. Will Katie show up to the parking lot after school? Zach gives me a facetious little wave like we're best friends, and I'm rethinking my choice not to give him the finger earlier when a voice beside me says, "Is this seat taken?" It's Lilly Kahale. I'm a little surprised to see her. I wouldn't have thought this service would be her kind of thing.

"I guess not." I move my backpack to the floor.

"No Matty?"

"He had something else to do."

"Ah." She flops down beside me, and I don't mind at all because one, she's downright sexy with big, shiny black hair and a full figure that fills her skin like a caramel latte eggplant (yeah, I really am that shallow), and two, you can always count on Lilly to speak her mind.

That's putting it mildly. Despite a host of freshman boys constantly hanging around her locker, she's famous for her bad temper. When she first appeared on-screen in Zach's gore fest, somebody in the audience whistled. Not to be outdone, a squeaky voice called out, "I wouldn't mind a piece of that." Mrs. Foster didn't have to say a word because Lilly stood up from her front row chair, whipped around, and said, "Fat chance, losers. Grow up."

That shut them up.

Lilly glances around the auditorium, then takes out her phone and starts scrolling through Instagram photos as if she's already bored.

"Looking for old pictures of Marisol?" I venture, more subtly this time because I know Lilly isn't Marisol's biggest fan after getting kicked out of journalism class for supposedly breaking Marisol's computer.

"Right." She snorts and crosses her very shapely legs. End of discussion.

When Mrs. Foster walks out on stage, the music stops. "I want to thank you all for coming today on this very sorrowful occasion," she begins. "Marisol Cowsill was one of North's rising stars, a friend to many, her bright light dimmed all too soon." She goes on with her sun and stars metaphors, basically implying Marisol was solely responsible for creating our award-winning journalism program, and I can't help thinking Mr. Cooper and her fellow reporters might not appreciate it. I wonder if Dan Daily will still show up now that Marisol is gone. He's due the day before Christmas break.

Many in the auditorium are sniffling and sobbing, and Lilly looks up from her phone. "Hypocrites," she hisses.

A senior turns around to shush her, but she says, "*You* shut up," and he does.

"What? The girl was a complete and total bitch, and everybody here knows it," she says, lowering her voice only slightly when she notices me looking at her. I raise my eyebrows and give her my best *Go on, I'm listening* expression. "I didn't break her computer on purpose. It fell over when I stood up and my backpack accidentally hit the table. But she just had to go and tell Mr. Cooper."

The journalism room has a whole new set of 27-inch iMacs, courtesy of a grant from one of the television stations after Marisol wrote an article about the controversial Pebble Mine project, kind of a fish versus jobs and profit sort of thing. The station picked up the story and even interviewed one of Marisol's sources, Camila's environmental science professor at the University of Washington. It was after that Dan Daily proposed adding North to his top ten list of high schools. And also why Marisol could do no wrong as far as Mr. Cooper was concerned.

"Mr. Cooper kicked you out because of that?" I ask, even though I already know it.

"She told him I got mad because she had to shut down one of my article ideas. It was bullshit. I needed that position. She wasn't the only one who wanted to get out of here and go to a decent college."

"Girls, I really need you to take your discussion outside or be quiet," Mr. Ivy, the film club sponsor, whispers as he hunches over Lilly's shoulder in the aisle.

I say, "Sorry," and glance up guiltily at Mrs. Foster who thins her lips in disapproval at us from the stage. Lilly lets out a gigantic huff, then crosses her legs the other way and resumes scrolling through her phone. No one is going to take it from her because technically, school is out for the day. And who in their right mind would want to confront her?

Lilly's parents own a Polynesian restaurant in midtown, called Sefina's. They serve amazing poi and a BBQ beef bowl to die for. Lilly and her four older brothers all work there. It's so popular customers have been begging them to open new locations in Eagle River and Wasilla. It never occurred to me Lilly wouldn't want to help out in the family business after high school.

We listen to various teachers praise Marisol's work ethic, and then bow our heads for a moment of silence before the jazz band takes up, "Time to Say Goodbye." On the way out, I see my dad standing with the cross-county ski team in the back of the auditorium and experience a pang of guilt. Dad hates that I quit the team two years ago, but I'm just not into it anymore. I also see Pete in his dress uniform moving down the aisle toward Camila and her parents. So he made it. He's stationed at JBER, the Air Force side, and doesn't usually get off duty before four.

I drop a couple of books off at my locker and head out to the parking lot. I didn't state an exact location to meet, but I see Katie standing by the twenty-foot Tlingit Indian totem pole in front of the circle drive. Heat races up my spine, and I force my feet to stay steady as I join her. "Hey. Some service, huh?"

"What's this about, Virginia?" She glances at her phone, then turns sideways to survey the parking lot as if she's looking for someone, anyone, who might rescue her from me. I feel like throwing up.

"We haven't had much of a chance to talk since you got back, so first, I just wanted to say sorry about your dad."

"Thanks." Her voice is flat, and she folds her arms across her chest to let me know she's not interested in my sympathy.

When she first left Alaska for Bellingham, Washington, in the middle of our eighth-grade year, we talked on the phone every night for weeks. Then one day it stopped. She wouldn't answer my calls or texts. I was sure I'd done something wrong until Pete showed me an article about her father's trial.

"You need to give her time to heal. Imagine what that poor child has gone through. She'll come around," Mom said. But she didn't. I didn't even know she'd moved back to Alaska until I saw her at school a few weeks ago.

Katie glances at her phone again, and I steel myself, speaking in a rush. "Okay. You obviously don't have a lot of time so I'll get right to the point. I want to talk to you about David."

"Who?" Her brows knit together, and for a second the gorgeous dimples in her cheeks disappear.

"David Teal. You know, from our eighth-grade pre-algebra class?"

"I don't know who you're talking about."

"Dark hair. Always sat in the back and would never look you in the eye? He's Inuit, I think."

"Oh. Right." She shakes her head as if trying to call up memories of a guy who barely crossed our radar. "What about him?"

Deep breath, Virginia. "Well, the thing is, he was the last person to see Marisol before she died, and now people are saying that he killed her. I don't believe it, and I think you and I should get to the bottom of it. David's had it rough between being homeless and that whole awful thing with his sister. I mean, I know the police are saying Marisol's fall was an accident, but I just don't want to see him picked on. He's suffered enough."

I blather on in the same vein for a bit because, after all, Katie wanted to be a detective just like me, and I know she has a strong sense of justice. "So, if we can talk to a couple of her friends on the newspaper staff and maybe to David too, we can find out what happened."

Katie's eyes have been growing wider by the second until she finally says, "Virginia, are you serious? We're not in middle school anymore. We're not cops."

"I know, but—"

"No. Absolutely not. Marisol fell. It was an accident, and that's all there is to it."

"Don't you want to know what really happened?" I'm starting to sound desperate.

"I do know!" Katie drops her jaw. "Are you listening? Marisol fell and broke her neck on stairs that should have had better lighting. It will be a miracle if the Cowsills don't sue the district and get Mrs. Foster fired. But if you want to know what I really think, it's that this is some weird and pathetic attempt of yours to get us back together. So let me set you straight right now. It isn't going to happen. I liked you once when we were kids, but it wasn't right…or natural. Look, I don't want to hurt your feelings, but you need to move on like I have. I'm sorry."

And with that, she pushes away from the concrete base of the totem pole and heads across the parking lot to a beat-up gray Corolla. She doesn't look back, which is just as well because my eyes are stinging like crazy.

Good going, Virginia. You aren't too pitiful. Slowly, I walk to my own car. I toss my backpack into the back seat, slide behind the wheel, and start the engine and windshield defroster. I'm glad the windows are covered in snow so no one can see me when I lay my head against the steering wheel and cry.

CHAPTER SIX

KATIE

Three years earlier.

"It's a good offer, and I'm ready to start over," Dad says over the dinner table a few days before Christmas. His jaw is set in a hard line, but his eyes are pinched with hurt. No doubt something secretive and private that has to do with whatever he and Mom were talking about when I got home from school.

My mother's face is emotionless as usual, and she's hardly said a word other than to tell me to set the table and wash my hands for dinner. I wish I understood her better. Dad, I get. Prestige is his bread and butter. Whatever makes him look good. Mom's got a bit of a wild streak, but she keeps it locked up as if to let it out and express herself would do her in.

Once, we went to Wasilla to get some knives sharpened, and we stopped at a trading post where the owner had a hybrid wolf chained to a post out front. "Don't try to pet her, she'll bite your hand off. But she's a good watch dog," he told me.

I've never seen my mother so angry. "Owning hybrids is illegal." She clenched her teeth as if she wouldn't mind biting him.

"Only if you don't have a permit. I got a permit," he answered defensively.

We left without buying anything, and Mom wouldn't talk about it the entire way home. I still remember the animal pacing the length of its chain. Back and forth. Back and forth. I tried to talk to it, but it wouldn't even look at me, so desperate it was to get back to its brothers and sisters in the wild. Virginia said we should sneak back and free it. We made elaborate plans to buy bolt cutters and steal a car to drive to Wasilla, but of course it never happened. I wonder if the wolf dog is still there, or if it gave up one day and laid down in its chain and died. Is that how my mom feels? Trapped with a husband she doesn't love and a kid she never wanted?

I pass her the asparagus left over from our summer garden, and she doesn't even look at me. "When?" she says.

"Next week. Thursday. The sooner the better." Dad clenches his jaw.

I want to scream and cry and throw a tantrum. How will I ever say goodbye to Virginia? I wonder if the Eatons will let me live with them. But even if they agreed, my father wouldn't let me. He uses me to keep Mom in check, to make sure she doesn't gnaw her own leg off to free herself from her chains.

* * *

Later, after I go to bed, I feel someone shaking my shoulder. "Wake up, sleepyhead. The Northern Lights are out. Get dressed."

"Where are we going?"

"McHugh Creek. We need to get out of the city to properly see them." Mom holds my clothes out for me, and in the light from the window reflecting off the snow, she looks almost happy. Make that *frantic*.

"Can Virginia come with us?"

Mom half laughs. Slightly hysterical, I think. "I don't see why not. Just make sure it's all right with her mother. And be quiet. I don't want to wake your father."

We tiptoe past my parents' bedroom. Outside, I can just make out Mrs. Taylor sitting in the passenger seat. Her little boy, Josh, is buckled into a car seat behind her.

Virginia is ecstatic, even though this sort of late-night wilderness adventure is normal for her family.

"Thank you for inviting me," she says, sliding into the back seat beside me. "My mom sent brownies."

"How thoughtful of her," my mother replies in a tone that says she'd sooner eat dirt than partake of a store-bought brownie mix.

Mrs. Taylor says she'd like one, and after a moment Mom relents and holds it in her lap as we drive down the Seward Highway toward Girdwood. Stars sparkle in the sky and a milky green river is forming overhead. Mom and Mrs. Taylor talk about the science behind the Aurora Borealis while Josh sleeps. It strikes me as funny because Dad says Mrs. Taylor is an airhead who doesn't know her ass from a hole in the ground. It can't be totally true because Mrs. Taylor is actually Dr. Denise Taylor, a biologist with the Alaska Fish and Wildlife Center.

Virginia takes my hand and gives it a gentle squeeze. "This is magical. I can picture us doing this together when we're old."

"What are your parents doing tonight?" I ask to change the subject. I don't want to spoil the moment with my news.

"Being boring. Watching from the backyard."

I can picture them together, holding hands on the back steps. Mrs. Eaton's head on her husband's shoulder. They're romantics like Virginia.

Mom pulls into a fairly crowded parking lot and stops the car. The thing about Alaskans is they all talk as if they've seen the Northern Lights a million times, but they'll get up in the middle of the night and take a hundred pictures just like tourists. The same goes for spotting moose. Most people say they're a nuisance, but let one cross the road and all traffic stops while people get out of their cars to watch them amble by.

"Stay close," Mom warns as Virginia and I head up a trailhead away from other people.

We find a rock where we can sit together, and I lean into Virginia's arms the way I imagine her parents doing. The sky has purple streaks now, fanning like a window curtain in a breeze. If you listen, you can hear them crackle, even over the sounds of water from the Turnagain arm of Cook Inlet lapping the nearby shore.

"Magical," says Virginia, nuzzling my neck.

"Enchanting, just like you." We kiss for a while, and then I finally tell her. My heart is about to burst, and I'm crying as I force out the words. "We're moving. Dad has a new job in Bellingham. I don't want to go."

She sobs with me, and we promise to call each other every night. She'll visit me first, and then I'll stay with her family in the summer. How can my parents take me out of school in the middle of the year, she wants to know. Don't they know how hard it will be for me to start over without friends? Without her?

We hold on to each other tight. "Will you write?" she asks.

"Of course." I don't tell her that I've already written her one letter. It says how much I love her. How I think of her day and night. How when her hand finds mine or when our lips meet, it's the only time I feel whole. I'll send it to her in a week, or maybe a month, so she won't forget me. I already feel lost just thinking of being without her. We stay out there a long time, hours, until our butts are numb with cold.

"Your mom is probably worried about you. We should head back," she says in a tired voice. We're both exhausted from so much crying.

All the other cars are gone when we reach the parking lot. As I come around a boulder-size rock, I see my mother and Mrs. Taylor by the car. Their arms are wrapped around each other in a full embrace, and their faces are wet with tears.

CHAPTER SEVEN

VIRGINIA

Thursday, December 12, 7:30 p.m.

Weird and pathetic, that's me. Oh my god, how could I have been so stupid?

I'm sitting cross-legged on my bed, balancing my laptop on my knees and googling David Teal. Most people probably don't know how easy it is to get someone's criminal history. All you need is a proper name. Alaska state records provide criminal convictions, court orders, warrants, charges, even aliases. The problem is David is a minor, and it's practically impossible to find out stuff about anyone under eighteen. David's father, David Teal, Sr., however, is wanted for theft and taking indecent liberties with a minor. His last known address is Utqiagvik. Not helpful. That's so far north it's practically another country.

I shut the laptop and fall back against my pillow, replaying my conversation with Katie for the hundredth time. What was I thinking? I should have planned it better. Started it off by saying I was sorry about her mother, not her father. The online photos of Mrs. McRanes were horrible. Beaten within an inch of her life. Shot in the face. I texted Katie many times to find out how she was doing, but she must have blocked my number. "I liked you once when we were kids, but it wasn't right or natural," she told me this afternoon. How could she believe that? I thought we loved each other.

I should give up this idea of finding Marisol's killer. David doesn't need my help because the police believe Marisol's death was an accident. *Leave it alone, Virginia. You need to move on like I have.*

I get up and wander into the living room, feeling restless. Mom and Dad and Reggie are watching TV. Mom scoots out from under Dad's arm and comes over to where I linger in the doorway. "Sweetheart, what is it? Are you okay?"

I can barely stand up straight. "I talked to Katie today."

"Oh, sweetie." She takes my hand and leads me to the new, white granite island in the kitchen. "It didn't go well?"

"You could say that. She hates my guts. She told me to leave her alone."

"I'm sure she didn't say that." Mom hands me a folded tissue from the supply in her pocket, and I blow my nose. She puts a plate of chocolate chip cookies fresh from the package on the island in front of me. "Tell me what happened."

Mom believes food can cure everything. Katie and I were kissing in the garage the first time Mom saw us. She was pulling in from work. She got out of the car, her eyebrows shooting up about a mile a minute, and went inside. To think about it, I guess. Katie and I froze. We didn't know what to do. Thirty seconds later, my mother came out and invited Katie to stay for dinner. She must have told Dad because he never asked. Pete, not surprisingly, gave me a hard time at first, saying it explained the Belle Brockhoff and Anastasia Bucsis posters in my room. "They have a name for that," he said.

"Pete," Dad warned, passing by him in the hall.

"What? I was going to say kickass girl athletes." Then he threw a dirty sock at me from his laundry basket.

No one in my family cared who I wanted to kiss, but Dad was worried I might get hurt. He knew Katie's father from a fish and game board they both served on. "The man's too macho for my tastes. A trophy hunter should not be allowed to serve on a wildlife committee," I heard him tell Mom once.

I take a cookie and nibble around the edges just to make Mom happy. "I don't think Marisol's death was an accident, and some people at school are blaming David Teal."

"I see. And that concerns you and Katie exactly how?" she asks.

Well, crap. We both know it really doesn't. "I just thought we could help. You know, get other kids off his back. He's been through a lot. His dad's disappeared, and everybody still talks about what happened between him and his sister."

"Everybody?"

"Other kids at school." My eyes bore into the table, the broken cookie clutched in my fingers. I don't want to get into this because I already know what my mother thinks. The ugly truth is most Alaska Natives have trouble fitting in at North. They're usually quiet and don't mix with the rest of us. Once, when we were taking the PEAKS test, a girl asked the room monitor what a tire was. She was just down from the bush and didn't understand that cars ride on tires. She'd only seen them on the sides of docks to protect boats from breaking up against the pilings. Mom says it's our fault. Well, not ours specifically, but everyone who's come to Alaska and imposed their cultures on Natives, beginning with Russian fur traders.

"You said you could find out more about him." I drop the cookie on the plate and fold my hands in my lap.

Mom sits back in her chair. "I can and I have, it's David's father who was accused of assaulting Ahna. My understanding is that David tried to protect her and turned his father in."

"Then why did they take her out of school?"

"That I don't know. Perhaps to protect her from gossip just like this. And as you said, that poor boy has been through enough, so I hope you won't make this worse for him by calling attention to what happened in the past and fanning the flames of gossip by investigating this on your own."

She knows me far too well. But I can't just let it go. "Don't you think it's possible Marisol was pushed?"

"Yes, I do. But I don't know why anyone would suspect David. Honey, it doesn't sound to me like Katie is on board with this. And I'd hate to see you hurt again. Whatever happened to that nice girl, Tally?"

I reach for the cookie again. "We broke up." Tally and I dated on and off at the beginning of the school year. She was fun, but she wasn't Katie.

"Well, isn't there someone else you could hang out with? Yoon-hi?"

"She's straight."

"Right. How about—"

"Mom, don't."

She nods and falls silent. Picks up a cookie herself.

I know she's right. I should get on with my life. David Teal is used to notoriety. He doesn't care what any of us think. I should just let him be.

CHAPTER EIGHT

KATIE

Thursday, December 12, 8:00 p.m.

Rocky texts me after dinner. *How did it go?*

He means my meeting with Virginia. I send back a thumbs-up and stare glumly at my phone. A second later, he sends: *Want to hang out?*

Can't, I reply. *Watching Josh.* It's an excuse, and Rocky probably knows it, but he's a decent guy for the most part and usually tries to give me my space.

Ok. Wish I didn't have to go to Fairbanks this weekend. See you tomorrow.

The hockey team has a game this weekend, and girlfriends aren't allowed to go unless they drive because there's not enough room on the plane. It's not that I love hockey, because I don't, but it's a bummer because it leaves me on my own. I should be used to it. While Mom was in the hospital I stayed with our next-door neighbor who worked the night shift at a telecommunications business. She was a nice lady who always left a hot plate in the oven for me and took me several times a week to see my mother. Mom was unconscious for two full days, and when she did recover, she had to learn to speak all over again.

I wish I could have talked to Virginia back then, but my phone got broken in the scuffle. Or to put it more accurately, Dad threw it across the room. By the time the cops showed up courtesy of our neighbor's phone call when she heard the noise, I was hiding in my room, too scared to come out. It was not my proudest moment. After that, I had to see a counselor who kept telling me not to be ashamed. It wasn't my fault my father lost his temper. Most of what happened that night is a blur now, and I prefer to keep it that way.

Rocky sends another text. *Taking a shower. Wish you were here*—along with a photo of his junk. I delete it right away. Wouldn't want my mother accidentally seeing it. Why do guys think that's appealing? What does he expect? *Be right there*, and a picture of my boobs?

I consider sending *You might want to heat the water*, but decide on, *Looking good!* With a smiley face emoji. I set the phone on the stack of books that serves as my nightstand, wishing not for the first time that we had more furniture. At least it's a room to myself. When we first moved back to Alaska, I had to share a room with Josh. Mrs. Taylor had moved into a two-bedroom apartment on Muldoon, not the greatest part of town, but then she and Mom pooled their money and we got a bigger place off Dimond and I switched to North. This apartment is still a far cry from the house we lived in before, but I'm glad to be back.

The old house makes me think of Marisol, and then naturally of my meeting this afternoon with Virginia. God, that girl is beautiful. She's all angles. Lean and sinewy, though she moves about, like the proverbial bull in a china shop. Rocky gets turned-on when I tell him stories about how in eighth grade we used to kiss. He's mentioned more than once how he'd like to try a three-way. Please, is that every guy's wet dream?

"Katie, would you mind giving Josh his bath?" my mother calls from the living room. Even after nearly two years of rehab, she's still hard to understand. And her depth perception is terrible. Without her right eye, she's constantly bumping into doorframes. Mrs. Taylor says her eye patch makes her look like a pirate.

"Okay. When's dinner?"

"In a bit."

I find Josh playing on the floor of his room with his tambourine drums. They're fake animal skins stretched over bent willow wood frames. At only three, the kid already has some talent, taking after his mom more than his father—some old white guy who took off before Josh was even born.

"Kay-tee." Josh giggles, holding out his arms for me to carry him to the bathroom. It's our nightly ritual. When he was a baby in his car seat, he was always throwing up, and frankly, I thought he was kind of gross. But now I adore him. I hold him in my arms and kiss his sweet head. He smells like pumpkin and my mother's homemade green bean stew. His gold skin and thick dark hair remind me of David Teal's.

It's ridiculous that people would think David had anything to do with Marisol's death, and it makes me mad every time I hear that stupid rumor about him and his sister. David, Zach Pratt, and I were assigned to the same small group in eighth-grade pre-algebra. One day when Zach was absent, I looked over and saw David drawing a topographical map instead of working the variables and fractions problem. Honestly, after the first day, I'd stopped trying to make conversation with him because he'd never answer my questions, and Zach did enough talking for all three of us. But with Zach gone, the silence was awkward. "Is that your homeland?" I asked, probably sounding like a total noob.

"My home is wherever I lay my head at night," he answered. Well, thank you, Tonto. He sounded like a Hollywood Indian right out of an old Western.

But then we started talking in earnest. He wanted to be a land surveyor, hence the map. Ahna, who's actually his twin but a year behind in school, hoped to be a dentist. He knew all about wilderness survival, including which kind of mushrooms were safe to eat and how to get a fire going with wet wood. We talked about *Into the Wild*, the movie about a kid who came to Alaska, traveled illegally into Denali, and lived in an old bus until he died from eating the wrong kind of berries. There are always news stories about tourists getting attacked when they get too close to bears while trying to take their pictures, and hikers who get lost because they think Alaska is like the lower forty-eight with a convenience store on every corner. David hadn't seen the movie but agreed it was dumb to think you could find your way around the wilds of Denali just because you'd hiked and camped a few times on family vacations.

I thought we'd be great friends after that, but the next day Zach was back and his usual chatty self. He rudely sneezed on David when David glanced up from his map. Still, sometimes David would offer me an almost-smile when we'd pass in the hall and I was able to catch his eye.

Josh slaps the bath water, obviously thinking I'm not paying enough attention to him. "Kay-tee read?" he asks.

"After dinner." His favorite book is *Goodnight Moon*, but sometimes I'll read him my class notes if I'm getting too far behind. He doesn't care what it is as long as I hold him in my lap. In eighth grade when Virginia and I used to study together, she'd hold me and I'd pretend she was my husband.

Virginia. How can that girl still affect me after three long years? I probably sounded harsher than I meant to this afternoon. Yet, our past is our past. I will not be like my mother.

CHAPTER NINE

VIRGINIA

Friday, December 13, 7:15 a.m.

The next morning, I find Matty waiting at my locker. He looks fabulous as always, today sporting "Nearly Me" breast enhancers under a low-cut chiffon top that will surely earn him a trip to Mrs. Foster's office if any of his teachers look at him too closely. He's also wearing a midwaist denim jacket. Camouflage, I suppose, for his unusually curvy figure.

"They come with hip pad boosters, but I thought I'd try out the boob enhancers first," he says, jiggling a fake breast with his hand. "How was the service yesterday?"

"Fine." I want to be mad at him for bailing on me, but I can't stay angry for long because what would be the point? Matty is who he is, self-absorbed, but also one of the most loyal people I've ever met. "Why didn't you come?"

He shrugs. "Oh, you know. Homework, that kind of thing."

"Homework?" I tap a foot, letting him know I don't intend to stop until I find out where he was.

"Holy Christmas, Virginia. Don't you think it's hypocritical to pretend we liked Marisol? That anyone will really miss her?"

Hypocritical. It's exactly what Lilly Kahale said yesterday. It's hard to explain what it was about Marisol Cowsill that could make you so dislike her. When we were kids, the answer was obvious. She was mean-spirited, always looking for ways to make herself feel superior to everybody else. She was relentless with Katie who was often bothered by her stupid "dyke" remarks. Mom said Marisol had an inferiority complex on account of Camila being the superstar of the family. And Pete overheard their mother once ask her why she couldn't be more like Camila. Ouch. Um, because Camila's five years older? It would be like asking Reggie why he can't do an ollie as well as Pete.

Marisol got worse as she got older. Still driven, still with the superior attitude, but more subtle with her insults. She'd get you when you weren't expecting it, which would make you want to run the other way if you saw her coming toward you in the hall.

Matty takes a few selfies for his blog, and then Yoon-hi joins us just as David Teal makes his way in our direction down the hall. Two girls I don't really know spot him, and one says, "Did you see the pic? It's gotta be him. Why don't they just arrest him?"

"I know, right?" says the other. "I guess in the bush, it's either your sister or a mountain goat."

David keeps walking like he either didn't hear or can't be bothered, but Yoon-hi looks at me and says, "What?"

I shake my head. "Nothing. It's stupid." Although I don't get the pic comment at all.

"But what does it mean, a mountain goat?"

"That there aren't enough girls to go around in some of the villages," Matty mutters, then to my surprise, yells at the girl, "Why don't you shut the fuck up, you stupid whore." Which is what I wish I'd said.

She glances at her friend and finds the courage to reply, "Why don't you mind your own business, drag queen?"

"Is that supposed to hurt my feelings?" He stomps a foot in her direction, and she shrinks back. In ninth grade, Matty weighed about a hundred pounds. He's at least six feet tall and pushing 230 now. Yeah, I'd be afraid too, I think to the girl as she slams her locker door and the two hurry on up the stairs.

I put my hand on Matty's shoulder. "Easy, tiger."

He wiggles his hips and does a pirouette. "Hear me roar."

CHAPTER TEN

KATIE

Friday, December 13, 7:30 a.m.

Everybody standing by the bus is talking about some Instagram photo that was apparently posted a couple of days ago but is just now getting noticed. They say it's Marisol and David right before he pushed her. I haven't seen it. I'm scrolling through my phone to find it.

"Who posted it?" I ask a girl who's also waiting for the hockey team to board the bus. Rocky says girlfriends and fans sending the team off with cheers before away games brings them luck.

"Somebody named Anon. Here." She hands me her phone.

Anon. I chuckle to myself. No doubt short for Anonymous. The photo's cast in shadows, but it's obviously taken on the wide landing in the film club stairwell. Marisol's back is to the stairs, and a figure in a hoodie stands in front of her with arms outstretched. With a back to the camera, I can't see the other person's face, and the photo is too dark to read Marisol's expression. She looks like she's holding something in her left hand.

Just then, the hockey team emerges from the gym, and the crowd breaks into applause. "Have you seen this?" I say, holding out the phone when Rocky joins me on the sidewalk.

"Yup. David Teal." He leans in to kiss me, but I draw back, still wanting to talk about the picture.

"How do you know?"

"Everybody knows. Look, North Face logo on the shoulder. It's DT's jacket." He spreads the photo with two fingers to show me.

"So? It's one of the most common brands. It could be anybody, even you," I argue, because I don't want it to be David. I don't want to believe my eighth-grade friend-for-a-day had anything to do with Marisol's death.

Rocky frowns, unbecoming on his typically placid features. He has a square jaw, smallish eyes, and a kind of Viking-style haircut, parted in the middle and chopped off halfway down his neck. Most girls think he's handsome, and I guess he kind of is. "It isn't me. See, logo on the front." He points to his own jacket, and then back to the Insta post. "Come on, babe. You're embarrassing me."

For a second, I don't get it. Embarrassing him because I'm looking at a photograph? The caption underneath it reads, "What are you up to, Marisol?" I don't know what it means.

Rocky's voice brings me back. "For godsakes, we're supposed to be kissing. Everybody's watching!"

Not true, except for the girl who's got her hand out because she wants her phone back. I pass it over and start to peck his cheek.

He turns his face to meet mine, his lips crushing mine so hard our teeth bump. He grabs my hand and wraps my fingers around his crotch. "That's better. I'll be thinking about you every second I'm away."

Ugh. It's all I can do not to jerk my hand away. Rocky is the team's junior captain. The other players love him, and if they keep winning, he'll probably have his pick of college scholarships.

Something I could use. With my grades the way they are, I'll be lucky to get into a trade school. It was hard getting back into the school groove while Mom was in the hospital.

A player on the bus pulls down a window noisily and hoots, "Way to go, Rockman," as Rocky boards and turns back to me to wave.

"Wish me luck. Love you, babe!"

"Good luck." Why do guys get such a kick out of watching their friends get over on girls? I wait until the bus pulls away before wiping my palm across my jeans.

Poor David. I can't let this stand because he doesn't deserve it. Which means I need to find Virginia.

CHAPTER ELEVEN

VIRGINIA

Friday, December 13, 9:00 a.m.

I'm in the middle of an early final for Spanish when Mrs. Foster's secretary comes on the intercom. "Will David Teal please report to the front office?"

Lilly Kahale inhales a sharp breath beside me, and someone in the back row titters.

Our teacher looks up from her desk and frowns as if she's about to say something, then changes her mind and goes back to whatever she was doing. I know the announcement has to be about the Gram post, but I still haven't seen it because if I try to take my phone out before I turn in my test, she'll think I'm cheating.

"It's a picture of Marisol and David before he pushed her," Matty told me just before we were instructed to get out our #2 pencils. I glare at Matty's back and think: You asked me about her memorial service but fail to mention an incriminating photograph?

A couple of years ago, the district upgraded security in all the high schools by installing video cams in halls and classrooms. Not, however, in bathrooms or stairwells. I get that bathrooms should be private, but stairs? Isn't that where most in-your-face bullying occurs, out of sight of teachers? I feel sorry for David, and for a second I think again about starting my own investigation, but then I remember what Katie said. "We're not in eighth grade anymore. We're not cops."

In other words, we should let the professionals handle it.

I finish my test and wait for Matty by the door until he and Lilly are the only ones still working. I understand why Lilly's still at it, given her comment about wanting to go to college. But Matty couldn't care less about his grades. He sees no higher education in his future, not when he can make a million bucks from advertisers on his blog.

I wait until I'm afraid I'll be late for my next class and head out to the hall, nearly bumping headlong into Katie.

"Oh!" we both say at once.

"I'm sorry, I was just—"

And she interrupts with, "I've been looking for you."

"Me?" The warmth I've experienced every time I'm near her since seventh grade starts to seep through me even as I tell myself: It's not what you think, so knock it off.

She takes a step back. "Were you serious about wanting to help David, Virginia? Because if you are, I'm in. Like you said, we need to get to the bottom of this."

Just then, Matty and Lilly come out. Matty slips by, but Lilly stops and I follow her line of sight in time to see David Teal coming out of Mrs. Foster's office, flanked by the cops from Marisol's service. He's not in handcuffs, but his head is down, and he looks more dejected than I've ever seen him. This, from a guy who could play Dejected Guy #1 in a movie about teenage suicide.

"Shit," Katie growls. "I was afraid of this."

"Will you excuse me?" says Lilly, more politely than I've ever heard her.

I move aside. Katie's holding out a piece of paper when I glance back.

"Have you seen this? It's a flyer—they're posted everywhere. I just pulled one off of my locker. People say it's David, but I'm not so sure. Listen, if you meant what you said, then we need to do something about this. I mean, even if it is David, it doesn't prove he pushed her."

She goes on about some map he drew in middle school and how he can catch a snowshoe hare with his bare hands. I'm hardly listening. I can feel the color drain from my face. "Is that the infamous Gram photo?"

"It is. The original said something about Marisol being up to something. But this is so much worse."

She's right. Handwritten, in thick black ink across the bottom, it says, "You won't get away with it, DT. Rot in hell."

"DT. Rocky calls him DT," Katie mutters to herself.

I shrug because I've heard others say it, and I even manage to sound fairly lucid when I say, "This seems personal, like whoever made these really hates him. But why does everyone think it's him?" I can hear the tremor in my voice, and I stuff my hands in my pockets to hide the fact they're shaking.

"It's the jacket. The logo on the back. Did you notice he was wearing it a minute ago when the cops took him out?"

I find myself nodding absently, although my thoughts are racing a mile a minute. David probably has a single set of clothes. Unlike the dozens of pants, shirts, boots, and jackets in my closet...including a vintage black North Face hoodie. Katie keeps pointing at the one on the flyer as if inviting me to examine it up close.

The thing is, I don't need to because I already know the jacket in the photo is mine.

CHAPTER TWELVE

KATIE

Friday, December 13, 6:45 p.m.

Weekend nights you can usually find me selling tickets at the midtown Cinemark theater. I earn a little money of my own, and it gets me out of the apartment, away from Mom and Mrs. Taylor. Also, I get to see all the movies I want for free.

Virginia and I have made plans to meet at a place called Caseo's Coffeehouse after my shift, and I'm trying not to feel too excited about it as I head home to change into my cashier's uniform. I've done my best to ignore it all day, but I can't deny the familiar spark that passed between us this morning. When I first returned to Alaska, I really did want to see her. Not because I wanted to renew our romance—I'm done with that. My mother's life of secrecy? No thanks. Because if she hadn't cheated on Dad with Mrs. Taylor, none of what came afterward would have happened. But three years ago Virginia was my best friend. And maybe, just maybe, we can be friends again. I see her with Matty and Yoon-hi Park, and I envy the ease with which they talk to one another. Rocky's fine as far as guys go, but at the end of a date he doesn't want to cuddle or analyze the latest episode of *Crime Stoppers*.

Sometimes, when I'm with him, I think, let's just get this over with already. It's like a game of how much I'm willing to give and how much he wants to take.

The first time I saw Virginia when I enrolled at North, she was kissing a girl in the upstairs hall. She didn't see me, and I don't think she saw my mother and Mrs. Taylor the night we drove down the Seward Highway to view the Northern Lights. To be fair, Mom jumped away the second I came around the boulder, but for a smart girl, Virginia has a tendency to be oblivious. I mean, sure she and the girl were in an otherwise empty alcove. But come on, anyone coming up the stairs would have noticed them right away. I don't think she knows the meaning of discreet. Then again, why would she when her parents are cool about everything? I doubt her mother ever hung up a phone the second Virginia walked into a room. Or was always going over to a neighbor's house for gardening advice when the woman didn't have a garden.

The woman in question stops by my room as I tug my black Cinemark uniform shirt over my head. She opens and closes her mouth as if she's surprised to see me. "Your mom's not here."

"I know." I can hear the stiffness in my voice. I make no secret of the fact that I don't like Mrs. Taylor, even though I liked her well enough three years ago. I can't help but blame her now for everything that happened between my mother and my father. Her and Mom, both. I will say she flew to Bellingham the minute she heard about the fight, and she doesn't shirk at the sight of my mother's disfigurements the way some people do.

She stands in the doorway as if she's waiting for an invitation to enter. Not happening, lady. "Is there something else?" I say, staring her down.

"Well, actually there is. Your father called a few minutes ago. I told him you were out. I thought you were."

"He...what? Dad called?" My knees shake, and I drop heavily to the side of my single bed. "Does Mom know?"

Mrs. Taylor hesitates, and then comes in to sit beside me. "No. I'm not sure I should tell her. What do you think?"

I'm taken aback because—an adult asking my opinion? That's gotta be a first. I'm also stunned by the mention of my father who I try never to think about. "Don't tell her." I honestly don't know what my mother would do. She was nearly a year into physical therapy by the time his trial started and she had to testify against him. We both did. It was one of the worst experiences of my life.

Dad was given ten years for attempted murder. He's serving his time at Airway Heights Correction Center just outside Spokane.

My father called. I still can't get over it. "Did he say what he wanted?"

Mrs. Taylor pauses again, the outside corners of her eyes drawn downward in an expression of concern. "Just that he wanted to talk to you."

"Me? Not her?"

"And to let you know he's sorry."

With those few words, my entire world comes crashing down. Mrs. Taylor folds her arms around me as I burst into tears.

CHAPTER THIRTEEN

KATIE

Two and a half years earlier.

Mom calls Dad and me in for dinner just as I finish another letter to Virginia. I haven't sent the others because I'm planning to mail them all together. This one has news that Dad says if I behave myself and get good grades, he might let me visit her in Alaska when school is out in a couple of weeks.

I'm already thinking about the trip and fantasizing about meeting her in the airport. I can hardly wait. I picture us running in slow motion into each other's arms, like a movie. Dozens of people will probably see us, and I won't care. Not in the slightest. I'm so over caring what other people think because that's how much I love Virginia. Maybe the bystanders will even applaud the notion of lovers torn apart and reunited. Who doesn't enjoy a good old-fashioned love story? Just thinking about it makes me want to tell her right away so I text: *I have a secret. We may be seeing each other sooner than we thought.* I add a row of kissy-face emojis.

I wait for the text to go through. I've been having trouble with my phone, a hand-me-down my mother gave me yesterday that I'm afraid to put a passcode on because it doesn't always unlock right away. It's still in her old case. Not a big deal, I guess, but I want to wait for just the right moment to ask my father for a new one. It's got to be when he's in a good mood.

Lately, he seems pretty content. He likes his job, although he says his new partners are a couple of liberal whackos, smoking dope behind the clinic every morning. He's been talking about buying them out since he says he brings in most of the business anyway.

Mom calls again, and I can't wait any longer for Virginia's reply, so I head to the kitchen, remembering at the last second to set my phone on the TV stand in the living room. My father has a strict "No phones at the dinner table" policy, and if I'm ever going to get a new one, or even a better hand-me-down from Mom, that's one rule I don't want to break.

The minute I get to the table, I can tell something's wrong. When I start to sit down, my father grabs me by the wrist and pulls me into his lap. "Your mother's not happy with us, Katie Kat. I don't think she loves us. What do you think we can do to make her happy?"

What I want to say is, "Buy her a new phone." But now is not the time when he's got an empty whiskey glass in front of him, and his breath reeks of alcohol and smoke from Tapa's Tavern where he stops nearly every night on his way home from work to shoot the shit with other big game hunters. I've peeked inside enough times on my way home from school to know they've got elk and deer heads strung with year-round Christmas lights on the walls, half a dozen pool tables, and a couple of dart boards in the back. No smoking is allowed inside, but the door is almost always propped open to accommodate scruffy-chinned rednecks wearing ball caps and flannel shirts, huffing and puffing away on the sidewalk.

I'm perched awkwardly on my father's knee, and if he had an ounce of common sense, he'd see how inappropriate this is. We're not a demonstrative family, but when Dad has a couple of belts in him, suddenly I'm his "little girl," the one he uses to try to get Mom talking when she's giving him the silent treatment.

"I don't know." I squirm away. "Maybe try talking directly to her?"

Fortunately, he lets this pass, and I take my seat at the table, trying not to be too obvious when I scoot my placemat away from him. My father's not a happy drunk. Or a neat one. Last time he did this, right before we left Alaska, he puked all over my dinner. I thought I'd never eat again.

"May I be excused?" I say to Mom who still has her back to us at the stove.

"No, you may not," she says. And my next words, "I'm not feeling well," die on my lips when she adds, "We'll eat together like a proper family."

"A proper family," Dad says softly, giving his glass a shake before dumping melting ice cubes down his throat. "What does that mean? Do you love me, Janet?"

"Of course I do." She whips around and slams plates of unseasoned roasted vegetables and overcooked potatoes down in front of us.

"When was the last time we had sex?"

Oh god. Can I die now? Please? Thankfully, my mother doesn't answer, and we eat for a while in silence. Then he starts mumbling about a "slut" secretary in his office who keeps coming on to him, which turns into more mumbling about Mom's "slut friend" in Alaska. By now, I've got Mrs. Taylor figured out, and despite missing Virginia like crazy, I'm almost glad we moved, if for no other reason than to get away from the homewrecker, Denise Taylor.

"Do you ever talk to her?" Dad asks.

Mom looks up from her plate and glares. "How many times are you going to ask me that?"

"Maybe a million, or until I believe your answer." He glares back, then throws his fork down and gestures to his plate. "I'm sick of this shit, all these crappy vegetables. Why don't you ever fix the game I bring home?" Without waiting for an answer, he stomps into the living room, and I can hear the liquor cabinet door open and the TV come on.

"Go fuck yourself," Mom whispers under her breath, staring at her plate. It doesn't surprise me because she's just as tough as he is. Then we hear a bang and a scream.

Mom and I glance at each other, startled, and we both jump up and run into the living room. The TV is lying on the floor, though oddly still playing, and Dad stands, holding out a phone. His face has turned bright red, and he's practically quivering with rage.

"You bitch liar! When were you going to tell me? All this time. You don't love me, and after everything I gave you. We have a daughter. Are you going to leave her, too?"

The rest of what he says is lost to me because I keep staring at the phone, at my undelivered text to Virginia. He hurls it across the room. It catches the side of my hand and crashes into the glass door of his gun cabinet. Shards of glass fly everywhere. The impact breaks my little finger, but I don't know it until later—I'm too numb with shock.

Mom's voice turns deadly quiet. "Go to your room, Katie. Now."

I'm a coward. Shaking all over because this one's totally on me. Mom and Dad yell at each other, and she says he's not man enough to give up and accept her for who she is. He says it's all that slut whore's fault, meaning Mrs. Taylor, I'm sure. And why did they ever get married in the first place?

We all know the answer to that one. Me. I was born five and a half months after they were married. My heart pounds in my ears as I scurry like a mouse into my room and close the door, trying to tune out the yelling and breaking furniture because all I can think about is that I'm not going to make it to Alaska after all. And I have no way to tell Virginia.

When the shot comes, like a car backfiring only louder, it's almost a relief because the house is finally quiet. It's several more minutes until I hear a siren and the sound of police breaking down our front door.

CHAPTER FOURTEEN

KATIE

Friday, December 13, 7:00 p.m.

It's been ages since I cried like that. Mrs. Taylor releases me as my tears gradually subside.

"I'm sorry to bring all that up for you, Katie. I can't imagine how hard it is. He—your father, that is—he gave me his phone number. Shall I throw it away?" There's an odd hesitation in her voice. She's usually confident as if nothing ever fazes her.

I force myself to my feet, smoothing the creases in my Cinemark uniform pants, and catch a glimpse of myself in the dresser mirror. My face is blotchy and swollen, and I'm pretty sure the slimy stuff on my collar is snot. I turn back to the bed, and take a look at her, almost as if I'm seeing her for the first time. With her long, black hair and smooth, brown complexion, I have to admit she's pretty in an unassuming way. Some women actually look better without makeup. Virginia, for one. Mrs. Taylor does, too. Also, I can see why Mom's attracted to her because it's certainly clear she loves my mother. She doesn't even seem to mind Mom's remoteness.

"No, I'll take it," I say, holding out my hand for the yellow Post-it Note.

She gives me a look as if to say she thinks it's a bad idea, but hands me my father's number at the prison and the hours he's allowed to take calls. Hi, Dad, I think, sorry to miss your call. How's everything? Try to kill anybody else lately?

After a minute, Mrs. Taylor makes her way to the door. "Well," she says as if that should about cover our moments of weird intimacy. "What time is your shift over?"

"Eleven. But you guys don't need to wait up for me. I'm meeting a friend after."

"Okay." She starts to leave.

"And, Mrs. Taylor?"

"Yes, sweetheart?" She's tried forever to get me to call her by her first name, Denise, and has finally given up.

I sound it out in my head. *Denise*. Almost there, not quite. "Thanks. For everything."

"You're welcome," she says, nodding. I'm glad she doesn't ask exactly what everything is because frankly, that's a list too long to rattle off before I have to be at work in—I glance at my phone—twelve minutes.

After she leaves, and I can hear her puttering around in the kitchen, I look again at the scrap of paper. Dad, I think, so many mistakes on both sides, but yours are unforgivable.

I tear the paper into tiny pieces and watch them flutter into the trash.

CHAPTER FIFTEEN

VIRGINIA

Friday, December 13, 8:30 p.m.

Part of me wants to burn my North Face hoodie in our backyard fire pit. *It's not what you think, I swear. Marisol was alive and well when I left her*, I can hear myself trying to explain to the police. What I ought to do is march myself into the living room and confess to my parents right now. I usually tell them everything, but this is different. I need to talk to Katie, even though she'll probably hate me for letting everybody at school think the figure in the photo is David.

With a sigh, I stuff the hoodie in my backpack and head out for the coffee shop. I have one stop to make first. Matty left school early, and I promised Mrs. Hicks I'd get his notecards to him this weekend. I finished my first draft on economic interests and the Civil War on time. (Yeah, call me lazy I went with that.) The next draft is due Tuesday, on the backs of our original notecards. The paper and our five-minute presentation on Thursday will serve as our first semester final. Matty's cards are covered with red ink, even worse than mine. I doubt he'll care, but if he chooses not to work on it, it won't be because of me.

The Browns live in a tiny house on Quinhagat, just off Dowling. Matty's father is a fisherman for one of the big operations at Bristol Bay. He works road construction off-season. Mrs. Brown is an elementary school teacher. She opens the door to my knock.

"Oh, hey, Virginia. Matty's at work. You just missed him. Do you want to come inside? I have a sweet potato pie in the oven. It should be out in less than a minute." She's a big woman with broad hips and a cheerful smile she spreads over wide-spaced teeth. Matty looks just like her, other than his teeth. His small choppers he got from his dad who waves the back of his hand at me from the couch where he's watching basketball on TV.

"Hey, Gin," he calls out, without turning around.

"Hi, Mr. Brown," I yell back. He's the only one who calls me Gin, but I don't mind because one, I like him, and two, who's going to argue with a man built like a pro linebacker?

Matty came out to his parents when he was four. The way he tells it, when he said he wanted to be a girl, his mother replied, "Tell me something I don't already know." And his father said, "Damn, son. You couldn't have mentioned it sooner?" Then he pulled out Matty's birthday present, a miniature pair of bright yellow Grundéns bibs. The bibs didn't go to waste. Matty decorated them with colorful stickers from his mom's kindergarten classroom, and when he got too big to wear them, he hung them on his bedroom wall. "Deadliest Catch Art," he calls it.

I think his father is a little disappointed that Matty has no interest in fishing, but I don't know how anyone could blame Matty. It's dangerous work, and even off-season, you can smell a fisherman nearby. The stink of dead fish never wears off.

I stomp the snow off my boots, then slide them off my feet inside the door and follow Mrs. Brown into the kitchen.

"Work? Do you mean film club?" I say, inhaling a delicious, toasty scent. Matty isn't a fan of Zach's, but after the reception

The Dead Can't Talk received at North's film festival, he put his personal reservations aside and agreed to appear in the sequel.

"No, honey, I don't think so." Mrs. Brown pulls a hot pie with homemade crust from the oven and tests it with the tip of her finger. "School activities were canceled tonight so the police can take a second look at the crime scene. Pretty sure Matty's at Misconceptions. He helps out with costumes."

Two things about this make my eyes cross. The cops are calling the stairwell a crime scene now? That doesn't bode well for David, and guilt surges through me once again. Also, Matty's working at Misconceptions? Why didn't I know this? It's one of Anchorage's most popular gay bars.

I tuck into a slice of pie, but my head's not into the conversation about unruly kindergartners who hide in the coat closet during lunch. I have another stop before I meet with Katie now. I'm going to a drag show.

CHAPTER SIXTEEN

KATIE

Friday, December 13, 8:45 p.m.

The theater is packed, which didn't make my boss too pleased when I showed up five minutes late to work. She handed me the cash box and told me to get out to a ticket booth, pronto.

I settled in pretty quickly, and between ticket-selling rushes I caught my breath and sat back to enjoy people-watching on the outdoor plaza.

There's a skating rink about a hundred yards away and an ice carving show a little closer. It's supposed to start tomorrow so the sculptors are busy putting the finishing touches on their masterpieces of bears, princess castles, salmon running upstream, and male moose locking racks in battle. Some carvers use hand saws and chisels, but for broader work, most use noisy chainsaws. I'm watching a guy chip away at a castle when I notice Rocky's younger sister Sonya coming toward my booth. The instant our eyes meet, hers slide away and she starts jostling one of her friends toward another booth. The other friend gives her a *what's wrong with you* look and says, "There's no line at this one," so of course Sonya has no choice but to join the two at my window.

"Hi, Sonya," I say, when she slides her money under the plexiglass shield between us.

"Hey...Oh, it's Katie right? Rocky's friend? I almost didn't recognize you. How's it going?" Rocky's *girlfriend*, I start to correct her, and then change my mind. Sonya's never liked me. Rocky tells me not to take it personally. She hates most people, according to him.

"Fine." I fake-smile. "I'm surprised you're not in Fairbanks with your family. Are your parents letting you stay by yourself?" Rocky and Sonya are as different as siblings can be. She's got dark, needle-straight hair to his wavy blond, and her eyes and skin are brown like most Alaska Natives. Rocky's parents started fostering her when she was a baby and adopted her a few years later when it became clear her biological mother would never be able to take care of her. I haven't talked to her much, mostly because she goes to her room whenever I come over.

Her gaze slips from side to side, and she answers simply, "Yeah."

Okay. She's a sophomore, so old enough to stay alone, I guess. But would it kill her to elaborate? To say why she isn't attending the biggest game of the season? Flying to Fairbanks isn't cheap. A ticket can easily run you five hundred bucks, but I know her parents would spring for it. They never miss Rocky's games.

When she turns away to enter the theater with her friends, I notice a wad of papers poking out the back pocket of her jeans. They're upside down and folded lengthways, but I can see the writing at the bottom of the innermost sheet. *Rot in hell.*

Well, what do you know? I think I know who's putting up the Marisol and David posters.

CHAPTER SEVENTEEN

VIRGINIA

Friday, December 13, 10:15 p.m.

Misconceptions has been around in one form or another since the late 1800s. At one time, it was a prospector's bar called Gold Rush Charlie's. Later, a strip club known as Sphinx. And when it burned to the ground in the early 1990s, it was rebuilt and turned into a gay bar. The most recent owner has renamed it again, adding red velvet curtains and a tufted leather door. Tourists on Fourth Avenue probably barely notice it, except when the queens come out like everybody else to throw purple beads and tubes of ChapStick during February's Fur Rondy celebration.

I've heard night crowds in adult establishments often don't show up until after midnight, so I'm not bothered to find the parking lot nearly empty. There's a heavyset Lady Gaga at the door collecting a cover charge with bills wedged between her fingers. I'd rather not pay if I don't have to, so I head for the rear entrance through an alley on one side. On the way, I grab a couple of empty blue plastic milk crates, then wait by the back door for someone to come out.

The harbor down the hill below me is stunning in the dark. Lights from the port form a colorful glowing necklace. The strain of country music echoes from a karaoke bar around the corner. I love the smell of Cook Inlet: a mixture of fish, oil from the big cargo ships, salt water, and the clear scent of promise. I've lived in Anchorage my whole life, and it still thrills me.

Presently, a guy comes out with a cigarette in one hand, a lighter in the other, and I jiggle the crates like I'm there to pick up something and ask him to hold the door. It's a trick I've learned from watching detective shows on TV—act like you have a purpose for being where you don't belong.

The kitchen and the first two dressing rooms down a dimly lit hall are empty so I stop a Cher coming from the other direction. "Matt Brown?" More crate jiggling.

"Who?" She's got a gravelly voice and an east-coast accent.

"Tall Black guy? Heavyset?"

"Oh, you mean Whitney. Second door on the right, just before the stage."

The narrow corridor smells of cooking grease and cheap perfume that's probably disguising something else. I find the door, open it, and set my props inside. "What time's your performance?"

Matty looks up into the mirror at his dressing table and blinks, the only indication he's at all startled to see me. Then he goes back to dabbing nearly white foundation on his cheeks, probably to make them look even more imposing. It's clear he isn't just sewing costumes. "Three minutes. Do you think I should work more on my eyes?"

"They're perfect just the way they are." His whole look is over-the-top, and I absolutely love it. His natural eyebrows are concealed with foundation and redrawn much thicker half an inch higher on his forehead. Midnight blue eye shadow makes his blue eyes pop. My gaze travels down his voluptuous figure. He's wearing padding in the right places, and his baby blue sequined studded jacket is spectacular. He's even got on blue, patent leather heels—kitten heels, he told me once. Short, but flattering to his heavily muscled calves. He tugs on a Whitney Houston wig over some kind of beige-colored skull cap and dips his chin, assessing himself in the mirror, then readjusting it. He could easily fool people into thinking he's in his midtwenties. Not seventeen and too young to perform.

"So." I cross my arms, taking a seat on the upside-down crates. "How long have you been doing this? And why didn't you tell me?"

"A month." He shrugs. "Give or take. Usually just on weekends. I'm the opening act." His tone is deceptively relaxed.

"And?"

Another shrug. "You've had a lot to cope with."

"Meaning?"

Matty turns around to me and sighs. "Are you really going to make me say it? You've been anxious and depressed, Virginia, mooning after Katie."

It's an upsetting statement from a friend who's always had my back, even if it's true. I shake my head, redirecting my focus to his activities here. Evidently, this explains Matty's recent absences from film club, and probably why he missed Marisol's service yesterday. "Did Marisol know?" I spread my hands, imitating his indifference.

"What? Of course not!" He protests a little too loudly, which tells me she likely did. The thing is, Matty's a terrible liar. It doesn't come naturally to him, probably because he's basically an honest person. His eyes flutter, and he fans his chin in a tell a child could recognize.

"I have a secret, too," I say, gripping my knees with cold fingers. I take a deep breath, then spit it out. "The other person in the Insta post is me."

He lifts his brows another inch. "I'm listening."

"That's it. I took a shortcut from the second floor through the stairwell. Marisol was coming up. I didn't push her, I swear." We eye each other for a couple of seconds, and then I say, "Your turn. How did she find out you perform here?"

He hesitates. "She never said. I can only guess she got suspicious because I was missing so much time on Zach's project. I found her waiting outside the back door last Saturday. She knew I'd get fired if the owner found out that I'm only seventeen."

"And so what? She wanted to do an article about it for the *Gazette*?"

"Yeah, but she never got the chance."

Maybe because she's dead? I'm getting ready to ask for details. Cher opens the door without knocking and sticks her head inside the room that's crowded with costumes, bolts of shiny fabric, wigs on Styrofoam heads, and bunches of other stuff. "You're on in thirty seconds, Whitney."

"Be right there." Matty shoos her out, then rises, twisting this way and that to view his striking sequined gown in the mirror. "How do I look?"

"Like a star." I feel a slow grin spread across my face. "Any chance I could stay and watch?"

He winks. "I'd be hurt if you didn't. Text me later?"

"I'm meeting Katie." My smile stays in place.

"Well, good for you, girl. I'm glad to hear it." He swishes his hips in approval. "In the morning then?"

"You got it."

I follow him through the stinky hall to stand semiawkwardly on the floor below the stage as music from somewhere in back starts and swells, and he struts out. The audience consists of two old guys with beards and half a dozen preppy, twenty-something girls. One wears a sash reading: "Bride To Be." Doubtlessly, a bachelorette party.

Matty plays to all of them, spreading his arms and shaking his fake boobs with everything he's got. He dips his chin and works his bright red lips to lip-sync around the lyrics of "Queen of the Night," like he's embodying the soul of one of the greatest performers of all time.

For more than a minute, I don't see the flat, worn-out carpet, the tiny, tipsy tables, the acoustic panel ceiling, or the scuffed, black-painted drywall that I'm leaning against.

The song is one of my mother's favorites. She used to listen to it while fixing dinner, often singing and bobbing along right with it. Whitney Houston at her finest before she self-destructed.

When Matty's done, the girls rush forward, and he bends so they can stuff dollar bills into his cleavage. The guys whistle and stomp their feet, and I clap my hands until they hurt.

Yesterday, in the cafeteria, Matty said Marisol was petty and vicious.

I'd been about to ask him where he was Tuesday after school, but now I'm glad I didn't. Matty is in his element. A fierce, six foot four, 230-pound-plus performer. My friend who wouldn't hurt a fly.

CHAPTER EIGHTEEN

KATIE

Friday, December 13, 11:15 p.m.

There's no sign of Virginia when I get to Caseo's Coffeehouse and for a half-second the idea of leaving flits across my mind... because is it really smart to pick the scab off an old wound? But then I think, I've been looking forward to this all evening. There's no reason we can't be friends as long as Virginia respects my boundaries. And I really want to tell her about the posters in Sonya's pocket. To get her take on why Sonya's so intent on smearing David Teal's reputation.

I order a caramel mocha smoothie at the counter and take a seat at a table in the middle of the café. The place is mind-boggling with pinball machines along both side walls and fantastic HD videos of Denali flyovers playing directly behind them. What looks like a computer motherboard occupies the ceiling. Green, with random switches, combs, and knobs. Teenagers mingle around an open doorway to an earsplitting arcade in back, while a couple of women with short hair play chess at a nearby table. Virginia likes this place? I can feel my nose wrinkle with disapproval, but after a couple of minutes I get used to all the jangling sounds and start to enjoy the friendly vibe.

A different girl from the one at the counter brings me my drink. She sets it down and asks me if it's my first time here. Two women own it, she explains, Silicon Valley types who gave up corporate stress to enjoy the beauty and peace of the wilderness, and yes, it is supposed to resemble the inside of a video game console.

The speech sounds a little canned, especially since Anchorage is hardly wilderness and this place is anything but peaceful, but the girl is kind of cute with her nose ring and spiky purple-tipped hair. I'm just beginning to think there's something familiar about her when Virginia charges in, drops her backpack on the floor and apologizes all over herself for being late. She pauses, glancing sideways at the girl, then doing a double-take eyeing her more closely. "Tally," she says. "I didn't know you worked here."

Tally offers her an impish grin. "You never asked. I just started."

That's when it hits me. This is the girl Virginia was kissing my first day at North.

Virginia introduces us, and Tally gives me a two-finger salute. "So, this is the notorious Katie."

What am I supposed to say to that? Hello, do you enjoy swapping spit with my ex-girlfriend? "Hi," I say. "Pleased to meet you." And I hold out my hand. God, what am I? Thirty?

Tally shakes it, trying not to laugh. "Pleased to meet you, too, Katie. I'm the rebound girl. Maybe not the only one." She winks at Virginia. "But I can assure you, I'm not competition." She waits for half a second, then adds, "So, I'll leave you two alone to get reacquainted. Virginia, I'll have your drink out in"—she peeks at the large black Fitbit on her wrist—"four and a half minutes."

"I'm timing you," Virginia calls after her as she heads back to the counter. "It's café rules," she says, glancing at my face and misreading my expression. "Drinks out in five minutes or they're free. See, service in here used to be like, really slow until some of us complained. Michelle and Monica are really good about taking customer comments seriously—"

"Rebound girl? Is this a gay place?" It suddenly occurs to me that most of the customers in here are female and that the two playing chess are holding hands under the table.

Virginia gulps and wipes her palms down the front of her jeans. "Not technically. Everybody's welcome. The arcade is pretty awesome…" She pauses and gets a look I remember from eighth grade. Defiance. "So, which are you mad about, Katie? That I had a girlfriend after you, or that I invited you to meet me at a gay-friendly coffeehouse?"

How many girlfriends? I almost ask, but don't because I don't want to give her the wrong impression. "Neither. I just didn't know this place existed." And for good measure, I add, "Rocky's never brought me here." Oh god, how lame is that? I'm not thirty. I'm twelve.

Virginia takes her coat off and slings it over the back of her chair. I try not to stare at her breasts, looking small and shapely in a tight, unbuttoned Henley. "It's probably not Rocky's kind of place. And anyway, it's kind of new. They've been open about a year now. They've got great pastries and sandwiches, and Michelle and Monica are really neat."

Neat. I'm glad she said that because it takes some of the coolness away from her. Still, did I really used to kiss this girl? Her lips look soft and full, tempting, but it feels like a lifetime ago.

I take a sip of the smoothie and fold my hands together on the table as she slaps her backpack on the chair between us, saying, "Ready to get down to business?"

"In a minute. Let's wait for Tally to come back with your drink." In truth, all I really want to do is stare at her. She wears her long brown hair in a low ponytail, tied back with an elastic band. Streaks of blond, probably from last summer's sun, frame her narrow face.

"Okay," she says. "Then how was work?"

How could I forget? "I know who's putting up the DT posters," I exclaim. "Sonya Dare, Rocky's younger sister. I don't know why though." I describe the papers I spied in Sonya's pocket and the shifty way she'd looked at me. "We aren't friends, not even close, so it wasn't like I could ask her about them. And I don't get how she knows David Teal, him being a year ahead of her and all."

The girl who took my drink order brings Virginia's coffee to the table. "Thanks." Virginia nods at her distractedly. "She doesn't, as far as I know. Although I guess she probably knew him a little because she was best friends with his sister, Ahna. Last year when they were freshmen, I used to see Sonya and Ahna together in the hall. Then Ahna left. But my mother says it was Ahna's father, not David, who molested her. David reported it to the Indian Ed Counselor who told the police. The father took off, but DCS put her in foster care to protect her just in case."

Wow. My heart goes out to the girl. And here I thought I had it bad. If it weren't for our Bellingham neighbor letting me stay with her, I would have found myself in the system. "Do you think Sonya blames David for keeping Ahna from her? Do you think she took the picture?"

Virginia frowns and fingers the zipper on her backpack almost nervously. "I don't mean they were *together* together. But I guess it's possible. I wish I'd turned around."

"Huh?"

"It's a lot to think about. Will you excuse me? I need to run to the restroom."

I keep my eyes trained straight ahead as she vanishes inside the noisy arcade in back. More customers come in, all women. Some are dressed in heels and skirts as if they've just come from work. Others wear typical Alaska gear. Heavy shirts and boots. Their noses run like they've been outside, jogging or biking in the cold of night.

Sonya and Ahna, I reflect. The picture on the poster is the same as the one on Instagram. Does that mean Sonya took it *and* pushed Marisol? Was it David she meant to hurt instead?

Apparently, gossip travels fast. During my break, my Cinemark manager who I know from East said she heard the police were taking another look at the stairwell. I tap my plastic cup in thought as the couple playing chess get up to leave. The woman who's been facing me rubs the other's back. It's a small, but intimate gesture I find fascinating. My phone pings, and I glance down at a text from Rocky. *Miss me?*

Part of me wants to ask him about Sonya and her flyers. Instead, I silence my phone and turn it over in my lap.

Maybe Virginia and I can puzzle this all out together.

CHAPTER NINETEEN

VIRGINIA

Friday, December 13, 11:45 p.m.

By the time I get back from the bathroom, I know what I need to say. I've known all along I have to come clean about being in the stairwell, but doing it is harder than I expected. I spread my hands on the table, hoping Katie won't notice that I'm trembling. "There's something I need to tell you before we go any further."

Katie frowns and waits.

"The figure in the photo is me, not David Teal." It's my turn to wait as a flicker of alarm crosses her face. I can just imagine what she's thinking. Why didn't I tell her before? What else am I hiding? And the biggest question of all, can she trust me?

Katie is sure to have major trust issues after all she's been through. I read everything I could get my hands on about her father's trial. The defense asserting her mother struck him first; him claiming he didn't know the gun was loaded. The prosecutor said both mother and daughter were recovering from years of emotional abuse by what sounded like a control freak. Which shouldn't be discounted by the fact Janet McRanes was having an affair behind her husband's back with a woman, their Alaskan neighbor, Dr. Denise Taylor. I remember how Katie hated to go home at night because her parents were often fighting, but she always refused to ask her dad to let her stay at my house. "It's no use. He'll just say no," she used to tell me.

I open my backpack and drag my sweatshirt out. Lay it on the table, my palms sweating even though I just washed and dried my hands. "David has a hoodie just like mine. But I never saw him or anyone else on the stairs. It was just me and Marisol."

Katie stares at it for a long moment. I hope she's reached the same conclusion I have, that the photographer, not me, was the last person to see Marisol alive. "You, not David," she says slowly.

"Right."

"And Sonya would have known that if she was the photographer?" She traces the right shoulder logo with a finger, and before I can answer that, she murmurs, "Curious."

"What is?"

"All of it. How people can so easily ruin each other's lives." I'm not sure what she means. Is she talking about David, or Marisol? Her father, or even me? "What if…" She pauses. "What if whoever did it didn't mean to kill her?"

She shoves the jacket across the table at me and blinks like she's just woken up. I stuff it inside my backpack, not certain if I should feel relieved. "It's a possibility, I suppose. An accident." *Not like shooting your wife in the face.* "What exactly are you thinking?"

"I don't know. It's just…why would Sonya take a photo, then knock Marisol down the stairs when it's plainly David she's mad at?"

It's an excellent point. "We need a plan," I say. Which takes me back to eighth grade and how we staked out the hall and kept interviewing potential suspects who might have bullied Lindsey Cole until we finally figured out it was no one.

I can feel my heart rate slowing, and I start to realize I'm enjoying this a lot more than I should, considering Marisol is dead and I'm probably in a bit of hot water myself with the hoodie. But I like sitting here with Katie, and I'm glad she isn't looking at me like I've grown a second head. We agree to meet at school in the morning and take a second look at the stairwell. And then, before I have a chance to overthink it, I say, "We could go cross-country skiing tomorrow afternoon when we're done. The team is cooking hot dogs at Connor's Bog and the trails will be freshly groomed." I hold my breath, prepared for disappointment.

Katie smiles, dimples creasing. "I think I'd like that. I've got to find my ski pants, but why don't we plan on it. See you tomorrow morning."

My heart sings a song. "Great. I'll see you then."

CHAPTER TWENTY

KATIE

Saturday, December 14, 8:00 a.m.

The minute I wake up I realize I forgot to return Rocky's text. *Miss you too*, I type. With any luck, he'll think the exchange got lost in a frigid time warp between Anchorage and Fairbanks. My weather app says it's -48 in Fairbanks, cold enough to freeze the hair in your nostrils, a balmy 24 degrees here. Perfect weather for a quick tour of the crime scene before hot dogs and skiing. I find my old ski pants in a box in the front hall closet and am just about to jump into the shower when my phone rings. It's Rocky.

"Hey, babe. Just want to make sure you're all right. I got a little worried when I didn't hear from you last night."

"Sorry. I got hung up at work. We had a huge crowd for the last showing of the *Star Wars* retrospective. People came in costumes. You should have seen them. Twelve Darth Vaders, three Han Solos, and too many little green Yodas with wrinkles and wispy hair to count. What's the big furry guy called? Never mind, it's not important. By the time I got home I was afraid

I'd wake you. So, how are you? Are you looking forward to the game this afternoon?" Holy crap. Why am I lying and adding so much detail?

"You bet," he replies enthusiastically, not seeming to notice anything amiss. "Lathrop's got a senior goalie who could go pro next year. But if we stay focused, everything should be fine. Start strong, stay strong. Coach is thinking about putting in one of the sophomores third quarter, but only if we're far enough ahead."

He talks hockey for a while, and I say the proper "uh-huh," "really," and "wow," at what I hope are the right moments. When there's a lull in the conversation, I say casually, "Sonya came to the theater last night."

"The late show?"

"Second to the last. She had a couple of friends with her, but she didn't seem herself." Like I'd know what that looks like? "I think she's missing Ahna."

"Who?"

"David Teal's little sister. I guess they were best friends or something for a while. Does Sonya ever hear from her?" I'm pacing tight circles in my room, desperately hoping Rocky won't ask me what I'm talking about.

"Ahna Teal? Mmm, not that I know of. That girl fell off the map. Enrolled in another school, I think. Sonya wanted Mom and Dad to try to find her, but for once they put their foot down. DT wasn't any help. He told Sonya it was for the best. Guess he's got his own troubles now."

I drop to the edge of the bed because I'm so worked up I'm out of breath. "I heard it wasn't him in the stairwell. Someone else has a jacket just like his."

"No kidding." Rocky's tone says he couldn't care less. "Listen, babe, I've got to go. We're headed out to the rink for warm-ups. Maybe if we get back early enough tomorrow night, you and I can get together. Just thinking about you makes me hard."

Seriously? "What? Be right there," I yell, pretending my mother's calling me from another room. "Sorry. I need to go, too. And you know tomorrow night is out. Ten o'clock curfew on a school night." Sunday night's a school night, right?

"Oh, yeah. I forgot. Then I'll see you Monday morning. Fieldhouse early. God, I miss you. Love you."

"Me, too," I reply, mustering every ounce of eagerness I can manage. We hang up, and I'm left feeling disappointed in myself.

Is this what Mom used to do to Dad? Lie to him and make him think he mattered to her? My mother told me she loved me exactly once, the time I fell out of a tree and got knocked unconscious. She must have thought I'd die. I don't think she ever told my father that she loved him. I never understood why he stayed with her, knowing how she felt.

Rocky deserves better because he's a good guy. Not like my father. And I don't mind kissing him, but how can I keep telling him I love him when I'm still attracted to Virginia? The realization hits me like I've sloughed off a down-filled coat in a hot steam room. But it's not the huge revelation one might expect, especially when I force myself to face the fact that I've never stopped thinking about her. And last night when I met Tally, I was jealous. Just like when I saw them kissing in the hall.

Self-awareness, however, isn't everything it's cracked up to be. "You're old enough to make your own choices," my therapist told me. So, I choose this: No matter what my heart tries to tell me, the one thing I know is I never want Mom's life of secrecy and being disconnected from the people who care about her. So I guess it is time to figure out what I'm going to do, and then stand up for what I want.

* * *

Virginia is sitting on the raised foundation of the totem pole, swinging her legs and hitting the heels of her hiking boots against the concrete when I get to school. "Is the building locked?" I ask, dropping my backpack several feet away. She's wearing a different North Face jacket today with a matching navy beanie pushed back on her head. Her brown eyes sparkle in the cold.

"I haven't checked. Although I did talk to Eddie, the weekend building manager. Do you know him? He says the cops no longer think Marisol's death was an accident. He overheard them talking about her body's trajectory." Virginia's got a cruller in one hand, a steaming Styrofoam cup in the other. She extends a white paper bag. "Want one? They're really good."

"What does that mean? Her body's trajectory?" No, I don't know Eddie, the weekend building manager, and her casual attitude makes me cross. Doesn't she feel like I do? My emotions are all over the place.

Virginia takes a slow sip from the cup. "That she fell much harder and faster than she would have if she'd simply missed a step. Also, she landed on her back. Common sense should tell us that if she'd stumbled, even backward, she should have ended up on her face or side as she tried to catch herself on the railing. I don't know how Officers Dietrich and Hess missed it."

Dietrich and Hess, two other names I don't recognize. Does Virginia know everybody in town? No, my head answers. But her mother knows a lot of cops. I take a seat on the short concrete wall across from her.

"Have a cruller," she says again, her warm breath blowing a cloud of condensation like smoke in the morning darkness. "They're really good. Caseo's makes them fresh every morning."

"Are they neat?"

"What?"

"Never mind." I sulk. "I'm not hungry."

"No, you're in a bad mood." She narrows her eyes at me assessingly, then picks up her stuff and joins me, setting a second cup of coffee between us for me. "What's wrong? Did you get up on the wrong side of the bed?"

What an odd expression. It sounds like something one of her parents would say. Is there a right side? After a second, I pry off the lid and take a sip. It's nice and hot. Then I help myself to a pastry. She's right. It's delicious, puffy and crisp with just the right amount of sweetness. "Did you go back to Caseo's this morning?" I say, aiming for a lighter tone.

"I did. Did you find your ski pants?"

"I did." We stare at each other for a long moment. I really want her to kiss me, but also I don't. Not yet, because I have to figure out what to do about Rocky. I wish I could be more like her, a person who has always been comfortable in her own skin. Virginia knows exactly what she wants. How nice it must be to never have doubts.

"I would like you to go to Caseo's again sometime with me and perhaps have a sandwich," she says carefully. "Would you be interested in that sometime?"

I hide a smile. "I might. I hear they're neat."

"Why do you keep saying that?" Her eyebrows wrinkle together, and suddenly I burst out laughing, my bad mood completely broken.

"Because it's what you said about Michelle and Monica last night. The owners? You said they were neat."

"Oh god, did I? I'm such a dork." She slaps her forehead and knocks her cap off, which makes me laugh even harder. She chuckles for a second with me before her face turns serious. "Katie, I missed you. And I'm sorry about what happened to you in Bellingham. I wish I could have been there for you. I know we'll never go back to the way we were in middle school, but do you think we can be friends again?"

It's a start. I put a hand on her arm, which feels warm through her jacket. "I'd like that. Let's be friends." I could use a friend. I haven't had one in a long time, unless you count the hockey players and their girlfriends whom I sit with at lunch. Can girls and guys be friends? I guess they can. Virginia seems close to Matty.

"Do you ever talk to your father?" she asks, holding half a flaky cruller in a napkin between her thumb and forefinger.

I stiffen, pull my hand away, and then force myself to relax. "It's funny you should ask. He called yesterday and wants me to call him back."

"And?"

"I threw away his number."

She nods as if I've given the right answer. Or maybe it's just a gesture of encouragement. Sometimes I'm too suspicious.

"That's what I'd do," she goes on. "Look, I don't want to pry, but I'm here if you ever want to talk."

"Thanks. By the way, I stopped by the Dares' house this morning."

"Really? Why?"

"I figured I'd ask Sonya about the posters. You know, confront her head-on."

"Oh, good idea. What did she say?"

"She wouldn't come to the door. I may try again later." I'm pretty sure I heard muffled noises in the house, but the curtains were drawn so there was no way to know for sure.

Virginia says she'll go with me if I'd like. We finish our breakfast and head inside. School buildings look different on weekends. The overhead hall lights are off, and the atmosphere is more relaxed with the front office empty and dark. Sounds ring out from the gym as we get closer. Girls yelling, balls bouncing, sneakers squeaking across the polished wood floor. An occasional whistle suggests an energetic volleyball practice.

"Marisol was on the volleyball team," Virginia says, as we pass an open double door with metal bleachers just inside.

"Journalism, NHS, and volleyball. Not to mention valedictorian." I tick off Marisol's achievements on my fingers. "How did she have time for everything?"

Virginia shrugs. "No personal life?"

When we reach the film club stairwell, the door is propped open with a muddy brick. I'm half expecting crime scene tape to indicate the police were here last night, but it looks like it always does, except for two gigantic tubes of white florescent lights caged off high on the ceiling.

"Sucks," says a voice at the top of the stairs.

"I know. Should we go somewhere else?"

"Suggestions?"

"The little auditorium? The choir usually practices on Saturdays, but they should be done by now."

Zach Pratt and Lilly Kahale come clattering down the stairs with Matty Brown jogging along a couple of steps after them. Zach's got a fancy camera with a Slurpee-size lens slung around his neck. Lilly and Matty are in full zombie makeup. Matty's wearing a bloody business suit, white shirt, and an ugly brown tie. A zombie businessman, I guess. Lilly's got on black yoga pants and a tight, yellow T-shirt that reads: "Ding dong, the witch is dead," with Dorothy pointing at a broomstick lying in a puddle.

"Hello, girls," says Zach. "Come to be in my movie? Head on up to the video lab. I've got a professional makeup artist in today. She'll get you all set up."

I find myself cringing, despite his friendly tone. There's something about the guy that isn't right. Every now and then he sits with us at lunch. Rocky hardly ever talks to him. He says they used to be kind of friendly, although he's never been to his house. A couple of weeks ago, Zach nearly fell off his stool laughing when a freshman tripped and dropped her lunch tray, falling headfirst into a bowl of mashed potatoes. "Bad influence," was all Rocky would say when I asked him what the hell was wrong with Zach.

Virginia curls her upper lip in what barely passes for a smile and says, "No thanks. We're not here for your movie, Zach. We're investigating Marisol Cowsill's death."

"Girl detectives." Zach smirks, wrinkling his nose and flashing brownish teeth. "Don't you have to have a license for that?"

"Not to look around," she replies, tossing her head and mimicking his disdainful expression.

Lilly releases one of her typical dramatic huffs, and Matty says, "Give it a rest, Zach."

"Whatever." Zach rolls his eyes and gives us a dismissive wave.

As they pass us, Matty brushes Virginia's sleeve and says, "She knows?"

"Not everything," Virginia whispers back.

When we reach the landing on the second floor, Virginia swivels back to study the scene. "I was standing here, and Marisol was right about where you are at the edge of the staircase. The door behind me was ajar, which means whoever took the picture was standing there." She indicates a corner partly hidden by the open door. There's still no surveillance camera, and even with the new ceiling lights, the area is in shadows.

I unfold a flyer I've pulled off David's locker to compare. Teachers toss them in the trash, but new ones keep appearing. "So, Marisol had to have seen the photographer, which means she must have known her...or him...since she didn't indicate surprise when she spoke to you."

"Right."

"But if it was Sonya," I go on, "why would she basically challenge Marisol in the Insta post, then tell David to rot in hell on the flyer?" I've thought about it since last night, and it still bothers me. We're both silent for a second, and then I can't help myself. "What did you and Matty mean when he said, 'She knows?' And you said, 'Not everything.' Were you talking about me?"

Virginia licks her lips and eyes the floor. "It's not what you think. He was asking if I'd told you about my hoodie and I said yes..." She shifts her weight from one foot to the other and can't quite seem to meet my eye.

"There's more?" I feel sick to my stomach, like the night on the Seward Highway when I saw my mother and Mrs. Taylor wrapped in each other's arms. I fucking hate secrets.

"Not about you and me. It's Matty's story, which I have no right to tell."

Hmm. "Okay. Let me get this straight. Matty knows you're the mysterious figure in the photograph. Are you saying he took the picture?" It doesn't make a lot of sense, but right now my brain is kind of scrambled.

"No," she starts. "I'm not saying that at all. Look, how about this. I'll ask Matty if it's okay to tell you, and then, if he says yes, well, then I'll explain."

"You mean I'll know what you know."

"Yes. Can you trust me until then? If I promise to ask him tonight?" Her beautiful brown eyes plead with me.

"I guess." I don't like it, but what else can I say? I don't want to go home, but all at once this investigation is a lot less fun. We stay a couple of minutes, then head for the video lab around the corner.

It's dark too, an interior space with windows facing out into the hall. A couple of dozen iMacs rest haphazardly on scattered tables, and two students hunch behind one with their backs to us. Two more kids move around a room in back, a boy swaying in a stationary makeshift boat on a slab of green carpet, and another squinting through a camera on a tripod and waving his arms.

Zach's makeup artist turns out to be a UAA college student studying cinema art. She seems to know him well. She sits just outside the door at a small table littered with lipstick tubes, powders, brushes, dirty tissues, and cosmetic dust. "I do Zach's makeup at no charge because it counts for homework." She knits too-black, heavy eyebrows at Virginia. "Would you like a free makeover? No zombie makeup. Maybe something a little more glamorous than whatever you're wearing now?"

She probably means well. I try hard not to giggle as Virginia gulps a quick, "No thanks." She's obviously embarrassed, but shouldn't be. She's pretty just the way she is. "We're trying to figure out what happened to the student who fell over there in the stairwell Tuesday afternoon," she mutters, stepping awkwardly around the table to peer inside the room.

"You mean the one they say was pushed? My gosh, how ghastly was that? Those savages have no sense of right or wrong. You wanna know what I think, they should stay in the bush where they belong."

Oh, no. She didn't seriously just say that. In less than a second my opinion has changed from thinking how nice it is of her to donate her time and skills to a bunch of high school kids making a movie to wondering how she ever made it into college. Virginia's eyes round in disbelief, but she manages to ask her if she was here Tuesday.

"Nope. Just Saturday mornings. Good luck."

"Good god, what an idiot," Virginia whispers as we head back through the scattered rows of computers toward the green room in the back.

I shake my head with disgust. No wonder this so-called artist and Zach Pratt are friends.

We find Mr. Ivy, the film club sponsor, inspecting fancy cameras on a plastic cart and making notes on a clipboard. His desk is on one side of the door, a bunch of four-drawer black filing cabinets on the other. Virginia and I have agreed we'll take turns asking questions, so I introduce myself and ask if he saw Marisol Tuesday afternoon.

His eyes stay focused on his clipboard. He doesn't look up. "I didn't, and you're not in film club so you shouldn't be here." It seems I lack Virginia's finesse. Crushed, I start to turn away, then he adds, "As long as you're here, make yourself useful and grab a couple of batteries for me from the fridge."

I glance around. "What fridge?" Virginia sticks her tongue out and makes a face at me behind his back.

"Behind the green room, girl. Get going. Rechargeable, double-A."

Virginia follows me halfway back, then stops to listen to the boy in the boat tell the one with the camera about why it's important to always wear a life jacket when you're on the water. Some kind of public safety announcement, I guess.

There's all kinds of stuff in the rear of the room. Costumes. Fishing rods. Tennis rackets. Three large trunks and massive lights in big umbrellas. Along the way, I have to step over cables, recorders, old flip cameras, and all kinds of other equipment I don't recognize. The cluttered metal shelves on either side of the refrigerator look ready to tip over. I find the batteries. Six boxes, twelve in each, beside a half-eaten sandwich and an open bottle of Mr. Pibb that's run down the side and congealed on the glass refrigerator shelf below it. I grab a box and take them back to Mr. Ivy, who's still standing by the cart, but has turned his attention to combing his moustache with what looks like an eyelash brush.

"No shave November," he says as if that explains it.

Two things wrong with that. He has no beard, and it's December. A lot of Alaskan men grow out their facial hair in winter, especially during the Iditarod and Fur Rondy. It's kind of a thing, but still. I hand him the batteries. "So, about Marisol—"

"Can't help you. Barely knew her. Never saw her. Now run along."

I try one more time, holding up an online yearbook photo of David Teal on my phone. "Any chance you saw this guy Tuesday after school?" He scarcely looks at it. "Or her?" I quickly locate another of Sonya.

He sighs. "Are you still here?"

"Waste of time," Virginia complains when we get back out to the hall.

"Totally. How weird was that?"

She flaps a hand in agreement. "Movie people are weird."

Our next stop is the journalism room on the first floor. It's empty and locked. We cup our fingers to the glass, staring into another room of computers and a photocopier the size of an air conditioner compressor. The *North High School Gazette* is published online and sent out in weekly emails to students and their parents, but the staff prints ads and game scores, posting them on colored paper on lockers and in the bathroom stalls. There's an easel pad with a list on the far wall, but it's too dark inside the room to read it.

"I don't suppose Sonya is in film club," I wonder out loud because it's the first time I've thought of it.

"I don't see how. Wouldn't Mr. Ivy have said so?" Virginia frets.

"Yeah. I guess you're right." I'm beginning to think detective work is a lot harder than it looks. Mrs. Eaton used to make sniffing out shoplifters at Pinella's sound so easy. Then again, she's trained and knows what to look for.

"Where to next?" Virginia glances up and down the empty halls.

"We could talk to the volleyball players or see if Mrs. Hicks is here." Mrs. Hicks is the NHS sponsor who knows everything and practically lives at school. She also teaches civics.

"Oh god. I haven't even started my second draft on causes of the Civil War," Virginia groans, throwing a hand up to her forehead.

"Do you need to get home and work on it?" I ask, hoping she'll say no.

She gazes at me with an expression that nearly stops my heart. "I'd rather go skiing with you."

Before I can answer that, her phone rings and she grabs it from her pocket, mouthing "Mom," at me, then putting it to her ear. "What's up?" A minute later her face grays and her bright brown eyes go dull. "Give me ten minutes. Yeah, I'll hurry." She hangs up. "I'm sorry. I can't go skiing after all. Pete's had an accident. I've got to get home right now."

CHAPTER TWENTY-ONE

VIRGINIA

Saturday, December 14, 12:00 p.m.

"An active shooter drill," Mom says, quickly adding, "Don't worry, sweetheart. Pete wasn't shot. It was just a drill, but you know how quickly things can go wrong if someone panics. His vehicle hit another and rolled. Not Pete's fault; he wasn't driving. In any event, I need you to stay with Reggie. I'm going to meet his ambulance at the base hospital."

I can think of several things to say to that. Like, Reggie's twelve. Can't he stay by himself? Or, Why can't we both go with you? But there's no use arguing with her when she gets like this. It will just delay the inevitable, meaning me getting cut out of her plans.

"Go skiing without me," I tell Katie, shoving my phone back in my pocket. "And please don't say anything to my dad until we know more about Pete's injuries."

Katie's eyes fill with worry, but she manages to nod calmly. "Will you text me later and let me know how he's doing?"

"Of course." We exchange phone numbers, which seems odd that we haven't before, and I take off.

Mom's standing next to the car with the motor running in the driveway when I get home. "Your brother's got some lacerations on his face and torso and possible swelling in his spine," she says, her cool tone not betraying the anxiety I know she must be feeling. "When your father gets back, tell him to bring you and Reggie to the hospital. I'll call the minute I know more."

"Was anybody else hurt?" Pete can be a pain in the ass. He still calls me names and likes to grab me around the neck and rub his knuckles across my scalp, but he genuinely cares about the well-being of others.

Mom fishes a small water bottle from her purse. "Not that I know of. I'll call later. I promise."

I go inside, fix sandwiches, and Reggie and I eat lunch on the couch. We play a couple of his video games. My head's not in it, and he kills off a couple hundred of my droids before I've finally had enough. I should work on my civics or calc AB assignment, but I can't concentrate. Was this how the Cowsills felt when they got word of Marisol's fall? How awful it must feel when you realize your daughter isn't coming home. That you'll never see your child again.

Mom calls just as Dad pulls into the garage. "How's Pete?" I ask, waving at Dad to stay in the car.

My mother is not one to beat around the bush. "Awake and alert. But the doctor's concerned because he can't move his legs."

Oh, shit. The ride to the base takes forever, even longer as the gate guard checks our IDs. When we get to my brother's room, I nearly freak at the sight of all the machines feeding his arms like he's some machine himself. He lifts his head off the pillow and tries to smile. "About time you all got here."

Reggie moves in as if to hug him, but Dad holds him back. "You've given us all quite a scare, son. Do you feel like talking about what happened?"

Mom and Dad did their best to hide their disappointment when Pete chose a military career over college even though he takes classes part-time with the Air Force picking up the tab. They're proud of everything he's accomplished now, and we're all glad we get to see him most holidays and weekends.

"Can you still snowboard?" Reggie asks in a small voice when Pete finishes his tale about how the lockdown got chaotic and one of his buddies panicked and ran the vehicle into someone else's at an intersection. He doesn't say it, but I've got to think his friend's military career is probably over. Losing your nerve isn't allowed in the Air Force. What if it hadn't been a drill?

"I hope so," Pete replies. "I think I can move my toes now."

Our eyes instantly swivel to the bottom of the bed. A sheet covers his feet. I don't see any movement, but Mom says, "That's great!" And Dad nods happily like Pete's already out doing a wildcat at Alyeska.

Camila Cowsill comes in a few minutes later, and Pete has to tell the story all over again. She takes his hand, and for a second it feels as if the rest of us don't exist. "Jesus, Pete. Don't ever scare me like that again."

I'm fully expecting him to say something stupid like, You're scared? How do you think I felt? But instead he rubs a thumb along her wrist and says in a low voice, "No, I won't. I'm sorry."

Evidently, they've rekindled their high school romance, which makes me happy for them. Camila's got her parents' elegance and even temperament. Her father is a pediatrician, her mom an obstetrician, with old-school Puerto Rican values. In a few years, Camila will probably join the family practice. And if she and Pete marry...

A doctor in a lab coat enters and cuts short my thoughts. "Just want to check a couple things before my shift ends." He fiddles with one of the machines, makes a couple of notes, and gazes at an iPad in the crook of his arm.

Dad says, "Virginia, why don't you and Reggie go on down to the mess hall. You can bring your mom and me back something to eat."

Reggie affects a stubborn pout. "I want to stay here."

"I'll go with Virginia," Camila volunteers.

We take their dinner orders and head for the cafeteria. It feels strange being alone with Marisol's sister. I'm pretty sure it's the first time. "So," I say. "You and Pete."

She offers me a tentative smile. "I know, right? We've kept in touch since high school. Texts, emails, even old-fashioned phone calls. I always liked him. I just didn't see how it could go anywhere with us living so far apart. But the other day when he showed up at Marisol's service at North, it was like all that time apart never happened. We went out afterward and talked for hours. He's just so sweet. Sounds frivolous, I guess, with everything else going on."

"No, it doesn't. He's always cared about you."

"He has?"

I think about my brother in high school, how he used to spend hours getting ready for their dates. He hasn't seen anyone seriously since. "Definitely. Listen, I'm really sorry about Marisol. She was…" I don't know how to finish the sentence. *A good student?*

"Difficult?" Camila supplies for me, her gaze darting over to meet mine.

"Well." I wiggle my shoulders self-consciously. Luckily, we enter the mess hall at that moment. When we reach the cashier's station, Camila insists on paying for all our meals, even Reggie's and my parents. We take seats at a picnic-style table to wait for our food to be packaged in to-go containers, and Camila stares silently at the table. I've lost my appetite. Then, because I can't think of anything else to say and Camila isn't talking, I say, "Marisol adored you."

"I know," she murmurs. "Worshipped the ground I walked on." My brows shoot up. "That's what Dad used to say. My parents were always telling me to be nicer to her."

"I get that."

"Do you?" She frowns in thought. "Virginia, you and your family…I don't know if you all really understand how special you are. You actually like each other. Marisol—" Camila shakes her head as if calling up a painful memory. "It sounds terrible to say, but I rarely thought of her as anything other than a pest. She was always spying on me. Dad said it was because she wanted to be like me, but it felt more like she wanted to get something on me. If I came in late from a date, she could hardly wait to tell our parents how I'd broken curfew."

One of the dining hall staff sets a couple of white paper bags on the table. Thinking Camila's done, I pick up the closest one and start to rise, but after a second, she says, "I hope, with time, I'll come to regard my sister more fondly. When I try to analyze our relationship, all I can come up with is how insecure and cruel she was. The only time she was embarrassed or sorry about anything…" I wait, expecting her to go on. "Never mind." She attempts a smile. "Listen to me. My parents would hate this. I shouldn't have said anything at all."

I can hardly keep from squirming, not that my opinion's any different. "I'm sorry. Your family service is tomorrow?"

"Angelus at two. It's private, but I know my parents would love it if you came since you were friends."

God, if Camila thinks that, she truly didn't know her sister at all. "Oh, well." I squirm some more. "You know maybe. If Pete is feeling better."

Camila's cheeks turn pink. "Oh gosh. Pete. I didn't think of that. Of course you can't come. I shouldn't have asked."

Now, I feel even worse. We head back to Pete's hospital room in silence. His face lights up at the sight of Camila, but he says to me, "Yo, little brother, folks are hungry. It took you long enough." So not funny.

"Hey, jackass," I reply. "I was just talking to Camila here about going all *Misery* on your legs since you probably won't feel it." Camila blinks, clearly startled. But Mom and Dad sigh and shake their heads. They've given up telling us to stop talking smack. Being close doesn't mean we're always nice to one another.

Reggie practically jumps up and down. "Show them, Pete! Show them how you can move your toes now."

Pete grins. "Not sure I should with Kathy Bates in the room."

"Oh, come on!"

"Fine." He pushes himself upright, strains until his face reddens, and wiggles his toes.

CHAPTER TWENTY-TWO

KATIE

Saturday, December 14, 10:30 p.m.

Camila actually said that? Where was she Tuesday afternoon? As soon as I hit send, I realize how absurd it sounds. Marisol and Camila may not have gotten along, but it's ridiculous to think Camila would show up at North just to shove her younger sister down the stairs.

Three little gray dots appear. *Do you want to talk instead of text? It might be easier.*

Sure. I'll call you.

Virginia's text updating me about Pete's health was waiting for me when I clocked out from work. Now that the *Star Wars* retrospective is over, the theater isn't as busy, and I got to go home early. "Be prepared to work Christmas Day though. It's the busiest day of the year," my manager warned me.

I don't mind. I'm not looking forward to a family holiday with Mom and Mrs. Taylor—Denise—I've been trying out her first name in my head. I did buy Josh a set of plastic dinosaurs and a toy lawn mower that shoots marbles into a bubble at the top for Christmas. Mom will complain about the noise, but he's going to love it.

"So Pete's really okay?" I ask when Virginia picks up. I'm on my bed with my pillow in my lap, and I've already changed into my nightgown. I've got my usual pad of colorful folding paper beside me. Pinks and purples, some with adorable tiny paisleys. It's an exciting life I lead when Rocky's out of town.

"The doctor says with luck he should make a full recovery. He's already his old obnoxious self. How was skiing?"

I think of all the words I could use to describe the afternoon and settle on "Incredible," because no words can come close to the feeling of traversing the quiet, snowy trails through the woods. At first, I was apprehensive about going. Connor's Bog is a multi-acre park off Jewel Road. In the summer, people bring their dogs to fetch balls and swim in the lake. In late September, it freezes and you can walk or ski across it. Visitors to the park light fires in metal barrels around the shore, and the trails are often groomed. North's cross-country ski team was already there when I arrived, lined up on the logs that serve as benches and eating hot dogs and chips on paper plates in their laps, their ski equipment propped against their cars. A girl I didn't know moved over to make room for me and offered to fix me a plate. Coach Eaton had brought some extra skis and boots and went with me for the first mile or so until I found my legs. I could have stayed out forever, tasting the scent of pine and snow and enjoying the serenity. Unfortunately, the sun goes down around three thirty, and I had to get to work.

"Dad said to tell you you're welcome to join them whenever you like," Virginia says in a dreamy voice that reminds me how much I've missed her the last couple of years. "I wish I could have gone with you."

"Me, too. How about tomorrow?" The words are out of my mouth before I can stop them.

"Oh, I'd love to!" she says at once. "Mom's going with me in the morning to talk to the cops, but maybe we can go tomorrow afternoon? Unless she makes me go to Marisol's service. I never should have told her about Camila's invitation."

"No kidding. You must have lost your mind." I half-laugh, despite it being the truth. The service at school was bad enough with teachers saying what a fine example Marisol was for the rest of us, not bothering to acknowledge that no one really liked her. "You're going to tell the police about your jacket?"

Virginia groans. "I have to. I've waited too long as it is."

I slide down on my bed, and we fall into making plans to interview other students on Monday, beginning with the freshmen girls who found the body. Virginia writes up sample scripts—what we'll ask and how they might answer. Adjusting as we think of possible responses they might give.

"And just so you know," she says a couple of minutes later. "I talked to Matty, and he says it's okay if I tell you what he's up to."

I've been thinking about that. "Well, don't," I say. "Not unless it has to do with me or Marisol. Matty deserves his privacy."

I can almost hear her smile. "You're right. You're really going to like him once you get to know him. He's funny and kind and totally full of himself, but in a good way, if that makes any sense. And anyway, he'll probably want to tell you himself. Or *show* you," she adds with a hint of mischief in her voice.

"Now you've got me curious." What could it be? I already know about his blog. Some new outfit he's previewing for subscribers?

"Just you wait." She chuckles. "I guarantee you'll be impressed."

We talk for a while longer. About our classes. About our favorite foods. About a field trip we took in eighth grade along the downtown planet walk. It was a tedious, six-hour hike that ended in Earthquake Park, late enough to watch the sun set over the water. By the end, my feet were killing me. But you don't see gorgeous sunsets like that in Bellingham, not in my old neighborhood.

"My phone's dying. Should I get my charger?" Virginia asks after a minute or so of silence. I glance at the clock, startled to see it's almost three a.m. I must have been dozing for a while.

"We should hang up. Talk more tomorrow?" I yawn.

"You bet." She pauses. "This was nice, Katie, just talking to you on the phone. I've missed it."

"Like old times." We hang up, and I plug in my own phone. Then I drift off, feeling better than I have in a very long time.

CHAPTER TWENTY-THREE

VIRGINIA

Sunday, December 15, 11:00 a.m.

Mom has been coming into my room every ten minutes for the last hour, telling me I need to get up. It's late morning, and I can hardly keep my eyes open. "If you don't get up this minute, I'm going to send Reggie in to throw cold water on you." Exasperation rings through her voice.

It sounds more like something my older brother would do. Nevertheless, I yawn and stretch and sit upright, dangling my legs off the side of the bed. "Have you heard from Pete?"

"A little while ago. He took his first steps this morning. He's coming home for a few days to recuperate. We'll see him later at the base. Now, it's your turn. Get up and take a shower." She stands in the doorway and taps her watch. "We're leaving in twenty minutes."

To go to the police station. I know I've got to get this over with, explaining what I was doing in the stairwell, but I'm not looking forward to it. What's worse, when Mom heard that Camila invited me to Marisol's funeral, she insisted we go together. If we visit Pete after that, there won't be time to ski with Katie.

My groan turns into a grin, however, as I think about last night. My cell phone battery was down to less than ten percent by the time I finally mentioned it. I'd been watching the battery drain for nearly an hour, but I didn't want to say anything because I could have talked to Katie all night. And I'm pretty sure she enjoyed the conversation as much as I did.

* * *

Forty-five minutes later, I'm showered and dressed. I've had an energy bar and two cups of coffee. A third, resting on the table in front of me, is getting cold as Mom and I sit side by side at a metal table in a windowless room at the downtown police station. Mom doesn't know Officers Dietrich and Hess, but plenty of others said hello to us when we came in. She makes friends easily, so even civilian employees she'd only met once or twice greeted her like a friend.

"Good afternoon, ladies." Officer Hess comes in to take a seat across from us. "Diet's on a call, so I'm afraid you're stuck with me."

He's one of the cops from Marisol's service. A stocky white guy with overly long sideburns that put me in mind of a werewolf. A whiff of Dark Temptation Axe, Reggie's favorite, tickles my nose as he drops a folder on the table and leans forward in his chair.

"Now then. You said on the phone this is regarding the Cowsill case?"

Mom nods at me, and I take my cue to pull the hoodie out of my backpack. She had me drop it in a plastic bag along with one of Sonya Dare's posters when I told her about it yesterday. "It's me, not David Teal in the photograph," I say, pointing to the poster. "I was headed to my car and took a shortcut down the film club staircase. Marisol was coming up. We met in the landing, and stopped for a minute and talked. Then I left. I didn't see David, and I never turned around."

My mother puts a reassuring hand on my arm because I'm shaking slightly. I'm telling Officer Hess exactly what she told me to say.

"You and Marisol were friends?" Hess lifts a bushy brow.

"Not really, but we knew each other. My brother dated her sister." *Dates.*

"Camila Cowsill?"

"Right."

Hess eyes the hoodie. "May I keep this for a while?"

"Yes."

"All right then." He pushes back his chair as if to get up.

Is that it?

Mom says, "Is there anything you can tell us about the investigation?"

Hess blows out coffee-breath. "Mrs. Eaton, I'm sure you can understand—"

"Carol. Please call me Carol."

"Carol," he repeats with a hint of impatience. "I'm sure you understand that in an ongoing investigation we're not at liberty to share information until we know what's pertinent and what's not."

"Has David been arrested?" I ask as Mom's hand tightens on my forearm.

"Not at this time."

"Glad to hear it." I grit my teeth. "Because the one you should really be looking at is Sonya Dare. Or at least her cell phone. She's a sophomore at North and a one-time friend of David's sister, Ahna. Sonya is the one putting up these flyers." I pull the paper out of the plastic bag. "My friend saw her at the theater Friday night. She had a whole bunch of these in her pocket because she blames David for his sister being forced into foster care when their fa—"

"Virginia, that's enough." Mom cuts me off, which is just as well because I'm babbling.

Hess studies me for a second and taps the flyer with a stubby finger. "This photo was not taken with a cell phone camera."

"How do you know?" I start to say, but Mom's one step ahead of me.

"Resolution?" she says, more to herself.

He bobs his chin. "And lighting."

"Less control with the shutter on a cell phone camera," Mom explains to me.

"Did you see Sonya Tuesday afternoon?" Hess asks as I attempt to process this new information. Not a cell phone? What then? One of those expensive cameras from journalism or the video lab? Who else has a genuine camera? I'm guessing they're not that common unless you take a class or are into photography on your own.

I shake my head. "I didn't see anybody other than my friend Tally outside the library until I met Marisol in the stairwell." Where was David, I think, frowning to myself. He had to be there somewhere since the cops chose to question him the morning after Marisol's death, before people even started noticing the Gram post. Did he slip into a restroom? Why didn't I see him?

"What did you and Marisol talk about?" asks Hess.

Oh, sure, now he's interested. I'm tempted to lie, but think better of it. Mom knows anyway. "Nothing important. I was trying to discourage her from doing a story that would out bisexual students."

"What made you think to do that?"

"It was on her list. I saw it a day or so earlier when I walked past the journalism room."

"I see. And did she agree to your request?"

"She didn't agree or disagree," I say, affecting a careless shrug. "She said she'd think about it." Actually, Marisol told me to get the hell out of her face. She was in quite a mood, more nasty than usual, but I'm not going mention that because I don't want to bring Katie's name into it.

Hess scratches the side of his face and asks again, "And Sonya Dare, you didn't see her before you left school? Either in the parking lot, or in the upstairs hall before you entered the stairwell?"

Mom gives me an elbow nudge, and I search my memory once more. I hadn't been to the parking lot yet, but I do remember passing the video lab and seeing Lilly Kahale and a couple of other students sitting at computers. Mr. Ivy was at his desk, or was he? I really can't recall. Maybe he was in back. There might have been students at the other end of the hall, but I never turned around and looked. "I don't think so," I say. "Have you asked her where she was that afternoon?"

Officer Hess pushes back his chair for real this time and stands, hooking his thumbs on his belt. "Thank you for coming in, Miss Eaton. I'll get your jacket back to you as soon as I can."

Mom also rises. I'm surprised to see they're the same height. "Have you talked to Sonya, Officer Hess?" she asks, using her getting-down-to-business tone, the one she employs when she's decided to stop being friendly because she's not going to pretend she believes some shoplifter's story anymore.

Hess lets loose a sigh that sends an unexpected chill through me. "We will. As soon as we find her."

CHAPTER TWENTY-FOUR

KATIE

Sunday, December 15, 1:30 p.m.

Josh and I are having lunch when I receive Virginia's text: *Sonya's disappeared.*

What!

Officer Hess let it slip. Her parents are still in Fairbanks. They called this morning, but she didn't answer her phone.

Which might just mean she's with a friend. I think about the girls I saw with Sonya Friday night, Natives like Sonya. I'm beginning to think Sonya doesn't like white people, which is more comforting than believing it's just me she doesn't like. Because what have I ever done to her? Except cheat, emotionally, on her brother... Well shit. I push that thought aside. Where is she? I'm almost positive I heard her in the house yesterday morning.

My phone beeps again. *About skiing. Mom's making me attend Marisol's funeral, and then we're going to visit Pete. I'm sorry. I really wanted to go. How about coffee later?*

Is Virginia blowing me off? "Juice. I want juice," Josh calls from his high chair and bangs the tray with his spoon.

"Just a sec, sweetie." I set the phone down, pour more apple juice into his Sippy Cup and let him out of the chair. Mom and Denise are out cutting down a Christmas tree for our apartment. They didn't even ask if I wanted to go with them. Probably because I've declined most of their invitations.

Josh toddles over to the doorway and slurps happily as I pick up my phone and text: *That works. Although we could go to a movie. I can get us in for free.*

Sounds great. Which one?

There's a crime caper that's been out for several weeks, which means it won't be overly crowded. We settle on a time to meet. Just as I drop Josh's plate in the sink, our landline rings. We only keep it because Denise uses it for work. I pick up without thinking, and a voice on the other end says, "Will you accept a collect call from Airway Heights Correction Center?"

"No!" I shout.

Another garbled voice speaks, but before it can go any further, I slam the phone against the counter and yank the cord free from the wall. My heart is beating so fast I have to sit down to calm myself. Dad, you motherfucker. Don't you get it that I never want to talk to you again?

The last time I saw him was in court. I refused to look at him, and when his attorney asked if he had ever deliberately hit me, I said, "Every day. He beat me from the inside out." I could tell he had more questions, but good old Dad, clean-shaven and looking clear-eyed for once, wouldn't let him. As if years of putting me between him and Mom could be wiped away by being selfless for a single day. My therapist called it passive-aggressive behavior and said it wasn't unusual for kids to find themselves caught between two dysfunctional parents.

Josh can see I'm distressed, and after a second, he patters over and lays his head in my lap. "Kay-tee cry?"

He's so cute. I pick him up and hug him. "Not today, little man. Let's go build something with your Legos."

* * *

Virginia and I both get to the movies early. As we sit in the near-empty theater waiting for the trailers to begin, I tell her about my father's latest phone call and how it pissed me off.

"What would you say to him if you did talk to him?" She gives me a sympathetic look and tosses popcorn in her mouth.

"I'd tell him to go to hell."

"Sounds healthy. What does your mom say?"

"She doesn't know." It isn't that I didn't consider telling her, but she looked so happy when she and Mrs. Taylor—Denise—came back with the spruce they'd cut down themselves in the Chugach National Forest. It scraped the ceiling of our tiny living room. The three of us worked together clipping branches and sawing down the trunk until it fit into a corner next to the window. I ended up helping them decorate it, which pleased them both to no end. "It's like we're a real family now," Mom said, plugging in the tiny, multicolored lights. "Oh!" She shot me a guilty look. "I didn't mean that the way it sounded."

I put my arm around her waist. "It's okay, Mom. You have a right to be happy." And as I sit here with Virginia, it occurs to me that I do, too.

"You know," Virginia says thoughtfully when the trailers start rolling. "I always felt sorry for your mother. She seemed so unhappy."

"She was."

"And now?"

"Things are better. She's…" I pause, giving it some thought. "I'm still not sure Mom's life turned out the way she wanted, but having Mrs. Taylor around really helps." I know it's true the moment I say it. Denise—I'm still getting used to saying her first name—is naturally content. She loves my mother, and she doesn't try to control her. If my mother decided to flake out, Denise wouldn't try to make her stay.

Four elderly people come in and sit a few rows in front of us. The women sit together, their husbands on the outside. A couples' date. The movie starts, a twisty tale about ex-cons planning the perfect diamond heist. There's a greedy jeweler looking to unload a handful of fakes who complicates their scheme. At one point, Virginia reaches for more popcorn and her knuckles brush the back of my hand.

"Are you trying to get fresh with me?" I tease.

She stiffens. "What? No! Sorry, I just—"

My fingers close around hers, and I can feel my lips curl upward at the corners. "Don't say that. Don't be sorry." I lean over so our shoulders touch, telling myself again that I deserve to be happy.

CHAPTER TWENTY-FIVE

VIRGINIA

Monday, December 16, 6:15 a.m.

Katie flirted with me last night.

That's a good thing, right?

Yeah. I'm just not sure she knows what she's doing. I can picture Matty rolling his eyes as he reads this.

Three dots appear, then: *Mom's got breakfast on the table. Can we talk about this at school?*

I send a thumbs-up emoji and make myself sit up. It's after six. Several minutes past my usual wake-up time, but it's always harder to get out of bed in winter. The sun won't be up for another four hours, and if it weren't for the moon reflecting off the backyard snow, I think I might go blind, like those fish in underground caves that never see daylight.

Mom knocks on my bedroom door. "Virginia, if you don't get into the bathroom right this minute, Reggie's going in before you."

I spring into action, grabbing a clean sweatshirt and a pair of jeans from the closet. We have a strict bathroom schedule in our house. I get to use the shower first because my school day starts before Reggie's. If he gets in there ahead of me, all bets are off if I can get to school on time. For a twelve-year-old, he spends a lot of time in the bathroom. And he never looks that dirty... I stop midthought. I definitely don't want to pursue that line to its logical conclusion. When I was twelve... Nope, don't want to go there either.

I shower and dress, slipping on one of my favorite pairs of rainbow TomboyXs before pulling on my jeans. My mind is on Katie. When we said good night at our cars in the theater parking lot, I wanted to kiss her. To taste her breath and feel the heat of her body pressed against me. It was all I could think about, but I didn't because despite holding hands for an hour and a half, I still don't know what she's thinking. Or honestly, if she even knows what she wants. As far as I can tell, she's still dating Rocky. I'd like to ask her to break it off with him, but after all that trauma she went through in Washington, I should be more sympathetic. My god, who wouldn't be confused after that? I always thought her parents were strange. Her dad made too many jokes, and her mom was so aloof. She'd talk to you, but it was more like she was just going through the motions. As if she thought it's what parents were supposed to do with their kids' friends.

* * *

We meet inside North's front door as planned and immediately head for freshman hall. "So...good movie last night," I say, bouncing on the inside as I wait for her reaction.

"The best." Katie smiles and skims her hand against mine, and of course I instantly melt. There isn't time for anything else, however, as the two girls who discovered Marisol's body step out of the restroom in front of us. Katie feigns surprise. "Hey, aren't you guys in Mr. Cooper's newspaper class? I've got an idea for an article. Do I tell him, or is there a suggestion box?" All part of our plan.

"That was Marisol's job," replies a pretty blonde with a topknot bun, the one with red lowlights.

"But we can take it," says the other, also blond, with dangling silver earrings.

With most classes, all you have to do is sign up with your counselor if you're interested. Mr. Cooper's newspaper class is different. You have to write an article on spec, and then he interviews you with Marisol sitting in. I've often wondered if he can take a shit without her. I guess he has to now. The class is one of a few that's not all upperclassmen because older students train the younger ones on what a good online newspaper should look like. It's not for dummies, so these two must be pretty bright.

"What's your idea?" asks the Topknot, ready to take notes on her phone.

"It's about Dan Daily from NBC. He's still coming, right? End of this week? I was thinking how the *Gazette* could do a profile on him. Maybe a special edition to post on lockers? You know, like how he got started in the business? I bet he'd be flattered, and then students would know enough about him to ask intelligent questions during the assembly."

Originally, the band was going to play for Daily and his news crew out by the totem pole Friday morning when he arrived, and then we were to have an all-school assembly. Marisol set the whole thing up. Finals end on Thursday, with makeups Friday morning. Usually, we have games in the gym in the afternoon with grade-levels competing against each other.

I step aside as two more girls come out of the restroom. "Is Mr. Daily still coming?"

Dangling Earrings shrugs and makes a face. "We don't know. It's such a mess. With Marisol out of the picture, Cooper's thinking about canceling the whole thing. We don't even know if Mr. Daily still wants to come."

"Shoot," Katie says, shifting her backpack up her shoulder. "Marisol was your editor-in-chief, right? Who's going to take her place?"

"Do you have any openings on your staff?" I add, as if I'm interested in a position.

The first bell rings, and locker doors begin clanging open and shut as the freshmen who've been standing around likely talking about homework and dates start making their way to class. Dangling Earrings cups an ear to hear over all the noise. "You can apply after Christmas. Lilly Kahale is filling in the rest of this semester. You might want to talk to her."

"Are you serious?" Katie and I exchange a fleeting glance. "We heard she got kicked out."

"Yeah, well, she came in Friday afternoon, begging for another chance. That movie guy Zach did, too. But he doesn't have the experience, and honestly, Lilly deserves it. She's got great ideas, and that beef she had with Marisol was so messed up. Marisol didn't have to go and tick her off like that. Cooper's got her back on strict probation, but I wouldn't be surprised if she gets a permanent spot after Christmas. I'm glad he let her in."

"Me, too," the other adds sincerely. "I'm not gonna lie, Lilly's actually nicer to the rest of us. She doesn't just pretend to listen to our opinions."

Katie and I nudge each other's elbows and say, "Thanks."

"We'll pass your idea on to Mr. Cooper," one of them says over her shoulder. "It's not half-bad."

"Better than half-bad. Great!" Katie grins at me the second they're out of earshot.

"I know, right?" I feel like we're starting to get somewhere. We head back for our own hall at a fast clip, not wanting to be late for class. "See you at lunch?" I call out hopefully, before veering off for Honors English. Katie's locker is straight ahead, and I can see Rocky lounging against it. For a second, I almost hate the guy, and then I think about his sister, Sonya. Have the cops found her? I don't know if she had anything to do with Marisol's death. Regardless, her parents must be worried sick about her.

Katie's got her eyes on Rocky, and she sounds distracted when she says, "See you."

CHAPTER TWENTY-SIX

KATIE

Monday, December 16, 7:30 a.m.

Oh crap. I was supposed to meet Rocky at the Fieldhouse. He texted yesterday afternoon to remind me, and I still forgot. I fake a smile as I shove a shoulder between him and my locker and spin my combination. "Hey, you. What's up?"

"Sonya's missing."

Still? "What happened?"

Rocky glances down the hall for a moment, looking lost. "No idea. The police think she might have run away. Jesus." He looks back, shaking his head from side to side. "She's got exactly two friends, and neither one of them has seen her since Friday when they went to the movies. My folks are trying not to panic. They talked to her Saturday afternoon. Yesterday morning, she wouldn't answer her phone. Which isn't unusual by itself, but now that one guy, Officer Hess, seems to think she had something to do with those stupid DT flyers."

"What do you mean?" I'm trying to sound innocent, even though I know exactly what he means.

"That she put them up. Like she's got something against DT, I guess. Man, it's so fucked up." Rocky frowns and rubs his chin. "Babe, you were supposed to meet me ten minutes ago. Did you forget?"

And just like that, he's stopped worrying about his sister. "I did," I say. "I'm sorry." Rocky considers it one of our traditions that the day after he wins a game we hook up behind the Fieldhouse for a five-minute quickie in the cold. God, why did I ever agree to that? I never loved him. I ran into him the day I saw Virginia kissing Tally. He was sweet and asked me out, and I suppose after that it was easier not to think about anything at all.

As I reach into my locker to get a book, he makes a clumsy grab for my breast. I jerk away before he can really get a hold of me, but all he does is wink. "Tell you what. You can make it up to me at lunch. We'll meet out at the trails." He's referring to where the ski trails start. There's a cove of trees protected from the wind just past the football stadium. It's a popular spot for student hookups when the Fieldhouse gets busy with gym classes.

"I can't," I stammer. "I'm meeting Virginia for lunch. We're working on our civics project."

Rocky frowns, and for a second I think he's going to start in about all the time I've been spending with her, like Dad would have with Mom, but instead, he says, "The Civil War thing? Got mine covered. Zach's doing my paper for me. I'm paying him," he adds, misreading my startled expression. "He's really good at that kind of thing."

Of course, he is. Everybody knows Zach Pratt is smart, but I thought Rocky was done with him. The whole Bad Influence thing. "Maybe I'll see you after school?" I say.

His eyes twinkle. "Sure. I'll be at the rink. Can't wait. Love you, babe."

CHAPTER TWENTY-SEVEN

VIRGINIA

Monday, December 16, 11:30 a.m.

By third period, word is out that the cops are working off a new theory, that Marisol's death wasn't an accident. That she was deliberately shoved down the stairs by person or persons unknown. People have been talking about it all morning, every chance they get. Nobody is saying anything about Sonya Dare.

At the end of the hour, our substitute rises from behind his desk and clears his throat. "Excuse me, class. I just received an email from your principal, Mrs. Foster, asking me to read the following announcement." He angles the computer to better see the screen.

"Students. By now most of you are aware the police are opening a new investigation into the events surrounding Marisol Cowsill's death. I'd ask that you please go about your business as usual. If you have any relevant thoughts or information you'd like to share, you may speak with Officers Hess and Dietrich who will be in the building all afternoon. Or, if you'd feel more comfortable, you may stop by my office and talk with me privately."

One of the football players sitting in the back jumps up. "I gotta go see Mrs. Foster," he says. His friends snicker as he lowers himself back into his seat.

The kid next to him coughs, "DT did it," inviting more low laughs and whispers.

I can't stand it. I leap to my feet and spin around, my blood pressure spiking. "You guys are idiots! That's me, not David Teal in the Insta photo. He didn't have anything to do with Marisol's death." The buzz in the room ceases, and a roar of silence fills my ears. Before I can go on, the bell rings. Several people glance my way as they make their exits, likely already posting how I went off in class because I lost it after killing Marisol.

Finally saying it out loud should make me feel better, but it doesn't. I let David take the heat when I could have stopped it.

"Have you noticed how Mrs. Foster doesn't like making announcements?" Matty says, plopping onto a stool beside me in the cafeteria a couple of minutes later.

"Just the bad-news kind. She probably thinks having teachers read them in class is more reassuring," Yoon-hi offers. She's brown-bagging it today, ham and cheese on multigrain bread. So different from the little bulgogi bowls in dainty porcelain dishes she used to bring from home a couple of months ago.

"If anyone wants to know what I think, and I'm sure you do"—Tally pauses for effect—"I believe we've got a serial killer on the loose." She sets her tray down with a clatter across from Matty. A few weeks ago she began eating lunch in the library when she started crushing on the young new librarian. Today is her first day back. "First Marisol, and now Sonya? Statistics show that one out of every five Americans is a serial killer."

"Bullshit." Matty flips a bright pink boa in my face.

"Bullshit, yourself." She pokes a finger at the thin slice of pepperoni pizza on her paper plate. "I'm not making it up. Well, maybe it's a potential serial killer. The point is, it's always the ones you least suspect. The innocent-looking ones like Ted Bundy in Florida."

"Or Aileen Wuornos, also in Florida," says Yoon-hi.

"She was hardly innocent-looking. Wasn't she like some kind of schizoid prostitute?" Matty picks a feather off my chin and flicks it to the floor. "You're awfully quiet, Virginia. Don't tell us you don't have an opinion. Haven't you been watching Netflix's true crime series?"

He knows I do. We talk about it almost daily. That, and the latest Apple and iHeart podcasts. "Sonya's only missing. But good thing we don't live in Florida," I say quietly, keeping my eyes on the hallway door. I'm trying not to appear too obvious about it. My heart rate ramps up when Katie walks in and makes her way toward us. Relief flushes through me as she passes Rocky's group and keeps going. There's not an empty stool at his table anyway. His fellow hockey players fill the seats, a girl on either side of him. Brooke Teasdale sits so close she might as well climb inside his jersey. He looks up, watching thoughtfully until Katie stops behind me.

"Sorry, I'm late," she says as Yoon-hi slides over to make room for her.

Tally bounces a brow and gives me a less-than-subtle wink. "Hey, Katie. Good to see you again. Welcome to the table of misfits."

"I prefer eccentrics." Matty sticks out pink-nailed fingers for Katie to shake. "We passed each other in the stairwell the other day, but we haven't officially met. I see you know Tally, and obviously my BFF, Virginia. I'm Matty, a.k.a Brown Sugar, a.k.a Whitney Houston, performer exotica at Misconceptions." When did he come up with all that, I wonder idly. "And this"—he goes on, flapping a wrist—"is Yoon-hi Park, North's only underachieving Asian."

"Fuck you, Matty," Yoon-hi says without rancor. "Nice to meet you, Katie." She's definitely adapting to her new Alaska life. She's even cut her hair into a short angled bob, that's becoming to her pale, pretty face.

Katie says, "Nice to meet you all. I lived in Anchorage a couple of years ago. My family moved to Washington, and now we're back. I went to East at first, until my parents moved to this side of town." Her parents? Meaning her mom and Denise Taylor? That's a step in the right direction.

"We know." Matty lifts his chin, ignoring the toe of my boot bumping his shin under the table. "Promise me you'll come to my performance, Katie. At Misconceptions? I'm quite gifted, in case you haven't guessed. A fierce and fishy talent. Are you free Saturday night?"

"I haven't told her yet." I keep a subtle eye on Katie's bemused expression.

At the same time, Tally snorts, "Isn't that a cliché? A truly gifted Black dude? I suppose you're well-endowed in all the right places, too."

"Fuck you, Tally. You don't know the places I'm endowed." Matty gives her a mock sweet smile before turning his attention back to Katie. "Well?"

"Um. I work Saturday nights."

"No worries. How about tonight? Business is pretty slow on weeknights. If Lady Gaga's at the door, I'll get you in free. All of you." He gestures, flashing his nail polish again to include Tally and Yoon-hi. So much for him only performing weekends. And his anxiety about getting fired seems to have vanished. Almost like he's saying: *Take that, Marisol.*

"I'm in," says Tally.

"Sounds good to me." Yoon-hi makes a quick note in her phone calendar, which is nothing less than I'd expect because she's always so well-organized.

"Gaga?" Katie gazes at me, puzzled.

"You'll love it if you're up for it," I say. "But why don't we let it be a surprise?" I don't know why I added that. Am I worried she won't want to come? Matty is a lot to take. I loved his show, but I know drag isn't for everyone. And Katie still seems a bit delicate.

She's barely touched her salad in a jar, but lunch will be over in ten minutes, and we'd planned to talk to David. I need to, I have to set the record straight with him. "Are you ready? I don't want to rush you," I say, tossing my own half-eaten sandwich in the trash.

Katie stuffs her plastic fork and dressing-soaked mason jar back into her lunch sack and follows me to the door. "You guys should check out the trails," Tally calls loudly after us.

The tips of my ears heat, and neither of us looks back.

David isn't at his locker, or in the Indian Ed counselor's office where four girls with straight, dark hair, wearing oversized, white sweatshirts sit around a table eating lunch. They talk quietly amongst themselves, clamping their jaws tight when we peek in and ask if they've seen David. The closest one glares, but she also looks a little fearful as if we're there to bust them for having fun by themselves.

"Try Mrs. Foster's office," the counselor suggests, pushing through the door with a plate piled high with mac and cheese and three slices of buttered brown bread on the side. He's a big white guy who wears T-shirts, shorts, and flip-flops even in the middle of winter.

"Thanks."

Sure enough, David and Mrs. Foster are just coming out of her office as we turn back into the main hall. Mrs. Foster, who's got a hand on David's shoulder, says, "Honey, I don't want to tell you your business, but I think you're making a mistake."

"So you said," he answers in a surly voice, shaking her off and heading in the direction of his locker down the hall.

Katie starts up after him. "David, wait. Can we talk?" He keeps walking, and she has to trot to catch up. I jog along behind her. "Virginia and me, we just want to say we're on your side. I know what it feels like to be a pariah. Please don't tell me you're quitting school. Nobody wants that to happen."

"By nobody, you mean everybody?" He pauses to twist the locker dial. "I didn't touch her."

"Who?"

"Marisol *or* Ahna, you pick. Am I forgetting Sonya? Not her, either. I appreciate the vote of confidence, but get lost." When he opens his locker, I jerk backward at the sudden stench. Somebody has smeared shit all over his books and coat. It's everywhere. A crumpled paper sack, stained damp and shiny on the bottom, tells me where it came from. Dog crap, from the smell of it. It's so disgusting.

David stands there for a millisecond, then slams the door. "Guess I won't be taking anything with me, after all."

"We'll help you clean it up," I say quickly. "We're trying to figure out what really happened in the stairwell Tuesday afternoon. Do you mind telling me about you and Marisol? What she said to you? Look, it was me in the North Face hoodie. I've already confessed to the cops. I promise I'll let everyone know." To admit I feel like a jerk for not saying something earlier would be an understatement. I could justify myself by saying I didn't know anything about the photo or the posters until Friday, but that still gave me hours to confess to everyone at school. I should have asked Mrs. Foster to make an announcement, or tacked up my own posters acknowledging my guilt.

"Officers Hess and Dietrich shouldn't even be looking at you anymore," I continue in my half-assed way.

David gazes at me with sorrowful, round eyes that make me hate myself even more. "A little too late, don't you think?" I can tell he's debating whether to answer my question, but he's clearly a better person than I am. "Tuesday after school, Marisol stopped me in the first floor hall and said she wanted to do a feature on me. Naturally, she meant my father and Ahna. All I wanted to do was protect my sister. Look how that worked out. I left the building directly after."

So, that's why I never saw him. I'd gone up the main stairs to the library to return a couple of books and had come across Marisol on the back staircase moments later.

David's eyes turn even darker as he glances to the door, unfocused. "There was just something about her, Marisol...I needed to throw up."

"I get that. Please," I beg. "Isn't there something I can do to make this up to you?" I motion to the inside of his locker.

"I think you've done enough."

"David. Let us help," Katie says softly. "You and I were friends once."

"Is that what you think?" he scoffs.

Her face pales, and I can't help flinching right alongside her as she asks him where he's going to go now.

"Nowhere. Anywhere. Back where I belong, maybe. I'm done with this place, this school, this city." He looks her up and down, ignoring me. "For what it's worth, I don't blame you. You're not the problem, only part of it. This city is toxic."

We watch him storm out of North's main entrance to the parking lot. "God," Katie breathes. "Who would do this to his locker?"

I can think of a hundred people who wanted to believe David Teal was guilty of something just because the color of his skin is different. "I don't know," I answer, my voice thin and breaking. "I don't know."

CHAPTER TWENTY-EIGHT

KATIE

Monday, December 16, 1:15 p.m.

I didn't think I could feel much worse after the conversation with David, only now I keep thinking about Rocky. Replaying all the things I should have said in my head. Seeing David, getting a glimpse at the mess inside his locker, was a wake-up call. I've always thought I was a decent person, but am I any better than someone who would do that to David? I mean, what kind of person lies to a guy who cares about her?

Part of me wants to keep telling myself I'm not gay. That I never intentionally used Rocky as a crutch. As a beard. Part of me wants to say: At least I never painted the inside of somebody's locker with excrement. But do bad deeds really have a hierarchy? Can a pickpocket claim to be a decent person when he only stole an old lady's purse and didn't beat her?

I remember hiding in my room when I was little and wishing for a normal life. For parents who didn't slam doors and break dishes. For a father who didn't drink and a mother who would actually talk to me. I didn't know what normal looked like until I met Virginia and her family. I fell in love with them. I even enjoyed observing their squabbles. Pete giving his stupid noogies. Reggie with his head always buried in some lame video game. Mr. and Mrs. Eaton who so obviously loved each other and all their kids. The first time I met Virginia, we were cross-country skiing in Russian Jack Park. It was icy, and I slipped. Everyone else skied on obliviously, but Virginia held out a hand and laughed good-naturedly when I scrambled to my feet, then promptly fell again. She took off her glove to help me up, telling me this was called classic cross-country skiing, which made me classically uncoordinated. I called her a bitch, smiling around the word because I knew I had to look ridiculous lying on the ground, tangled in my borrowed skis. Seeing her face, wrapping my fingers around her palm, it took my breath away. The way she looked at me made me want to kiss her. We were in seventh grade, and I could tell she wanted me, too. When we moved to Washington, I hoped I'd grow out of my feelings because it was just so hard being away from her. Sometimes it's easier not to feel anything, and I was just so mad about everything.

My thoughts cycle back to Rocky. And then on to the horrible things I said to Virginia in the parking lot a few days ago. I go through the motions of taking notes in English. Of solving equations in math. Of washing my instruments in chemistry.

"You missed something," my chem lab partner, Amy Meeks, says, coming up behind me at the sink. She drops a glass beaker in the soapy water, swishes it clean, then sets it on a damp gray towel to dry. She's cute, with freckles, braces, wavy red hair like a movie star, and pixie features. Each week we take turns cleaning and putting away our equipment. We didn't choose to be lab partners, but she's new to North like I am, making us class friends.

"So have you got Christmas plans?" she asks conversationally when we finish.

"Not really. You?"

"Flying to the Big Apple to see my father. To meet his latest girlfriend. The last one was barely out of diapers. It's a new one every month."

This feels like an invitation to talk about my family, but I'm not biting. "Diapers?"

"She's twenty-two. Pretty sure he took her out just to piss off my mother. Mom moved me and my little sister to Alaska to escape him. The day before we left, she told him she'd sooner drown herself in a bucket of water than spend another minute with him."

"Seriously?"

"He told her he'd help."

I'm not sure Amy's kidding. She checks the burner to verify it's off. When we return to our table to await the bell, she says, "Parents, right? I'd like to drown them both."

I fight back a smile. Apparently, we have more in common than a class.

CHAPTER TWENTY-NINE

VIRGINIA

Monday, December 16, 3:00 p.m.

I'm all focused on the investigation now, though my between-class pursuits proved fruitless. A conversation with Marisol's volleyball co-captain and senior reporter for the *Gazette*, Fatima Mann, yielded nothing other than a grudging acknowledgement that Marisol was a pretty good setter but could use more work on her hits. Mr. Cooper told me to mind my own business before I had a chance to even ask him about Marisol's other story ideas. The easel I'd noticed last week was put away, so I got nothing there, either.

After school, I sidle up to Yoon-hi at her locker as she takes her camera out of the snow boot in her locker and sharpens a pencil with it.

She catches my look and lifts her chin. "What? You thought this was a real camera?"

"Sorry, it's just that Officer Hess said the Insta pic wasn't taken with a smartphone camera."

She tosses me her pencil sharpener. It's as light as an empty water bottle. "This one's shit for calls and photos, but it doubles as a coffee mug. You want it? I didn't kill her, Virginia, although we were planning to run away together."

She's putting me on, making me feel guilty for suspecting her. I set it back on the floor of the locker and say, "See you later." I am *so* not in the mood to be teased.

With everything else going on, Katie and I neglected to make plans to meet after school. And when I go by her locker, she isn't there. I wait for a couple of minutes, then head for Mrs. Hicks's room, finding her rearranging student desks into a circle. "Can I help?" I offer, dropping my backpack inside the door.

"Absolutely," she replies. There's a post in the center of the room and outlets on the floor we have to work around.

"Getting ready for an NHS meeting?" I say when we finish, hoping to start a conversation that will eventually work its way around to Marisol.

"Not until after Christmas. Then, I suppose, we'll have to choose a new president." She sighs, then gestures to the chairs. "This is to facilitate better class discussions."

"So we get to choose who won the Civil War?"

"Very funny. I said discuss, not vote. You have your brother Pete's sense of humor. Why aren't you in NHS, Virginia?"

I shrug. "Not smart enough, I guess." I like Mrs. Hicks even though her assignments are too hard and she doesn't mind putting kids on the spot if she believes they aren't paying attention. She's one of those teachers who wants to be friends with everybody, which can be annoying, but somehow it works for her.

"That's a cop-out and you know it," she argues, refusing to let me off the hook. "I suppose it's also why you quit the ski team?"

"Exactly. It's an intellectual sport."

"Oh, you know what I mean." She waves a hand in semi-irritation. "You don't want to compete with Pete's reputation. And you quit skiing because Katie doesn't go with you anymore."

My god, does this woman know everything about me? She and her husband are friends with my parents, but it's still unnerving to think she knows me that well. I'd like to argue about Pete, but she may be right. He was a champion athlete in high school and in National Honor Society both his junior and senior year. He and Camila were North's golden couple. She was valedictorian just like Marisol, but with a higher GPA and doubtlessly better liked.

"If I promise to apply to NHS in the spring, will you get off my back?" I say.

"Are you promising?"

"I'll think about it."

Her lips twitch. "Then I'll think about it, too."

We leave it at that.

On my way back down the hall, I see Officer Hess leaning on the counter in the front office. He looks bored, so I stick my head in the door, get a waft of his obnoxious aftershave, and ask him how the investigation is going.

He rests his chin on a fist. "You know I can't tell you that."

"So no confessions? No arrests?" What I want to say is, "You do know you're responsible for the shit in David Teal's locker?" Because I feel like blaming someone else, and he's an easy target since he never told anyone that Marisol and David had their little encounter on the first floor, not the second.

He does a slow blink, probably thinking the same thing— that it's my fault. "I can't tell you that, either."

I huff a noisy breath, making sure he hears it. Fine. Be that way.

I check Katie's locker one more time, then send her a text: *Heading out.*

No response.

An uneasy knot shifts in my stomach. We were fine at lunch. My friends were their usual nerdy selves, but that didn't seem to bother her. Tactless Tally suggested we might enjoy some alone time at the cross-country ski trailhead, but I don't think Katie got it. Was it the nasty mess in David's locker then that turned her off? Or the realization I'm a coward who lets someone else take the fall for my mistakes?

I stand by her locker for another full minute as if I can magically make her appear. Then, feeling foolish, I spin around and stride back to the front office.

Mrs. Foster has joined Hess at the counter. She looks up as I enter. "Is there something I can do for you, Virginia?"

"I'd like to speak with Officer Hess. Alone, if you don't mind."

"All right." She goes back to her office and shuts the door.

Hess regards me noncommittally. "Yes?"

I put on my best imitation of Mom's no-nonsense face. "What kind of camera was used to take the photo in the Gram post?"

He shakes his head. "We have no way of knowing."

"But you're sure it wasn't a smartphone camera?"

"Yes."

"So, something more professional then, like one of those used in the video lab or by the newspaper staff?"

"Possibly."

"Is it your belief that Person A took the picture of Marisol and me in the stairwell and posted it online, and that Person B, someone else, used the same photo in the poster that blames David Teal?"

For a second, I don't think Hess will answer. He taps his fingers on the counter in quick succession, like he's running scales on a piano. It's a gesture of impatience. "That's our working theory."

Okay. That makes sense. But it still doesn't explain why the photographer would post the pic at all. Unless a third person, C, is responsible for that? But how could that be possible? "Is Person B Sonya Dare?" I ask.

"Miss Eaton—"

"Virginia."

"Virginia." He sighs. "I know you want to help. But will you please just let me do my job?"

Which is what, standing around acting like you're our new hall monitor? "Have you found Sonya?"

"We're looking. Now do you have something you want to share? Some news or a revelation I don't know about?"

At this point, I'm not sure I'd tell him even if I did. I stomp out and make one last circuit by Katie's locker. Relief washes over me like warm bathwater when I see her coming toward me in the hall. It's not until she gets close that I notice how worried she looks.

"Oh, there you are," she says. "I thought I'd missed you."

"Everything okay?"

"Yes. Well, no." She bites her lip. "I just talked to Rocky. His father is organizing a search party for Sonya in Valley of the Moon Park. I'd thought I'd join them. Do you want to go with me?"

Uh oh. This is serious. "Just let me grab my coat," I say.

CHAPTER THIRTY

KATIE

Monday, December 16, 3:15 p.m.

I had every intention of breaking up with Rocky after school, but when I found him, he was on the phone with his father.

"Yes, sir. I'll be right there," he said, punching off and sliding it into the breast pocket of his army jacket before addressing me with a troubled expression. "Sorry. Can't stay to talk. My father's stroking out. He says this theory about Sonya's running away is rubbish, and the cops aren't doing enough to find her. I'm supposed to grab a couple of the guys and come help look for her."

"Didn't you say she's run away before?" I asked, recalling him telling me once that his dad had forbidden Sonya from having contact with her biological mother when her mom, an alcoholic, tried to see her a couple of years ago. Sonya had wanted to live with her, but he wouldn't even consider it, saying something like, "She didn't want you when you were a baby, why should she get another chance?" Sonya moved in with a friend until they got things sorted out. Mr. Dare's a tough man. Loves his kids, but doesn't let them get away with much.

"This is different. Anyway, Dad's not taking no for an answer." Rocky beckoned to a player out on the ice who skated over, turning his blades in the nick of time and spraying ice dust at our feet.

"What's up?"

Rocky explained the situation, and the player agreed to help.

"I'd like to help, too," I found myself saying, though the conversation wasn't turning out the way I'd hoped. Which is how I ended up heading to Valley of the Moon Park with Virginia.

We leave my car in North's main parking lot because hers is somewhat newer and no doubt more reliable. By the time we get to the park, forty or so people have gathered around the multi-tiered rocket ship in the middle of the playground. Rocky's mom is handing out high-powered flashlights, and his dad is directing groups of eight to spread out on the trails.

"Stay an arm's length apart, no more, and don't lose sight of each other. Remember, any little thing you see could be important. A scrap of clothes, a boot. Let's find Sonya," he shouts into a bullhorn.

The hair on the back of my neck rises, and I get an itch in the small of my back. Matty, Tally, and Yoon-hi join us, and I notice some of the kids from film club and the ski team gathering in other groups.

Virginia glances over my shoulder toward the parking lot. "There's my mom. I'll be right back."

"I don't get it. Why this park?" Matty says to the rest of us.

He has a point. The playgrounds and open spaces are pretty enough, but tarps and tents for the homeless are clearly visible just inside the woods. It's not a terrible neighborhood, but it's nowhere close to the Dares' estate on the northwest side of town, and I seem to recall that a couple of guys were shot to death a few years back along one of the bike trails.

"Sonya meets her mother here," Yoon-hi replies.

We all turn to look at her with various degrees of disbelief on our faces. "How do you know that?" says Tally.

Yoon-hi crosses her arms. "I'm not just a pretty face. I hear things."

Virginia comes back a second later. "Let's stick together. Mom's going out with Dad and the ski team."

Amy Meeks walks over and introduces us to her mother and her little sister and asks if they can join our group. Rocky and a few members of the hockey team head out with Rocky's father.

Mr. Dare has the park well mapped out. We're each given a handful of flyers with Sonya's yearbook picture, a phone number, and HAVE YOU SEEN HER? typed in large letters at the bottom. There's no description of her clothes, probably because no one knows what she was wearing. Her friends haven't seen her since Friday night. Her parents talked to her Saturday afternoon, which means she must have disappeared sometime between late Saturday and Sunday morning when they tried to reach her again. I fold the flyers in half and stuff them inside my coat. Are we supposed to hand them out to homeless people? Because everyone else here appears to be engaged in the search.

We start on one of the designated trails as instructed, searching around large rocks and snags—dead spruce trees that are left upright and decompose naturally. Many have brown needles indicating they were probably killed by beetles, although it's not unusual for full-grown live trees to topple over in windstorms. Tree roots don't grow very deep in Anchorage due to permafrost.

We pass close by a homeless camp of tents, sleeping bags, and trash but see no signs of life, and I wonder if the occupants have scattered, more afraid of us than we are of them. Every few seconds we take turns calling out Sonya's name, our pace no faster than a crawl because we don't want to miss any possible clues. As dusk approaches, Virginia moves closer to me and holds out her hand. I take it, and we walk holding hands and occasionally stumbling until it's completely dark.

"How long are we supposed to do this?" I hear Amy's little sister whisper.

"Let's turn back. It's too dark to see anything," her mother replies.

A second later, someone shouts, "I found something!"

When we get back to the big blue rocket in the playground, Zach Pratt looks triumphant, holding a small black item aloft in his gloved hand. "I think it's Sonya's phone!" he shouts, passing it to Rocky's dad who examines it with a flashlight. Mr. Dare's big, square face sags, and all at once he looks ten years older. When he speaks, his voice is flat. "Thanks, Zach. It is."

CHAPTER THIRTY-ONE

VIRGINIA

Monday, December 16, 6:30 p.m.

I didn't realize how much I'd been hoping to see Sonya until I find myself staring at her father desperately clutching the phone's black case. The atmosphere of an exciting treasure hunt has changed. It's quiet now, just a few low murmurs and the sounds of feet shuffling about in the muddy snow. I'm numb with cold and disappointment even though all along I kept telling myself we shouldn't get our hopes up. "She ran away. She must have," I mumble to myself, wanting to believe Sonya left to be with her mom because the police were on to her, and she didn't want to face the music.

Mom steps over and slips an arm around my waist. "Come now, honey. This is a good sign. She was here. It means we're on the right track. We won't give up."

We will for the night. Mr. Dare hands the phone to Rocky who's taken off his gloves and is busily punching it with his thumbs, trying to unlock it. "Still got a little battery left," he mutters. "Well, crap. No texts, no calls, or search history." I'm surprised he was able to unlock it.

"Thank you all for coming," Mr. Dare says graciously, lowering the bullhorn. "If you still have flyers, would you mind putting them up around your neighborhoods? And at school and any shops you frequent? I think we're done here for the night."

Several people offer to take more flyers. Others head silently for their cars. A squad car rumbles into the parking lot, spewing gasoline vapors, and Officer Dietrich climbs out of the driver's side. He says something into his radio and starts walking toward us, his shoes crunching on the ice. The Dares head over to meet him, their silhouettes illuminated in his headlights. After a moment, Zach joins them, and the group confers at the edge of the parking lot.

"She's probably with her mom." Katie grimaces beside me.

Mom puts her other arm around Katie's shoulder and pulls her close. "I'm sure that's it." It isn't exactly a happy thought, given Sonya's mother's track record, which Mom seems to realize. Her grim expression changes like a flight attendant who suddenly understands passengers are watching her to see if they should be afraid during an especially bumpy flight. "You know what?" she says, giving my waist a squeeze. "It's been a long day, and we're all cold and tired. Why don't you all come over to our house, anyone who wants to, and I'll make some nice hot soup. How does that sound?"

Amy's mother says they need to get home, but all my friends are up for it. "My car is still at school," says Katie.

"I'll take you back to it after dinner." I hold my breath.

She gives me a small but gorgeous smile. "Let me call my mother."

* * *

When we get to the house, I discover Dad's invited the cross-country ski team for dinner, too. Only six showed up, but he takes one look at kids spilling out of our living room and into the hall and kitchen and decides we needs more food. "How about fried chicken?" he asks Mom.

"Better get a couple of buckets. And don't forget to pick up Pete."

"Do I have to?" he jokes.

"And if Camila's with him, ask her if she'd like to join us."

Dad snatches his car keys from the hook by the door to the garage, and Mom starts opening cans of Progresso chicken noodle soup. When she sees me standing in the doorway, she shoos me out. "Go be with Katie. I can take care of this."

How did I get so lucky to have her as my mother?

Both couches and Dad's wingback are taken up by guests. They sit everywhere. On the arms of our sofas, the coffee table, the floor in front of the television, even on the windowsills. Katie motions me to squeeze in beside her on the fireplace hearth.

"Are you trying to freeze us out? Turn it on." Matty gestures to the gas logs behind me. I twist around and light them, and before long, he's entertaining the group with stories about how he got started with his blog. Matty loves an audience.

"Can you tell me where to find lime green snow bibs?" Tom Glass, the newest member of the ski team, asks him when he pauses.

"That depends. REI's are great, but if you're looking for true lime green—"

"I am. Forest or navy would be okay, I guess, if it's all I can get." A look passes between them, and I hide a smile for Matty. He hasn't had a boyfriend since sophomore year when Jason Gonzales moved to Talkeetna to help out with his dad's boat tour business.

The mood has definitely lightened, and I'm quiet for once, just enjoying the conversations and sitting next to Katie. After a moment she prods my knee with her elbow and says low enough so that only I can hear, "I'm not sure if I'm in love with you or your whole family."

Everything else fades into the background. My face flushes and my heart skips a beat. "What's that now?"

When she turns her head to look at me, the fire dances in her eyes. "This, Virginia. Your mom, your dad, your friends. This is what I always imagined having a real family would look like."

My mouth is so dry I can hardly speak. "I love you, Katie."

The corners of her lips lift, creasing her dimples. "I know. Or at least I think I know. I was hoping."

Of course I want to kiss her. I want to fold her in my arms and never let her go. With a house full of people watching, I hold out my hand between us, and she lays hers on top of it. Then slowly, ever so slowly, her fingers slip between mine, and she squeezes. It's different from when we went to the movies and when we searched the woods. More intense. The warmth begins in my fingers and extends up my arm and into my face and chest.

It's her. Katie McRanes. The girl I've loved since seventh grade. She stares into my eyes, and I know she feels the same.

Tally catches my eye and puckers her lips in an air kiss, before shifting her gaze back to Matty. I don't think Katie sees her. All I can think is that all this time I never stopped caring about Katie.

When Dad comes back with Pete, Camila, and several buckets of KFC fried chicken, my friends and I find our way into the kitchen. I help Mom dish out chicken noodle soup into plastic mugs and bowls and set a big empty plate for the chicken bones in the center of the island.

"You make the best soup, Mrs. Eaton," Matty says happily, slurping directly from a mug.

"You young charmer." Mom pats his back, and then leaves us to join Dad and the ski team in the living room.

I sit as close to Katie as I can get.

"So," says Matty after a few minutes which we spend sucking down soup and noisily chewing chicken. "I don't want to be crass—"

"Why start now?" says Tally.

"But I don't suppose anybody's still up for Misconceptions?"

"What exactly is that?" Katie asks.

Yoon-hi tosses a bone at the platter. "It's a drag show. And yes, I'm in. I think we deserve it after what we've been through. Nine o'clock, you said?"

"I should have been there an hour ago, so I need to leave right away. Got to go do my makeup. You guys can take a few minutes. Finish dinner and meet me there. I really hope you'll come." Matty directs his piercing blue eyes at Katie who looks a little dazed.

"He's really good," Tally adds, which I guess means she's already seen him perform. Why am I the last one to know of my best friend's secret life? I get that I've been distracted the last few weeks, but I still find the thought unsettling.

We drop our plates and mugs in the kitchen sink, throw the chicken bones back in the empty bucket and pile into Tally's ancient Land Rover that she inherited from an older sister who's away at college. Fat snowflakes splatter the windshield. The gravel constantly tossed on roads to keep them from getting slick crunches under her car's nearly bald tires. The black sky sparkles with diamond stars, and as Katie and I sit holding hands in the back, I recall a similar night in eighth grade when popsicle colors melted overhead.

There's so much we need to discuss privately, but with Tally and Yoon-hi chattering away in the front seat, it will have to wait. For now, I'm content to push all other thoughts aside, snuggle with my girl, and hope the night lasts forever.

CHAPTER THIRTY-TWO

KATIE

Monday, December 16, 9:30 p.m.

Over and over I swallow a dry lump in my throat. There's a guy sitting in the corner who's a dead ringer for Rocky in a few years. This place is not at all what I expected. It's gross and seedy and reminds me of Tapa's Tavern, my father's favorite Bellingham hangout.

"Get ready for the time of your life, Katie," Tally told me cheerfully, pulling the car into a littered downtown parking lot a moment ago.

Down the hill, the harbor lights shine like a garish carnival bracelet. In front of us sits a squat, gray building with a picture of a long-haired, busty girl above the door, the kind you see on a long hauler's mud flaps. A fat man in a cheap blond wig waves us in when Tally says we've come to see Whitney Houston. The place is deserted, except for a couple in drag at a nearby table and Rocky's older lookalike in the corner.

"Don't be nervous. Try to have some fun," Virginia whispers in my ear.

"I'm not nervous." I can hear the tremor in my voice.

Our table is a few feet from the stage, and we listen to a sad, old queen tell the history of Alaska's Gold Rush, working it around to encouraging the audience to be generous with tips. Ten percent of this week's proceeds will benefit an animal rescue operation, which is the only good thing about this place. I don't get the appeal. The room reeks of alcohol and urine.

What am I doing here? I barely know these people at my table. I'm a junior in high school. I should be home studying for my finals.

"Katie, we don't have to stay," Virginia whispers, catching my sour expression.

"I haven't broken up with Rocky," I blurt.

She tilts her chin and stares at me. "I guess I knew that. I sort of assumed you would when you got a chance."

"I'm just not sure this sort of life is for me."

"Oh." Hurt lays bare across her face. "Oh. You liked me in middle school, and now that you're all grown up you realize our feelings for each other aren't natural? Like this place?" She gestures to the homely queens sitting in front of us. One of them is crying while the other glances up indifferently, then goes back to scrolling through her phone.

"It's not that." How can I explain how lost I suddenly feel? "Can we talk about this later?" I say.

"Yup. No problem." She swallows and turns back to the stage, like she's a million miles away from me.

I fold my hands in my lap. My life is changing by the second. It's one thing to sit in her comfortable house surrounded by the people who love and care for her. Another to be downtown with people my asshole father would just as soon as spit on. You'd think that would make me like them more, but I'm so confused.

"Shh," Tally says, though no one's talking. "Here comes Matty."

The overhead lights dim and the stage ones brighten. A short drum roll precedes Matty's entrance. He's dressed in a shimmering blue gown with short heels, elbow-length white gloves, and a Jackie O pillbox hat. With extra padding, he cuts a broad, hourglass figure. It's not an outfit I would have pictured Whitney Houston wearing, but he slays it.

The music swells to Houston's signature song, "I Will Always Love You," by Dolly Parton, and Matty begins with his eyes closed, then slowly opens them, making eye contact one-by-one with every single person in the audience.

I forget my insecurities for the next few minutes. I'm spellbound by the song because it makes me think of Virginia. When he finishes and the music fades away, I wish I'd never shown her my doubts. The thing is, I'm not sure who I am. What world do I belong to? Rocky's where I can hide? Or this, where I feel exposed but so alive?

I glance at Virginia and see tears glistening in her eyes. I'm furious with myself because I caused them. Is it too late to take back everything I said?

After the applause dies down, Matty clumps noisily down the stage steps and joins our table, ordering ten-dollar Coca Colas for everyone from the guy in the cheap blond wig.

"Well?" He looks at me. "Fab, or what?"

"Marvelous. Incredible. You're her." I mean every word, but Virginia offers me a stilted smile as if she thinks I'm lying.

He grins. "I know. Right? Marisol would have ruined it for me. Such a bitch. Ding dong, the witch is dead."

It takes me a second to catch up. "The Munchkins?"

"Lilly's shirt," Virginia mutters.

Right. The one she was wearing Saturday morning in the film club stairwell.

"I saw online that someone at school is selling them. Yellow's not my color. When I die, please remember me fondly and bury me in this." Matty indicates his gown by running his fingers sensually down his breasts to his waist. "By the way, how's the investigation going?"

We get our Cokes. Virginia sips, averting her gaze from me. "It took me forever to figure out one person must have taken that crazy pic. And another, likely Sonya, downloaded it for the DT flyer. Now I suspect someone else entirely must have uploaded it. Is there any way you know of to get information about the camera?"

He shrugs, fingering a couple of loose sequins at his breast. "Easy if you work for Instagram. Every DSLR records EXIF data that includes shutter speed, aperture, date, time, and the camera's serial number. Instagram and other social media sites strip the data from their sites to keep it out of the hands of pervs. They retain it for their own nefarious means."

"Nefarious?" I say.

"Tracking users for advertising purposes."

"DSLR?" says Virginia.

"Digital single-lens reflective. Expensive cams."

"EXIF?" says Tally.

"Exchangeable image file format." Matty finishes off his Coke and settles back, looking smug.

Yoon-hi rolls her eyes. "EXIF or whatever aside, wouldn't there be some other way to trace it? Oh, that's interesting." She's taken out her phone. "The photo of Virginia and Marisol isn't there anymore."

"The school probably asked Instagram to delete it," I murmur.

"Well, regardless, the photo's probably on the camera's SIM card, right?"

"SD," says Matty.

"What?"

"SIM cards go in phones. SD cards go in cameras."

Yoon-hi gives him the finger. "Is that relevant?"

"Does everybody know the figure in the pic is me?" Virginia sighs.

Matty's smugness turns to guilt. "Sorry. You never told me to keep it a secret."

She glances at Tally. "You know, too?"

Tally spreads her hands. "It's all over school now. Besides, we're friends, Virginia. All of us. Is it right to keep secrets from each other? Look, I hate to be the dumb one, but am I the only one not following this whole picture thing? What does it matter if Sonya did or didn't take the photo? We pretty much know she's guilty since she ran away."

Virginia's eyeballs pop. "We *don't* know that. And guilty of what? We only know she put up the notices slamming David Teal. I've been assuming that the photographer killed Marisol, then posted it as if to blame Marisol for her own death. What did the comment say?"

"'What are you up to, Marisol?'," I say.

Virginia continues like I haven't spoken. "It doesn't make sense. If the photographer snapped the pic, then argued with Marisol and pushed her after I left, there's no way he or she would post it because it would lead right back to him or her."

I'm following Virginia's logic now. Tally nods, indicating she is, too. "Okay. I get it. You mean someone else must have come across it later and wanted to…what? Make everyone think Marisol was having some sort of illicit meeting with David? Or you? OMG, now I'm lost again."

Me, too. The music starts, and a youngish performer wearing a high pony steps on stage to one of Ariana Grande's hits. Matty leans forward and says something about Sonya, but I can't hear him.

Virginia points to her ear, indicating she can't either, and Yoon-hi says she has to get home and study for finals. I guess we're done here anyway.

We leave Matty and head out to Tally's car. It roars to life, sending up a cloud of pale gray smoke. "Katie," Tally says, "do you need to be dropped off somewhere?"

I glance over at Virginia's clear, bright face in the back seat beside me. My car is still at North. I'm hoping she'll offer again to take me to it, but she doesn't say a thing.

I want to cry. "Just drop me back at school," I say.

CHAPTER THIRTY-THREE

VIRGINIA

Monday, December 16, 10:45 p.m.

My plan is to tiptoe, quiet as a mouse, inside the house because I didn't tell Mom and Dad where I was going. Not because they'd object to Matty's new career; they're not like that. And I figure as long as he isn't serving alcohol what he's doing probably isn't illegal. It was already late, however, when I left, and I'm going to be up even later finishing my civics assignment.

The house is dark when I slip my key inside the lock and twist the knob. The ticking of my great grandma's cuckoo clock in the hall sounds weirdly loud.

"Ten bucks and they'll never know you're such a sneak," a voice speaks from the living room.

"Hush." I slip my boots off in the hall. "Are you alone? Where's Camila?"

"She just left. Don't you know better than to follow one question with a second until the first one's answered? You'll never be a good detective that way."

"I'm going to be a veterinarian."

"Lie. You can't stand the sight of blood." Pete is stretched out on the couch, his slippered feet resting on an orange throw pillow. His crutches lay on the floor in front of the coffee table, and his face looks pale and sweaty. Typical Pete, he's pushing himself too hard, trying to get back on his feet faster than the doctor recommended.

I take in a wad of crumpled tissues between two half-empty beer bottles. "Jeez, Pete. Have you been crying? And should you be drinking if you're on medication?" That one was on purpose.

"No, *Mom*. Camila's having a hard time dealing with her sister's death."

"But she didn't even like her." I push his feet off the couch so I can sit on the other end of it. He winces, shifting them gingerly to the coffee table.

"Did anyone ever tell you you'd make a terrible nurse? And just because they fought doesn't mean Camila didn't love Marisol. Emotions can be complicated, little brother."

"Will you please, pretty please, stop that 'little brother' shit?" I beg.

"Sorry." With a grunt, he leans forward and wraps his fingers around the closest bottle. Takes a halfhearted swig. My brother has never been more than a social drinker. In high school, he'd take his own beer bottles, filled with water, to parties. "I prefer watching everyone else make fools of themselves," he used to tell me.

"Are we friends, little—Virginia?"

The question takes me by surprise. "Sure. I guess."

"Am I a good brother to you?"

"More or less."

He sighs. "I'm serious. 'Cause I want to be. I want to be a good person."

"You are." I cuff his shoulder with my fist. "What's going on? Let me have that." I take the bottle and set it out of his reach on the table. "Is this about Camila and Marisol?"

The cuckoo chirps as I wait for him to answer.

"Marisol didn't have friends. When she was little, her mother used to make these playdates for her, but she didn't know how to play or be with others. She'd throw awful tantrums if she didn't get her way."

"Camila told you this?"

He nods.

"And now she feels guilty because she thinks she should have been a better sister?"

"It's crazy, right? I want to help. People are who they are. Even kids. But Marisol, she was always different."

I don't know how to answer that. He's right, of course. You can be one person in one circumstance, someone else with other people. Marisol had a way of pissing people off. She'd bully them into getting what she wanted, and she always seemed so angry. But there was no denying how hard she worked at school. Or how she elevated North's journalism program. Other kids, especially younger ones, looked up to her.

"You're a good brother," I tell Pete.

"Am I?"

"Without a doubt. Camila's lucky to have you."

"Katie's lucky to have you. You're back together now?"

"Not quite," I mutter, recalling the expression on her face when she told me she was still dating Rocky. How could I have been so stupid to fall for that crap about loving my family when we came back from the park? And holding my hand at the movies, what was that all about? Evidently, it's Mom and Dad she cares about, not me.

"I'm not worried about either one of you. You'll figure it out." Pete slaps my knee. "So, don't you have finals this week, or are you done with that?"

I shake my head and groan. "I took my Spanish final early, so I've got only one exam on Wednesday. But four, back to back, on Thursday. And I have to finish my Civil War paper tonight, or else." I draw a finger across my throat. "Which reminds me, Mrs. Hicks said to tell you she misses you. She thinks I should apply for NHS so I can be just like you."

"You could do worse. Here, slide on over this way and let me rub your head for luck." He tries to wrap an arm around my neck, but I scoot away, managing to evade him. "Sure I can't call you 'little brother' anymore?" he says as I push myself off the couch and trudge off toward my bedroom.

"Jackass," I hiss back. It's too dark to really see each other, but I figure he's probably smiling just as I am.

* * *

"David Teal has officially withdrawn from North," Katie announces the next morning.

I fight back a surge of guilt. "Disappointing, but not surprising. How do you know?"

"I overheard the front office staff talking about it. They think he's gone to live with his father in Utqiagvik."

"Dear god, that would be awful," I reply. David needs to stay away from his father. Mom said her cop friends had told her he was couch surfing at his uncle's apartment before all this happened. I hope he hasn't left the city.

Katie was waiting for me at my locker when I got to school. The dark circles under her eyes suggest she probably got about as much sleep as I did. *Emotions can be complicated*, I keep telling myself, trying to ignore resentment creeping like icicles around the edges of my brain. Maybe I just need to give her more time. Although basically last night when I told her I loved her she said she knew, and then later went on to tell me she's still dating Rocky. And her expression, when she walked into Misconceptions—it was like a hare that's suddenly wandered into the middle of a wolf den. Is she scared? And if so, of what? I have to wonder if she's afraid of letting go of a safer, more "normal" life with Rocky, or if she really cares for him.

"We should make an investigation board," she goes on as I open my locker and grab a couple of books. "A list of suspects and where they were at the time of Marisol's death. Also, check the cameras in the video lab and journalism room. See if we can find out which ones were used last Tuesday afternoon."

It's a good idea, but all I say is a noncommittal, "Okay," before a poster of Sonya down the hall catches my eye. "How's Rocky doing?" I look back in time to see Katie's jaw tense.

"What do you mean?" She draws back warily.

What the hell do you think I mean? "Just that his sister is missing. Any word on her mother or where they might be?" I make my voice sound innocent, but she has to know there's more to the question.

"Not that I know of." She pauses and shifts from one foot to the other. "Virginia, about last night—"

The bell rings, cutting her off.

"Gotta go." I slam my locker door. "Talk later." I head off to civics to turn in my notecards, the ones I worked on most of the night. Is she reconsidering what she said? And if so, do I even care?

I recognize that I'm being petty now. I'd like to blame it on lack of sleep and brain fog. But I know well enough I can sometimes be a jerk.

CHAPTER THIRTY-FOUR

KATIE

Tuesday, December 17, 7:30 a.m.

Well, that didn't go the way I wanted. Virginia has every right to be angry. I've given a lot of thought to what I said at Misconceptions, and I recognize that yeah, we're young, and places like that are foreign and scary, but I was up most of the night thinking about it. When I got up this morning, I came to the realization that I need to give our relationship a chance. Because just being in Virginia's presence makes me happy. Better than I ever felt in Bellingham.

I shuffle like a zombie to my first hour, listening to a lecture on the so-called beauty of math equations and halfway fall asleep during a final review. When my teacher steps into the hall, I slip my phone out and text Virginia. *Re: cameras. I'll talk to Cooper. You talk to Ivy.*

No answer.

I try again during second period. *Check plastic cart in back of VL. Think I saw a sign out sheet.*

By the end of third period, I'm feeling fairly desperate. *Cooper says no cameras used Tuesday.*

Finally, right before lunch, she answers. *Ivy out sick. VL locked. Class meeting in library.*

Despite the delay, I'm weak with relief. *What's for lunch?*

There's a very long pause, then, *Come find out.*

At least she hasn't written me off completely. I haven't talked to Rocky since yesterday when he told me about the search party for his sister. Between finishing my civics paper, working on my last big art project, and dealing with my messed-up thoughts, I looked up Sonya's biological mother on the Internet. I remembered Rocky saying her last name was Henry, but it took a while to find her. Luckily, Sonya's Facebook page is public. And after scrolling through numerous posts about injustices done to Natives and references from a site called "Cultural Survival," I learned her mother's first name is Iga.

A picture of a woman taken next to the rocket ship in Valley of the Moon Park revealed a round, brown face, gray hair at the temples and frizzy braids reaching halfway down her back. "Rode hard and put away wet," Dad would have said in his typically insensitive way.

I opened another tab and looked her up in the Alaska Criminal Justice database. Iga Henry, age thirty-seven—which sounded about right—has served time for assault, petty theft, misdemeanor drug possession, and vagrancy. Last address, unknown.

Going back to Sonya's Facebook page, I then discovered pictures of Sonya with a girl I could only guess was Ahna Teal. I looked her up in last year's yearbook, and sure enough. One Facebook picture had the two licking ice cream cones in identical boilersuits and matching trippy floral Vans at one of the Anchorage Runfests. Another showed them mugging next to a stuffed grizzly outside one of the downtown tourist shops. A third revealed them swinging on a jungle gym at Valley of the Moon Park. "My bestie," Sonya had written under a photo of Ahna posted last spring. Ahna had styled her straight, black hair to look like Sonya's distinctive side braid. The two look enough alike to almost pass as sisters. The last post regarding Ahna was dated in May, had no picture, and said simply, "You took her away, DT. I'll never forgive you."

Unfair, I thought, as David was only trying to save his sister from their father. I did a search for Ahna, but could find no social media presence for her. David, either.

Was I getting off track? Surely, Sonya's gone somewhere to be with her mother. And what could she possibly have had against Marisol? Which made me think to check Marisol's Instagram account. She's been tagged in new posts from a garbled handle. One with cannabis leaves and the comment: "Good buds stick together." Is someone implying she was a stoner?

Schadenfreude, a German word I'd learned in a class in Bellingham, meaning enjoyment obtained from others' troubles, had popped into my head. No doubt Marisol made a lot of enemies. An investigation board with a list of potential suspects seemed like a good idea and an even better way to get Virginia to talk to me again. Can I still salvage our relationship?

I half-assed my civics project, then spent nearly an hour on my art final. The class is my favorite. Our final project is to design a functional piece of art with stuff lying around our houses. One kid is creating a wood steampunk box to hold a toaster. Someone else is trying to make a floor lamp double as a table. During therapy, my counselor introduced me to the art of origami. As cheesy as it sounds, I had something in mind to do with that, but not your typical cootie catcher or crane. I needed to do something different, something no one else in class would come up with.

Finally, I spent another thirty minutes thinking about Virginia again, before falling asleep fully clothed. I'm only half-awake now, with another idea percolating in my head.

"Katie. Please tell me that's not your phone and you're not actually texting in class," Mrs. Pugh says, sneaking up behind me and eyeing what is obviously my cell phone in my lap. When she's not actively teaching, she usually sits at her desk so I'd thought I could safely get away with it.

If I were Virginia, I'd look her in the eye and say: It's not my phone, and I'm not texting. Instead, I mutter, "Sorry."

"Well, then. Let me have it. You can come and get it from me after school."

"Are you giving me a detention?" *Please, don't.* I shut it off and hand it over. Learned the importance of that the hard way. Won't make that mistake again.

"Do you want a detention?" Mrs. Pugh gives me one of her sad, curious looks.

"Um. No."

"All right, then. Just pick it up after school."

The bell rings, signaling lunchtime, and Zach Pratt moves forward from his seat two rows behind me. "Come by after school and we'll talk ad nauseam about why you shouldn't have your phone out." He flashes his ugly, brown teeth.

"Really?"

"Count on it. She's a teacher. She loves to hear herself talk."

There's nothing I can do about it now. I grab my backpack and hurry out. I want to get to the cafeteria and meet Virginia before she joins the others.

The halls seem more crowded than usual, and as I run/walk and sidestep groups of students, I catch snatches of their conversations.

"I heard her mother's a criminal."

"Rocky's putting together another search party."

"DT's in the wind."

"Did you get a load of all that crap in his locker?"

"Yeah, that one girl—"

Apparently, they have nothing better to do than gossip. Virginia and I reach the cafeteria from opposite directions at the same time.

"Are you out of breath?" she asks, pausing at the entrance. Students stream past us heading for the à la carte and pizza lines. Her tone is more upbeat than last night, but her eyes still have a dead look like she's disappointed I'm not the person she thought I was.

Maybe I can change that. I inhale a breath and straighten my spine. "A little. I had a thought I want to share." She waits, narrowing her eyes. "Why don't you come over for dinner tonight, and I'll tell you."

"Your house?"

"My apartment. Mom doesn't cook much anymore, so Denise and I mostly do it. It's my turn, and I promise not to poison you. I'll fix something—burgers, or something else— and then we can make our investigation board and study for finals." I'm still holding my breath and talking way too fast.

"A study group, and you cook," she says. Her eyes are practically slits.

Does it sound that strange? Probably shouldn't have mentioned poison. "Right."

"Will your mother be okay with it?"

Three years ago the answer would have been, "No way." Friends never came to my house. It was embarrassing, never being able to initiate or reciprocate an invitation. Visitors made my mother nervous, although my father usually didn't mind. It gave him a chance to show off his big-game trophies. Like the lion skin on the wall from an African safari or the photo of him crouched next to a dead zebra—him holding the zebra's head beside his shoulder like they were friends who planned to go out for a beer after. Ugh. Mom threw all that stuff away as soon as she got out of the hospital.

"Mom's changed," I reply. A little anyway.

"Okay, well sure then. Um, should I bring something, like dessert?"

"Just yourself." Listen to us, sounding like two adults. I guess the invitation did seem pretty odd, but I'm glad I made it.

We start to move on into the cafeteria. The disembodied voice of an intercom announcement floats through the hall. "Will Virginia Eaton and Katie McRanes please report to the main office? Virginia Eaton and Katie McRanes, come to the main office."

Virginia glances over. "What the hell?"

I'm as stunned as she is. We swivel back and do as we are told.

CHAPTER THIRTY-FIVE

VIRGINIA

Tuesday, December 17, 12:00 p.m.

Mrs. Foster has pulled two straight-back chairs from the conference table to face her desk, inquisition style. Officers Hess and Dietrich stand behind her with their backs to the window. Dietrich leans against the radiator.

"Have a seat, girls." She sits down herself, resting her forearms on the shiny faux-wood surface in front of her. A can of well-sharpened pencils, points up, occupies a corner next to a Windows laptop, a dusty African violet in a pink and blue ceramic pot right behind it. She's an attractive woman with short gray hair and tiny, red bow earrings.

"I'm sorry to interrupt your lunch, and I'll do my best to be brief," she says. "First, please understand that you're not in any trouble at this point, but if you'd like to call your parents and have them join us, you're welcome to do so."

At this point? I glance at Katie. Her lower lip quivers. "What's this about?" I ask, sitting forward aggressively in my chair to let her know I don't intend to let her or Officers Hess and Dietrich intimidate me.

"Yes, well. Like I said, you're not in trouble." Mrs. Foster's hands fidget ever so slightly. I can almost see her give herself a mental shake. "I received an anonymous tip that you two put excrement in another student's locker."

WTF? "You mean David's locker?" I frown. "I can assure you that we didn't. How did you receive this tip and when?" I have to remind myself of Pete's advice to ask one question at a time. But seriously? Mrs. Foster knows me. She knows my family. She was crazy about my brother like every other adult at North.

"In the student confidential box. I check it every day before lunch. Officer Hess"—she glances over her right shoulder at him—"suggested I call you in right away."

Hess and I glare at one another. Dietrich, a thin man with sharp brown eyes and a droopy moustache, folds his hands in front of him and eyes me neutrally.

The confidential box she's talking about sits on a corner of the counter in the main office as a sort of invitation to anyone who wants to report bullying. Mrs. Foster instituted it two years ago when a freshman boy committed suicide after being tormented online. Periodically, she reminds everyone of its presence.

"You've got a surveillance camera in the office," I say. "Can't you look and find out who left the tip?"

She frowns. "I'm afraid you're missing the point, Virginia. I wouldn't, even if I could. It's anonymous for a reason."

"Well, how about the hall then? The footage from that?"

"It was offline for a bit." She looks away.

How convenient, I think.

Hess sucks in his lips, and for a second his mouth disappears. "You didn't smear feces inside David Teal's locker?" he says, giving me a hard, unfriendly frown.

Oh, come on. "I already said I didn't."

"And you, Miss McRanes?"

Katie swallows, but her voice is clear enough. "I didn't, either."

Dietrich readjusts his pose against the radiator, crossing his feet at the ankles. "Have you been to Mr. Teal's locker?"

"Yes," I say.

"Why?"

"To let him know we don't believe he killed Marisol Cowsill." *And to confess it's me in the Insta pic.*

They take a couple of seconds to digest this. Dietrich's next question surprises me. "Did either of you take Sonya Dare's cell phone and drop it in Valley of the Moon Park?"

"What?" we both say at once.

I shake my head. "Why would you think that?" No surprise, they don't answer. The tips of my ears grow hot. "Who's telling you this?"

"We're not at liberty to say," Hess answers condescendingly, giving his werewolf whiskers a good scratching.

"But didn't you just say it was an anonymous tip found inside the confidential box?" Thinking I've boxed them into a corner, I'm having a TV detective's aha moment, although Dietrich wearily shakes his head.

"I've heard enough. I'm not comfortable with this," Mrs. Foster interrupts. "Please, girls. Go eat your lunches and then head back to class." Her fingers pat the desk nervously like a blind woman searching for her keys.

Katie and I get up and walk out. I'm incensed. When we pass the counter with the cardboard box, I open my mouth to call Hess a jerk, but stop when Katie puts a finger to her lips and points to the door.

"What an ass! Please. 'We're not at liberty to say.' How lame is that?" I mock once we're outside the office. The bell rings. Katie doesn't move, just stares absently down the hall as kids emerge en masse from the cafeteria.

"You know what this means," she says quietly.

Do I ever. "That Marisol's killer is trying to deflect attention to us."

Her gaze flits away as Rocky steps around the corner. "More than that. The cops don't believe Sonya is with her mother."

That floors me. Where then, is Sonya Dare?

CHAPTER THIRTY-SIX

VIRGINIA

Tuesday, December 17, 6:00 p.m.

I've spent most of the afternoon after school fake-studying and trying not to make too much of Katie's invitation. I figure it's a gesture of friendship, not that big a deal.

Shortly before six, I brush my hair, secure it with a blue elastic hair tie, and select one of the few semi-fancy tops I own, a peach boho with dainty, faux-pearl buttons. The only other time I wore it was to my last end-of-the-year cross-country ski team banquet. Mrs. Hicks was right about the reason I quit. Still, I don't miss it. I like to ski, but I never cared much for the every-day practice routine.

I stare at myself in the full-length mirror on the back of my bedroom door, then grab a tissue and wipe off most of the makeup I just put on. Better. Got to be who I am. At a quarter after, I grab my books and laptop and get ready to head out. In the back of my mind, I'm still thinking about Sonya. Where is she if she isn't with her mother? I can't imagine a kid her age holed up in a motel or camping by herself in the woods in this kind of weather. Maybe she has friends the Dares don't know about. I hope Hess and Dietrich are finally taking her disappearance seriously.

Pete and Camila are in the living room with their backs to me on the couch when I walk out, her head resting on his shoulder. I turn and make my way down the hall to Reggie's room so as not to disturb them, and find him engrossed in a game of Minecraft. The kid loves computers, and this game is his favorite. Green and brown pixels appear, disappear, and move about the screen.

"Hey, Reg. Tell Mom I won't be home for dinner. I'm going to Katie's."

He doesn't look up.

"Reggie," I say louder. "Did you hear me?"

"What?"

"Heading to Katie's. Tell Steve I said hi."

Reggie blows a breath that lifts his shaggy bangs, his eyes not leaving the screen. "Virginia. Steve is a fictional character just like Jason and Alex. Herobrine is a noncorporeal entity—"

"Leaving now."

"Bye." He stays focused on his game.

I'll text Mom later in case he forgets. It's six thirty when I arrive at Katie's new address, a rectangular building with a twin beside it, each housing a couple of dozen units. The second floor hall smells of boiled potatoes and dirty socks. I can hear canned laughter from a TV coming from another apartment and somebody walking on the floor above. This place is a far cry from the well-kept two-story the McRanes lived in three years ago, but I can't imagine either Katie or her mother miss it.

I knock, and my heart nearly stops at the sight of a woman with stringy brown hair who opens the door. She's got a black eye patch and the right side of her face sags like it doesn't know the left is smiling.

"I'm here to see Katie," I manage to stammer while simultaneously arranging my own face into a less-shocked expression.

"Welcome, Virginia. Come on in. It's good to see you again." Mrs. McRanes sounds like she's had a stroke. The bullet from her husband's gun shattered her cheekbone and took out her eye, I remember reading.

Katie and another woman I recognize as their former next-door neighbor, Dr. Taylor, come up behind her. And before I know it, I'm being ushered into the saddest-looking living room I've ever seen.

Except it's not.

It definitely needs new carpet and drapes that don't look like they've been stolen from a haunted house, but there's a live Christmas tree in one corner, a speckled pink poinsettia on a makeshift plywood coffee table in front of a tattered couch, and a Santa dish filled with red and green wrapped Hershey's Kisses on the windowsill. A dark-skinned boy with straight brown hair crouches under the lighted tree, surrounded by colorful Lego blocks. He waves a tiny fist.

"Glad you could come. Katie's fixing halibut burgers and peach cobbler. We're having iced tea, but we can probably scare you up a Coke." I tune in to Dr. Taylor's offer to get me a drink.

"Iced tea is fine, or whatever is easy," I reply, glancing covertly at a piece of colorful canvas art on the wall. Acrylic, like a pour.

The McRanes liked nice things. Or at least Katie's father did. Genuine leather furniture, original art, granite countertops and matching stainless steel appliances. This apartment isn't nice. It's old and smelly and decorated in a kitschy style that might have been popular thirty years ago. And yet it's homey, with a happy lived-in feel.

Mrs. McRanes lowers herself stiffly to a wood chair at a small, square dining table in the kitchen, and I find myself sitting beside her, talking about my classes, telling her all about Pete's accident, and speculating about which members of the cross-country team have any hope of making it onto the U.S. Ski Team. She isn't the woman I remember. Despite facial injuries that make it hard to understand her, Katie's mom is joyful.

"Stop quizzing the poor girl and let her eat," Dr. Taylor fusses when everyone else is seated at the table with heaping plates of halibut burgers and sweet potato fries in front of us. Josh, Dr. Taylor's son, sits in a high chair beside his mom, his eyes darting at each of us and occasionally banging his spoon and talking randomly about his Lego trucks.

"Oh, Katie, this is delicious," Mrs. McRanes exclaims around a bite of fish that dribbles out of the right side of her mouth.

Dr. Taylor leans over to wipe it with her napkin, but Katie's mom gently pushes her hand away. "I can do it. They think I'm helpless," she tells me. "But how else am I going to get back my fine motor skills if someone else takes care of me? I can cook, too. I make a mean vegetarian lasagna with edamame noodles."

"No, you don't," Katie and Dr. Taylor say together. They all laugh, and Josh giggles, then demonstrates how he can hold a sticky fry between each of his chubby fingers.

"I used to love your smoked salmon on saltines," I say shyly.

Mrs. McRanes gives me a lopsided grin. "That's so nice of you to say. Really?"

"Really." I smile.

Katie keeps eyeing me nervously. I've barely finished eating when she stands, scoops up our plates, and stacks them in the sink.

"I'll take care of those, honey. You girls go on and study," Dr. Taylor says, coming up behind her and turning on the water.

"Thanks."

"Don't forget to massage your hand," Katie's mom calls after her as we head back through a narrow hall to Katie's bedroom.

She closes the door on a tiny room with a single bed, a nightstand made of books, and a closet without a door.

"Your hand?" I say.

"It's nothing, an old injury long healed. Mom worries about nothing."

"Show me." I frown.

"Later. I need to get something off my chest."

"Okay."

She gestures to the bed. "Will you sit?" I do, as she stands in front of me, licking her lips uncertainly and swaying like she's about to fall. "Last night I had a moment. Doubt, I guess I'd call it. I wish I could explain, but I'm not sure how."

"Try." I swallow, telling myself not to get my hopes up.

"There was a guy at Misconceptions who looked like Rocky, and I don't know, it's been years since you and I were together, and I just thought what am I doing here? We're so young. Even younger then, and so immature. What I'm trying to say is that I'm over whatever hit me last night. So, will you give me a chance? I mean, another one? Will you give *us* a chance? Maybe?"

CHAPTER THIRTY-SEVEN

KATIE

Tuesday, December 17, 8:15 p.m.

I'm blowing it. Virginia's expression is flat, telling me there won't be a second chance. Except she's here. It's got to mean something, that she showed up here at all.

I try to explain how I felt last night and how sorry I am for the horrible stuff I said last week in the parking lot at school. I've been yammering away for several minutes, and I'm running out of words. "I wish I had your courage," I say at last.

"What are you talking about?" Virginia tilts her head.

"Your nerve. Your confidence. Your willingness to be who you are. Have you ever had doubts? Reservations? Any uncertainty ever?" If she has, I've never seen it.

She gets up and wanders to my open closet. "Of course. Are you kidding? I'm not brave. I let David take the rap for the photo. I'm the reason he withdrew from North. Shit. Katie, come on. What happened to your hand?"

I hold it out. My shaking hand. My little finger slightly bent from the break. "My father threw a phone."

"The night he shot your mother?"

"He wasn't aiming for me. It just happened."

"Broken?" She doesn't wait for me to explain that Mom's concern is how she expresses her affection for me. It's the only way she knows how. "Katie." Virginia's eyes go soft. "None of it *just happened*. You know that, don't you? Your father was a psychopath who couldn't accept that his wife was gay. He was abusive and controlling. He—that motherfucker—he should have gone to jail a long time ago."

There she is, the girl who stands up for an underdog but doesn't let anyone get away with bullshit, even herself. "I know, Virginia. I *do* know. I want to show you something."

Before I let the moment get away from me, I reach under the bed and hand her a shoebox, the one I've been saving for the last three years. "Open it."

Inside, are a dozen letters addressed to her. My heart pounds. My head buzzes. Jolts like electric sparks shoot up my arms as she picks up a folded sheet of paper. "Start with this one." I motion to a wrinkled slip of pink stationery, and then I lay it in her lap. It's dated three years ago today.

Dear Virginia. My heart is breaking. I just found out we're moving and I may never see you again. If you don't yet know how much I love you...

"You wrote this before you left?"

"And this one on the plane." My eyes brim, and I hand her another. *I love you more than anything. I want to be with you...*

"Katie," she says quietly. "Why didn't you send them?"

"I planned to. I was saving them. You and me, we talked nearly every night, but I thought if you started to forget me—"

"I didn't!"

"I know that now. But I'm not like you. I don't have your confidence. The morning of my parents' fight, Dad told me I could visit you. I could hardly wait, but then he saw a message meant for you and assumed it was Mom texting Denise. I...I felt so damn guilty, like if I was different, stronger, I could have prevented it. None of that matters anymore. I love you, Virginia. I've always loved you...But for a while I lost my way."

Virginia's eyes go even softer, and she melts. She sobs and blubbers, while I turn into putty with snot and tears running down my face. Between the two of us we use about a million tissues from a box on top of my nightstand.

After a while, she leans in and kisses me. Hesitating at first, and then fuller when she understands it's exactly what I want. Her lips are warm and puffy, and I can taste her salty tears. I don't want to stop. Ever. We wrap our arms around each other, and it feels just right. As if together, we can make everything okay.

"Katie," she whispers into the softness of my cheek after several minutes. "If I say I love you, too, will you please not tell me that you know?"

I hiccup a giggle and release one arm from around her to snatch another tissue and blow my nose. It gives a mighty honk. We both fall back across the bed, laughing hysterically, but still holding on to each other.

"I know," I say, and we laugh some more.

For a long time we lie together, staring at the dirty popcorn ceiling in my tiny bedroom. I talk about my mother and father, the terrible fight they had, and all the hurtful things they used to say to each other. I tell her about the origami that I started doing originally for physical therapy but more to keep my thoughts occupied as I dealt with what had happened.

She tells me she saw my mother kissing Denise the night we drove out to McHugh Creek to view the Northern Lights.

"Why didn't you say something?" I ask as she nuzzles my neck, driving me crazy with desire.

"Like what? Did you know your weirdo mom is in love with a woman? Oh, hell, did I just say that out loud?"

"You did." I giggle. "But I don't mind. She is weird." Over the course of the conversation, my shirt has inched up my back. Virginia's fingers graze back and forth across my bare stomach, and I can hardly form a coherent thought.

"But happy?"

"Very. I didn't realize how happy they both are until tonight."

"Like us?"

"We're better." I prop myself up on an elbow to blow my nose again, feeling chilled without her beautiful, warm body pressed against me. "You never did tell me what you and Marisol talked about in the stairwell."

"Marisol. Are we back to that?" Her tone unexpectedly cools.

"Not if you don't want to be."

"But do you really want to know?"

Now I'm not sure I do. We're starting to paddle into deeper water, which the back part of my brain tells me is foolish when we're happy right where we are.

"Marisol wanted to write an article to out bisexual students," Virginia says in a regretful voice.

"Christ." I snort. "Wait. You mean me?"

"You know how she was. 'I should do a story about underaged drag queens.' 'I should do a story about Alaska Natives and incest.' That kind of shit."

I rise and pace to my closet. "That's so ugly. Shit. I'm sorry she's dead, but it doesn't stop me from disliking her. So, it was 'I should do a story about Katie McRanes. First she's a lesbian, and then she's not'?"

"Something like that."

"But, Virginia, I'm not."

"You mean you're not a lesbian because you only love me?"

"No! You're talking about that summer before eighth grade, aren't you? The day she threw dog poop at me? Virginia, please don't hold that against me. I didn't know what I was talking about. I love you, yes, but I'm not denying who I am. What I am is embarrassed and ashamed because I used Rocky to hide behind and to conceal my feelings, even from myself. But I don't love him. I haven't broken up with him because how can I when his sister is missing?"

Virginia nods, but not like she totally believes it. More like she's acknowledging that I'm still trying to work through all this. It kind of pisses me off. "What aren't you saying? You think I'm gutless?" I drop my fists to my hips.

"No, I don't."

"You do. Admit it. You just don't want to say it. You don't want to hurt my feelings, and you don't want me to be upset with you."

I can imagine her thoughts. If I really love her, why can't I just admit it to everybody else?

When I'm back at the bed, she grabs my wrist and gives it a coaxing tug. "I don't want to hurt your feelings *or* make you mad at me. I want you to sit beside me and kiss me like we haven't spent the last three years apart."

How can I resist? A few minutes later, she tickles my ear with her breath, and I whisper, "I'm stronger than you know."

I am. And somehow I'm going to find a way to prove it.

CHAPTER THIRTY-EIGHT

KATIE

Tuesday, December 17, 9:15 p.m.

It's after nine when I drag a sheet of posterboard from behind my dresser and scribble *SCHADENFREUDE* in big red letters at the top.

"What's that?" Virginia says lazily, with heavy hooded eyes that make me want to kiss her all over again.

"Taking pleasure from others' misfortunes."

"Oh. Good word." She takes the marker and writes *Marisol* underneath it.

"Next we list persons of interest," I say and write, *Sonya, Matty, Lilly,* and *Zach.*

"Because they all have access to cameras and the film club stairwell?"

"Right." We're sitting on the floor with the poster propped against my bed.

Virginia studies it for a moment, then twists to her knees. "Okay if I scratch out Matty's name?"

"Because you know he's innocent?"

"Well, no. Not for a fact. But I'm virtually certain he doesn't have it in him to hurt anybody."

I like Matty, too, but he did have motive and opportunity, especially after Marisol threatened to expose his new career. "Have you asked him where he was last Tuesday?"

Virginia's sexy look gives way to a frown. "What am I supposed to do, text him? 'Hey, Matty. Quick question. By any chance did you push Marisol down the stairs? NBD. Just asking.'"

I laugh, which comes out like a snort. I've been doing that a lot lately. "I'm thirsty. You want a Coke?"

"Sure."

I get up and go into the kitchen. Mom is finishing up the dishes. She puts the skillet away and turns to glance at me. Her eye patch has slipped, revealing the angry scar that ends like a knotted shoelace just below her eyebrow. She doesn't wear it unless she goes out or we have company. "Virginia is very pretty," she says as I break open an ice tray, fill two glasses, and add a generic cola that foams to the top.

"She is." I put the bottle back in the refrigerator.

"I like her," Mom goes on. "But you don't have to be like me."

"Good to know." I go back to my bedroom and hand a glass to Virginia. "My weirdo mother says she likes you."

Virginia slaps her forehead. "I can't believe I said that. I'm sorry!"

"Don't be. Like I said, she *is* weird." But getting better all the time, I add to myself.

Virginia has her phone out. She's put another name on the list: Don Lucky.

I cock my head and squint. "That sounds made-up."

"It isn't. He Insta-streamed Marisol's service with unflattering comments. Look." She shows me her phone.

A pimply red face fills the screen. "Who's crying now?" he cracks, then turns the camera to film the audience. The auditorium is about half full with kids on their phones, including a number who appear to be dozing. Mr. Cooper is picking his nose and staring blankly out the window. "Dig on up there, Coop. You almost got it," Don cracks again.

I wince, recalling how Rocky had his hand between my legs when Mrs. Foster was speaking. I hope Virginia didn't see it.

"I'll see if I can track Don down tomorrow," she murmurs, tapping a marker against her teeth. "Let's move on to the timeline. *The Anchorage Daily News* reported Marisol's body was found around three thirty Tuesday afternoon. I came up the front hall stairs at approximately three-fifteen, just a few minutes after school let out, and dropped off a couple of books at the library. And then headed for the film club stairwell where I ran into her on the landing."

"And passed the video lab on your way." I picture the hall. "Do you remember who was in it?"

"Lilly and a couple of sophomores. I don't know their names. Mr. Ivy must have been in the green room in the back."

"Should we cross Lilly off the list?"

Virginia curls her upper lip. "I guess." She draws a line through Lilly's name on the board.

"By the way, I looked at Marisol's Instagram account last night. Have you seen these?" I tap over to my app, looking for the cannabis leaves I saw last night. "Oh, that's weird. They're gone. There were weed pictures there yesterday, but they've been removed."

Virginia scoots closer to look at my phone, our shoulders touching. "Huh. Like the pic of me and her in the stairwell. What's the handle?"

"I can't remember. Something with a bunch of random letters and numbers. Not Anon. Was Marisol a stoner?"

"God, I don't see how she had time for it. But I suppose anything is possible."

She leans back on her elbows with her knees bent and fans them absentmindedly. It's a sexy movement that makes it hard to concentrate.

I eye the list and add Fatima Mann, the volleyball co-captain who told Virginia that Marisol needed work on her hits. It's probably a stretch to think Fatima would kill Marisol, although she was on the newspaper staff with her. When I turn back, Virginia gives me a heavy-lidded gaze and winks.

"You're looking very kissable right now," I say.

"What's stopping you?"

Sometime later, we take out our books to study. We are in different sections but take most of the same classes, except for my communications and art electives and Virginia's Spanish and Honors English. We quiz each other from our notecards for a while. My second final tomorrow is civics. I go through my paper, and then close my eyes and pretend I'm making my presentation. Juniors and seniors have two finals Wednesday afternoon, four on Thursday with no breaks except our five-minute passing periods and lunch. It's a complicated schedule because every class is longer than normal. Friday is a makeup day when Dan Daily is supposed to visit. We still don't know if that's going to happen.

"You've got to see this," Virginia says, interrupting my concentration. She's staring at her laptop with two windows open side by side.

"Which?"

"Twitter first. It's a poll on how many think Sonya ran away and how many think she's dead or kidnapped. Neck and neck so far. One guy swears he saw two men burying her in the C Street snow mountain."

The man-made mountain is one of several locations where Anchorage road crews dump excess snow from streets and parking lots. The trucks have made a winding road to the top of it, like an outdoor parking garage, three stories tall. In winters when snowfall is less abundant, they bring it back and pack the downtown streets to make a more exciting show for the ceremonial start to the Iditarod sled dog race. A second-go to bring in tourists.

"That's creepy." Poor Sonya. I hope to god it isn't true. "What's the other?"

"A new Gram post. More weed. Check it out."

I crawl across the floor to read over Virginia's shoulder, seeing a leaf under a profile picture of a giraffe's head photoshopped on a human body. Long Neck 51 says, "Where am I going to score now, Mar?" Three followers have liked the post.

"Is this how you study?" I ask Virginia.

She leans into me. "I'm having trouble focusing. Did you turn in your civics notecards?"

"This morning. My presentation is tomorrow afternoon."

"Mine is Thursday. My last final. Thanks so much, Mrs. Hicks." She wrinkles her nose into a scowl. "Do you know how boring it's going to be listening to everybody's five-minute presentations? They'll all be exactly alike."

"Not mine. I'm going Broadway." I snap my fingers. "How does a general, a statesman, son of a slave and a politician, dropped in the middle of a border state, by providence..." Hicks gives a prize every year for the best paper. It's usually not much. Last year Marisol won a fifteen-dollar gift certificate to the Moose's Tooth, a popular pizza joint. I'm guessing Zach will win this year.

Virginia's jaw drops. "You know *Hamilton*. Have you seen it?"

"Every year."

"Seriously?"

"Of course not." I can't imagine my father attending a Broadway show. He'd call the actors gay just because they sing and dance. Virginia gazes at me sheepishly. "Maybe you and I can go sometime," I say, bumping my shoulder against hers.

She kisses me and replies, "I'd like that very much."

CHAPTER THIRTY-NINE

VIRGINIA

Wednesday, December 18, 11:15 a.m.

The problem with our investigation board is our so-called persons of interest. A lot of people didn't like Marisol, but we don't necessarily know who they are. Don Lucky, for example. I never heard of him before last night. Is he a genuine hater, or just some kid clowning around at the service because he was bored? And then there's Long Neck 51, with his giraffe-morphed face. What's his deal? *Where am I going to score now, Mar?* Is he trolling based on the weed pic Katie noticed the night before? I think back to the original Insta post: *What are you up to, Marisol?* They sound a little alike. Was Anon hinting at the same sort of thing?

There was no mention of Sonya on the news last night. Dad fears the police aren't taking her disappearance seriously. Mom says there's probably a lot of stuff going on behind the scenes that we don't know about, but even she looked upset. When I got to school this morning, I heard buzz there's going to be another search party this weekend. Will it be too late?

As soon as Mrs. Pugh sits down at her desk, I sneak my phone out and take another look at the text Katie sent an hour ago. *Still love you.* With a big red heart.

I stayed up late again thinking about her. Remembering every kiss, every tender look she gave me, the way her body felt next to mine. Will she break up with Rocky before Christmas break? I hope so, but I've decided not to press her. I took her letters home with me and read them again before I went to bed.

"I'm scared I'll never see you again. Do you love me as much as I love you?" she'd written.

More, I think. The summer between seventh and eighth grade, she came over to my house nearly every night after dinner. We talked about actresses on TV and female athletes we thought were cute. She never talked about being gay, except the time she said she wasn't a lesbian. I didn't think much of it. I knew when I was little that I liked girls. It didn't seem like a big deal.

I glance at the text again and send back: *Wouldn't mind rehearsing.* With two red hearts.

When the bell rings, Matty stands up from behind his desk, spreads his arms out, and announces, "Another one bites the dust."

Technically, finals don't start until after lunch, although first semester Spanish ended last week when our teacher left for Mexico to start her break early. Mrs. Pugh is subbing for her and wearing her usual sour expression, but when I tell her I'll see her later, she says, "Good luck on your finals, Virginia."

"You're winning her over," Matty stage-whispers.

I shoot him my best *shut up* look.

Lilly moves on by us, saying something about her civics project to the guy next to her, and I realize this is when it starts in earnest. Junior year is when things happen, when our guidance counselors will call us to their offices next semester to talk about our after-high school plans. For me, that means college.

"I got lucky, so to speak, with Donald Lucky," says Matty, picking up his open laptop from the desk. "Dude's a sophomore band geek. Plays the trumpet. They had practice after school last Tuesday, but that doesn't mean he didn't take a potty break and slip out to the stairwell."

"You broke into the school records!" I say excitedly, assuming he looked at Don's schedule.

Matty rolls his eyes, cat-eyed tipped today with midnight blue eyeliner and a row of tiny crystals just below his brows. "Get real. I'm not a magician." He shuts the laptop and slides it in his backpack when we get out in the hall.

"You made it up?" My good mood deflates. Matty's got mad skills when it comes to creating websites, but I should have known he wasn't a hacker.

"Course not. I asked my new friend, Tom Glass." I gaze at him blankly. "Ski team, your house Monday night? Lime green bibs?"

"He's a sophomore?"

"What can I say? I like 'em young." Matty wags his brows. "Anyway, I think you're barking up the wrong tree with that one. Same with the drug angle, although I did come up with a way you could find out."

"I'm listening."

"Ask your brother."

"Reggie?"

"Pete, you goof. Ask him to ask the older sis to snoop out Marisol's room. Weed baggies in the drawer, you'll know she had a problem."

"I imagine the cops have already gone through her house. But I guess I can ask Pete to find out if Camila knows anything about it." I yawn as we head to the cafeteria. The halls aren't nearly as crowded as usual. It's not uncommon for kids to skip school the morning before finals. "What do you think, just put it out there? 'Hey, Camila, did Marisol ever say yes to drugs?'"

"That's what I'd do." Matty nods.

I go through the à la carte line for the Wednesday finals hoagie special. Matty makes his way around the corner behind the main counter to the commercial-size refrigerator where students store their sack lunches that need to be kept cold. While I wait for the lunch lady to unwrap a fresh tray and stick a sandwich in the warming oven for me, I text Pete.

Bad news.
What?
Rumor mill says Marisol was using drugs.
So?
Can you ask Camila?
No.

I tap my foot semi-impatiently as the cafeteria lady, a kind-faced woman who looks too old to have to work, hands me a plate with a steaming hoagie and wishes me good luck on my finals. A second later, my phone vibrates in my pocket.

Maybe. Need to take room temp. You're a pain in the you-know-what, little brother.

Jackass. Smiley face emoji.

I put away my phone.

Katie and Yoon-hi walk in just as Matty and I take our seats. Rocky's stool across the cafeteria is empty. It probably doesn't mean anything as we still have half an hour before finals start, but I can't help wondering if he's out looking for his little sister.

"Definitely need more rehearsals," Katie murmurs, sliding in beside me. Today, she's wearing ankle-length yoga pants and a tight, long-sleeved black T-shirt with "Artistic" written across the chest. A neon orange handprint below it has the forefinger extended as if it's just finger-painted the word. Her curly dark hair shines like it's just been washed, and her gray eyes sparkle. Instantly, I feel better. Our hands find each other's under the table and our fingers lace together. Hers is warm and slightly callused.

I pick up my sandwich with my left hand and between mouthfuls of roast beef dotted with horseradish and coleslaw, I fill everybody in on what we've learned about Marisol since our chat at Misconceptions. It isn't much. Mostly speculation.

Yoon-hi shakes her head, her choppy black hair falling back in place, when she hears about Long Neck 51's post. "Probably a troll. Or somebody with a grudge."

"Did she ever approach you with an idea for an article?" Katie asks her.

"No. You?"

"Nope." Katie swallows hard, her eyes darting sideways at me. She lets go of my hand and uses both of hers to pick up a halibut burger, probably left over from last night.

"Well, I can't stand sitting here and doing nothing. Let's check the cameras in the video lab," Tally says, after a couple of minutes of silence, punctuated by conversation bursts from other tables.

"It's locked. Mr. Ivy's still out sick," Matty replies, finishing off a carton of chocolate frozen yogurt.

"So? You're enterprising. Can't you get us in?"

I glance across the table at him. In my heart, I know he had nothing to do with Marisol's death, but I still haven't asked him for an alibi. Here's his chance to prove he has nothing to hide. "Don't you have a key?" I say.

"Not officially." He wads his paper sack into a softball, then lobs it at a trash can two tables away. It bounces off the lip and drops inside. "Okay, fine." He sighs. "Let's go."

CHAPTER FORTY

KATIE

Wednesday, December 18, 12:00 p.m.

The five of us traipse upstairs and down the hall in the direction of the film club stairwell. I don't know about the others, but I feel buzzed, as if we're a team of CIA operatives on the brink of solving an international mystery.

Then again, maybe I'm mistaking my heightened state for anxiety about everything else that's going on. My first final is art where I'll present a multi-colored construction paper bird of paradise that unfolds flat into a note when you pull two tabs disguised as petals above the head. It's my version of a pop-up card. This morning I showed it to Denise who threw her arms around me and said it was the most clever thing she'd ever seen.

"Thanks," I sputtered. She clearly overstated its worth, but I was pleased by her reaction. Origami calms my nerves.

We manage to reach the video lab without incident. Matty stops at the door, pulling a handful of keys attached to a big red leather M lined with purple rhinestones from his shoulder bag.

"Should we be doing this? What if the class comes back while we're inside?" Yoon-hi squints through a window at the rows of computers. A tinge of uncertainty has crept into her normally self-confident voice. No doubt she didn't sign up for breaking and entering.

Tally glances at the Fitbit partially covering a yin and yang tattoo on her wrist. "They're at first lunch like us. Come on, we've got eighteen minutes."

Virginia cracks her knuckles uneasily. "We could wait until tomorrow and talk to Mr. Ivy."

"He wasn't that helpful the first time," I remind her.

"You're right. Of course, you're right. Okay, let's do this."

The computers in the dark look like the backs of students hunched at desks. Matty unlocks the door and flips on the lights from a switch beside the fire alarm.

"Is that a good idea?" Yoon-hi asks again. The room has been straightened since the last time I saw it. The rows are neatly aligned with chairs pushed in and keyboards stacked underneath the monitors.

"We'll look a lot less suspicious with the lights on if someone walks by and sees us," Matty replies, moving quickly toward the back of the room.

We make our way single file to the plastic cart of cameras next to the green room door. There are twelve cameras, all neatly numbered by a label maker with matching numbers on the cart. A clipboard with a sign-out sheet rests on the four-drawer metal filing cabinet beside it, a pen dangling from a piece of dirty brown string on the clip. Matty wipes his hands down the front of his khakis, the only indication he might be nervous.

"Everybody grab a camera. Turn it on and press the playback mode. We're looking for a photo taken in the stairwell. Marisol and Virginia."

I pick up a fancy Olympus and twist it back and forth in my hand. Mr. Ivy has some nice equipment. Too bad the room in back is such a wreck.

A moment later, Virginia lets out a frustrated breath. "I'm seeing what looks like hundreds of photos and videos on this camera. How many does it hold?"

Matty glances up from his camera. "On a 32-gig card, maybe a thousand? Less with video."

"Yikes." She groans. "This is going to take forever. There's got to be a faster way to do this."

Tally takes a peek at her Fitbit. "We've got fifteen minutes till the bell."

"What if we plug them into the computers? Wouldn't it be easier to view the thumbnail rows from there?" Yoon-hi suggests. She perches on the edge of Mr. Ivy's cluttered desk. He's got a desk pad calendar, two dirty coffee mugs, an assortment of papers curling around the edges, a couple of USB cables, and two monitors. There's an old-fashioned tower under his desk.

"Do we have time?" I say. Everyone else's nervousness is rubbing off on me. Searching for a single photo among twelve thousand sounds more difficult than looking for objects in a hidden treasure game.

Matty narrows his eyes and gazes for a second around the room. "I think I have a better idea. We'll work backward. Look at the Internet browsing history on the computers. See who pulled up Instagram last week."

We all turn and gawk at him. "How?" says Virginia. "Every student has a unique login and password."

"In other classes, yes. But film club students use just one so we can access one another's videos and pics. Film club film club. Watch." He sits down at the closest iMac, shakes the mouse to wake it up, then types *filmclub* into the login space and again into the bar where the password goes. A close up of Mr. Ivy appears, frowning and pointing his finger at us as if he's warning us not to mess with his stuff.

"Cute." Virginia eyes the desktop with a smile.

She must be joking. Mr. Ivy is scary with his bristly little Hitler moustache and bushy eyebrows hooked together in a unibrow. He reminds me of an underworld crime lord from a black and white movie. I move closer to Virginia and lightly trace the inside of her elbow with a finger. She turns that striking smile on me.

"Next we open Chrome," Matty instructs. "Go to History at the top, then Full History, and scroll back to last week. Start with Tuesday and move forward."

Yoon-hi rolls her eyes as he demonstrates on a computer labeled "Ares." We all know how to do a history search. Previous searches pop up. YouTube, Adobe, Vampire Anthology, Zombies, Alaska Water Safety—I think of the boy in the green room boat—the DMV, TikTok and many others. The district blocks social media sites, but somebody always finds ways around the block.

"Not on this one," Matty mutters a minute later and glances at the rest of us. "Hello? What are you waiting for? Do you want me to comb through twenty-eight computers by myself? Film club film club, all one word and lower case," he calls out in a low voice as we scramble to the other computers.

Each computer is tagged in the upper right corner with the name of a Roman god. I sit down at Neptune. Virginia drops into the chair beside me at Minerva.

"I've got Apollo," Yoon-hi sings out from the row in front of us.

"Jupiter here. Eight minutes," says our self-appointed timekeeper, Tally.

"Spread out. Make sure you don't recheck a computer that someone else has already looked at," Matty advises.

Virginia finishes at Minerva and moves to the front row just inside the window. When a couple of students walk by glancing in at us, she calls out in a friendly voice, "How's it going?"

Ballsy. One of the many things I like about her.

"Five minutes," Tally tells us.

I check three more computers.

"I think I've found it," Yoon-hi shouts excitedly.

Matty shoves a chair back and hurries over. "Damn, girl. Good work." Tally, Virginia, and I join him. It's an Instagram login, the search dated last Tuesday, 5:08 p.m.

"Now what?" Yoon-hi asks, her fingers poised over the keyboard.

"One minute until the bell," says Tally, panic edging into her tone.

Virginia glances at me, then shakes her head with noticeable reluctance. "We'll have to come back after school."

CHAPTER FORTY-ONE

VIRGINIA

Wednesday, December 18, 1:00 p.m.

Matty had us stack the keyboards back under the monitors before we left the video lab. He rechecked to make sure the cameras had been returned to their rightful places in the cart and locked the room just as the bell rang for second lunch and Mr. Ivy's substitute turned the corner out of the film club stairwell. Students streamed out into the halls from other classrooms.

I could feel a prickle of sweat drip down my back. That was a little too close for comfort. Tally and Yoon-hi said they had other things to do after school, but Katie, Matty, and I agreed to wait half an hour after the dismissal bell to make sure Mr. Ivy's sub has left for the day, and then meet again outside the room.

Although it was a little out of the way, I used the film club stairs to get to my chem class on the first floor. I wanted to see if going there by myself would spark a memory I might have missed before. I paused for a moment on the landing, trying to recall the odor of marijuana. Nothing.

In the middle of my final, I feel my phone vibrate in my pocket, but I can't look at it until class is over.

I wish my teacher happy holidays, then grab and unlock my phone the second I step into the hall. It's a text from Pete: *No.*

No what?

No joints. The cops went over M's room days ago. Camila says no way would M do drugs.

"How did you do on the final?" Lilly Kahale asks, coming out behind me.

I slip the phone back in my pocket. "Pretty well. Wasn't sure about that coordination compound question. What did you put?"

"An ion bonded by covalent bonds to ligands."

Uh oh. "Is that the right answer?"

"Yep, I think so."

Well, crap. I should have spent more time studying. I like chem, but it's not my best subject. Lilly does well, but Zach Pratt almost always scores the highest. Our teacher posts exam scores by our ID numbers on the door the day after every test. The ID numbers are supposed to make it anonymous, but Zach signs his initials next to his grade, which drives the rest of us crazy. The guy's an obnoxious braggart.

Lilly and I stand and talk for a minute. Or more accurately, she complains about her dad making her work during Christmas break, and I pretend to listen. She ends up inviting me to their restaurant to try the new sausage and gravy dish sometime, and then we go our separate ways.

In Honors English with Mrs. Pugh, I feel more confident. But I still have trouble focusing, my thoughts wandering between cameras, Instagram accounts, and Sonya Dare. I saw a news van pull up in the circle drive a few minutes ago. Not sure if they're here for her or to get more scoop on Marisol. Mrs. Pugh, who is usually a sitter, has taken to walking up and down the aisles during tests. Like that will help me concentrate.

"Choose whether the author of the following phrase is attempting to evoke or influence a particular attitude." I have to read it twice.

"Enjoy your break, Virginia," Mrs. Pugh says when the dismissal bell rings and I lay my test on her desk.

"You, too." I think Matty's right. I'm winning her over.

Katie and I meet by her locker, and I'm so happy to see her I hardly mind when Rocky stops by with a sheaf of blue "Missing" flyers. The new ones have an updated picture of Sonya, along with her age: 15, height: five feet, two inches tall, weight: approximately 110 pounds, and a description of the clothes she was last seen wearing Friday night: a pink BTS concert sweatshirt, black jeans, white sneakers, and a green, down-filled jacket. "Please call 911 if you see anyone matching Sonya Dare's description," I read aloud from the flyers in his hands. My heart goes out to the Dares. What if Reggie went missing? I wouldn't be able to eat or sleep. I'd be frantic. Cops on true-crime shows are always saying the longer a person goes missing, the less likely they are to be found alive.

Rocky peels off thirty or so and asks if we'd mind posting them. "Here or around any businesses you frequent," he adds, his eyes creasing at the corners.

"How are your parents handling all this?" Katie asks, palming half the flyers.

"My mother's taking sedatives. Dad hasn't slept. The cops have an APB out for Sonya's bio mother. But her phone doesn't indicate any contact between the two. The one good piece of news is that one of Sonya's friends came forward and said she heard from Sonya Sunday morning, so at least we have a better idea when she disappeared. Sonya said she was coming to school around eleven to tack up more of those DT posters."

"Is the school open Sunday morning?" I ask.

"I guess. Apparently, one of the local churches holds service here. I just—" Rocky stops abruptly, swallowing hard. "Mrs. Foster's putting out a Google Voice asking parents for their help this afternoon looking in backyards and neighborhood parks, downtown doorways where some of the homeless hang out, that kind of thing."

Katie lets out a breath and lays a hand on Rocky's forearm. "I'm so sorry, Rocky. Is there anything I can do besides handing out these flyers?"

"No thanks." He gives her a long look, and I wonder if he knows she's seeing me again. Guilt flushes through me. I hope not. He needs to focus on finding his sister.

He shuffles down the hall to another cluster of students, his expression lost and upset. Much worse than when he was a sophomore and missed a winning hockey goal. The skin around his mouth is slack. His usually lustrous blond hair looks greasy. And ugh, the smell. When was the last time he bathed?

I ask Katie if she wants to go help him with the flyers. I can't read her expression when she holds up the ones in her hands and says, "Let's just take care of these."

* * *

Matty catches up with us when we're done papering the school's first floor lockers and bulletin boards and the windshields of the few cars left in the parking lot. I stick a few in the back seat of my car to tape in Caseo's window later.

"Just checked. The video lab is empty. Ready to find your photo?" he says, hiking up a pair of too-tight leather pants.

We follow him back inside. The gym doors burst open with a clatter, and six volleyball players spill out, laughing, chatting, and dripping sweat around their pits and the bottoms of their shiny shorts. Fatima is among them, wiping her face and the back of her neck with a terrycloth towel.

Matty holds me back as I start toward her. "Is now a good time? Wouldn't you rather your second interview with her appear more organic?"

He makes a good point, and he's probably eager to get to the video lab, and then on to Misconceptions or wherever. We move on up the stairs and into the hall, our shoes making slapping sounds against the vinyl surface. The first day of finals, and the school is practically deserted. Apparently, even teachers don't stick around if they don't have to.

Matty unlocks the video lab door and heads to the second row from the back to the iMac where Yoon-hi found the Instagram page. "Mercury, god of trickery." He glances at the label and mutters while typing in the film club login.

Katie stands behind him, shifting from one foot to the other. "So now you hack the Instagram account?"

"I don't have to," he replies, his blue eyes intent on the screen. "Hopefully." Mr. Ivy's picture pops up, reminding me of the old "Uncle Sam Wants You" posters. "The way this works in film club, well, in class too, I guess, after you take your photos and videos, you remove the SD card from the camera and insert it in this slot." His fingers run along the back of the monitor to show us. "The computer recognizes the device and the Photos app opens, asking you if you want to import them from the card."

"Which you do," I say, wishing he'd hurry up. I still don't feel comfortable being in here without a teacher.

"Uh-huh. Then you have a permanent copy of an image and can export it into iMovie or Adobe Premiere Pro." He demonstrates as he speaks, clicking on the Photos icon and showing how the photos are organized by date.

I suppress a groan. Dude, I don't need a movie lesson right now.

He goes back to Tuesday and finds the picture of me and Marisol. "I'm a genius." He sits back, lacing and flexing his fingers.

"You are," Katie acknowledges, clearly fighting off a smile.

The image stares me in the face, Marisol's last minutes of life. Her mouth is open, and her eyes look angry. It's probably when she yelled at me to get the hell away from her. On TV dramas, an expert would find a reflection of the photographer's face on the wall or in the metal railing. But the cinder block walls offer no such likeness, and the railing is painted black.

"So now what?" I step back.

"Please, Virginia, don't rush me. Let me work my magic. I don't suppose either of you lovely ladies cares to fetch me a diet soda?"

From the vending machines outside the cafeteria on the first floor? What are we, his personal gofers? I snort, imagining him channeling some 1960s business exec addressing a couple of naïve secretaries in polyester skirts and pantyhose.

I start to remind him that just this afternoon he told me he wasn't a magician, but Katie says, straight-faced, "I think there's a Mr. Pibb in the refrigerator in the green room.

"Great," he says. And when she doesn't move, "Well?"

"It's open. I'm going to guess Mr. Ivy drank most of it a few years ago."

I laugh out loud.

"Never mind." Matty scowls. He returns his focus to the computer while we high-five behind his back.

He exports the photo to the desktop and right clicks, opening in quick succession: Preview, Tools, Show Inspector, and the EXIF tab. "Here we go," he says dramatically, and we lean in again to see Date Time Digitized, Date Time Organized: Last Tuesday 3:18 p.m. The moment I must have encountered Marisol in the stairwell. I was there probably less than a minute.

My heart thumps as Matty takes a picture of the camera's serial number with his cell phone, and we all go back to the plastic cart. "Usually, there's a sticker near the tripod mount with the serial number, but if not we can find it on the lens," he mutters, picking up each camera one by one and comparing it to the serial number on his phone. "Oh, here it is." He holds out number eleven and asks me if I want to do the honors and find the picture on the camera's SD card.

There's not a single image on the camera. "What does it mean?" I ask, holding it out so Matty and Katie can see exactly what I see, which is absolutely nothing.

"A new SD card or the old one's been erased." Matty shrugs, pulling the clipboard off the cabinet. "Let's look at the sign-out sheet. Here's Tuesday, December tenth, camera number eleven. Checked out at three. Checked back in just after five, after the Instagram login."

We all stare at a loopy script, and for a long second no one speaks because clear as day, it reads: Lilly Kahale.

CHAPTER FORTY-TWO

VIRGINIA

Wednesday, December 18, 4:15 p.m.

Lilly Kahale had a big argument with Marisol over a newspaper story Marisol quashed. Lilly Kahale broke Marisol's computer and got kicked off the newspaper staff. Lilly Kahale was scrolling through Insta pics at Marisol's memorial service when she called Marisol a bitch and everybody else a hypocrite. Lilly Kahale is now editor-in-chief of the school newspaper.

Ding dong, the witch is dead.

Lilly Kahale took the photo and also posted it, which proves my entire theory about a third person wrong. *What are you up to, Marisol?* was the comment on what had to be her post as Anon. Is she also responsible for the other tags about pot? I go back to the picture on the screen. Marisol is holding something in her left hand. Did Lilly think it was a joint? She's got to know it wasn't. I'm almost positive it's just a pencil.

Returning to the cart, I take the clipboard from Matty and hand him the camera I nearly dropped. The sign-out sheet has five columns: Date, Name, Camera #, Check out time, Check in time. There are four sheets, three filled in. I take a picture of the top sheet with Lilly's signature on the very first line as distinctive and flamboyant as she is. An overly large L and K in cursive, middle letters gradually disappearing into a sloppy scribble, the last ones ending with a bouncy curl. I flip the page over and find her name once more on Friday, three days later. Same handwriting. There's no mistake.

"Don't touch that." Matty draws me out of my trance.

"What?"

"Mr. Ivy's cup. I know it doesn't look like it, but he knows exactly where everything is."

"You're kidding." I've moved to the rocking, swivel chair at his desk. The computer room looks neat enough, but his desk as well as the green room behind me is a mess with costumes on the floor and props spilling out of an open chest like there's been an earthquake.

"I'm not." Matty takes the coffee mug from my hand and returns it to its proper place as Katie leans on the end of the table that holds the Minerva and Neptune iMacs. She's got her sleeves pushed up past her elbows, her arms are crossed. My gaze travels down her legs, and I wonder idly if I could pull off yoga pants because she looks so sexy in hers. So not relevant to all this—I shake the thought from my brain.

Matty straightens the cart of cameras, which one of us must have knocked. After a moment, he drops to a chair at one of the other computers, pulls a compact from his purse, and pats his nose with a little white wedge sponge smudged with brown makeup on the tip.

None of us knows quite what to do. "Is there any way we could be misreading this?" Katie muses aloud, her gaze directed toward the green room. I'm not sure I'm reading anything at all. It makes no sense.

I rock back in Mr. Ivy's chair. "I could have sworn I saw Lilly sitting in here last Tuesday *before* I ran into Marisol, not more than fifteen minutes after school let out. There were a couple of other kids with her."

"Where was Mr. Ivy?" Katie asks me, pushing herself off the table and taking the clipboard from my hand.

"No idea."

"Well, you know what? I'm in the mood for poi. My mom used to fix it, but she always ruined it by substituting coconut water with tap. Isn't there somewhere around here we could find some good Polynesian food?"

Of course. I tilt my head, feeling a slow grin spread across my face. "I know just the place."

CHAPTER FORTY-THREE

KATIE

Wednesday, December 18, 5:00 p.m.

Matty had to work, but Virginia and I have agreed to meet at Sefina's, the Polynesian restaurant owned by the Kahale family, at seven.

"You're going out to dinner by yourself?" Mom asks, looking slightly appalled, when I tell her.

"Not by myself. With Virginia. We're celebrating the end of the first day of finals." A little white lie with just enough truth to make it plausible. For someone who has always seemed to enjoy solitude, my mother actually spends very little time by herself. My father, when he felt like messing with her, used to call her backward, saying he was the only one she ever slept with. Jeez, Dad, tell me something else I don't want to know.

I'm betting now that he was the only *man* she ever slept with. Once, she let it slip that she was hospitalized with a nervous breakdown during college. When I tried to pin her down on details, she told me she didn't want to talk about it, that it was the usual college stress.

I don't know the facts, but in my mind I've concocted an elaborate story about a girl she fell in love with. They broke up, or my mother's parents disapproved and wouldn't let them see each other. Both my grandparents have passed, so I can't ask them. Grandmother died when I was six. She came to visit us, and then went back home and shot herself, leaving a note that basically blamed Mom for not being a better hostess during the visit. Yeah, so screwed up. My therapist and I spent a month on that one.

"What did your art teacher think of your Strelitzia card?" Denise asks, coming up behind Mom in the kitchen and brushing a hand down the small of her back. She holds Josh on her hip. He's almost too big to be carried now. His chubby fingers gently tug her long, brown braid, then he reaches out both hands to me.

I take him, kiss his sweet-smelling head fondly, and set him on the floor. "I think she really liked it."

"Strelitzia?" Mom says, running her fingers through Josh's shaggy hair absently.

"It's the scientific name for a bird of paradise, my origami final for art." They don't grow here, but Denise knows all about botany.

"It's beautiful. The part I like best is the note. Show your mom," Denise urges, her eyes bright.

"I can't. Miss Langdon kept it. She's giving me an award for it at Friday's assembly." I rub the back of my neck, pleased, but embarrassed. I'm not used to praise. Having an awards assembly if Dan Daily doesn't show up is the current plan. It seems the district can't officially give us the day off before Christmas break. They require a certain number of what they call teacher-student contact days.

Mom claps her hands together. "Congratulations, Katie. I'm so proud of you. We'd love to come to the assembly if you'll let us."

Say what? If I'll *let* them? How many times in grade school did I wish my parents would attend my school events? My father was always too busy, and my mother made it clear she didn't want to. Mom glances pleadingly at Denise who instantly nods back.

"We'd love to, sweetheart. All of us. Just let us know what time, and we'll be there."

All of us: Mom, Denise, and Joshy—my new family. "Okay," I say. "I will."

I spend the rest of the afternoon studying for tomorrow's tests. Before we left school, Virginia and I worked out what we'd say to Lilly and how we thought it would be best to approach her.

Something about it doesn't seem right, and I think Virginia and Matty feel the same. Lilly is obviously impulsive. The fight she had with Marisol in journalism is legendary. Everybody at school likes to tell it. How one minute they were talking about new articles for the *Gazette*, how the next Lilly was swinging her backpack at Marisol's face and slamming a computer across the room instead. No wonder she got kicked out of class. But still, to push Marisol down the stairs, and then post the pic with Marisol and Virginia? How dumb is that? She'd have to know she'd eventually be a suspect, even disguising her identity with the Anon handle. And if it wasn't her, who did Virginia see Tuesday afternoon in the video lab?

* * *

Virginia slides her car in beside mine in Sefina's gravel parking lot. It's snowing again, but the restaurant is packed and brightly lit, with large windows across the front of the building, a big red sign on the roof, and a pink metal lotus flower above the double doors.

Virginia takes my hand, and we start for the door.

"Wait." I pull her back and cup my hands to her face to kiss her. "For luck." She tastes like blueberries and honey. Delicious.

She wraps her arms around me. "We have each other so we don't need it. To completing our investigation."

"To completing our investigation," I repeat.

Inside, a large man in a colorful Aloha shirt with palm leaves on the collar and across his chest shows us to the only empty table, which is next to the kitchen doors.

"You must be one of Lilly's brothers," Virginia says as he hands us laminated menus.

"How can you tell?" He offers a broad-faced, sweaty grin. "I'm Kemen. Are you a friend of my little sister?"

"We go to school together. I'm Virginia. This is Katie."

"Pleasure." His huge brown hand swallows each of ours in turn. "I went to North. Barely graduated. Lilly's the smart one in our family. Is Mrs. Pugh still there?"

"I have her for Honors Lit," Virginia tells him.

"My remedial English teacher. God, that old lady hated me. What a sourpuss. Would it kill her to crack a smile every hundred years? Don't tell her you saw me, okay? It would give her a heart attack." He chuckles. "I'll let Lilly know you're here. She's supposed to work the register tonight. But Dad's got her cooking, which she hates. And if you know Lilly, she's not quiet about it either."

The kitchen door swings open as a waiter who is probably another brother comes out, and then, as if on cue, a plaintive female voice snaps, "I'm not cleaning that up!" Pots clang, then, "Shit!"

Kemen catches my expression and chuckles. "Yeah. My sweetheart baby sister. Like I said, I'll let her know you're here. Try the sausage and gravy if you can't make up your mind what to order. It's new. Our regulars say they love it."

Most of the regulars appear to be Pacific Islanders like the Kahales. The restaurant crackles with chatter and the clinking of silverware on china plates.

Another guy, even heavier than Kemen and wearing a matching shirt, takes our order and we wait.

"Have you been here before?" I ask Virginia.

"A few times. Dad usually gets takeout. They don't accept reservations, and on weekends there's often an hour or more wait." Her knee touches mine under the table. I smile, reach down, and rest my hand on it.

We haven't talked about Rocky all day. I hope she knows it's her I love. Seeing his face when he handed us the "Missing" posters—I just couldn't have the conversation with him then. Where is Sonya, I wonder.

Presently, another guy delivers our food. "Hope this is enough," he says. "If it isn't, just let me know. We don't want any of our customers going home hungry."

I can't imagine that happening. He sets two steaming bowls piled high with sausage swimming in a thick brown gravy and two sides of poi on the table. It's easily enough to feed six people.

We're almost done eating when Lilly bursts forth from the kitchen. She yanks off her apron and rips a hairnet off her head. She rolls both in a careless ball, tossing it on a tray stand of recently bussed dishes by the door. "Holy shit, I'm tired. Scoot," she tells Virginia, plopping down opposite me and taking up more than half the seat. "I'm really glad you guys decided to come. Was it good?" She gestures to my bowl.

"Delicious." I pat my belly to show her I've eaten all I can.

"Glad to hear it. Tell Kemen I said to give you the friends and family discount when you leave. And if you give us a good review on Yelp, Dad will give you another twenty-five percent off the next time you come in." She flops against the padded vinyl booth. "So, Katie. I saw your art final."

"You take art?" I don't know why I'm so surprised.

"Not this semester. I couldn't fit it in my schedule. But I was in the journalism room when Langdon came running in to show Mr. Cooper after school. I'm not much into origami, but I have to say it was truly amazing. You could sell that stuff on Etsy."

"Oh, thanks. Did Miss Langdon unfold it?" I'm hoping she didn't. I want Virginia to see it first.

"You mean to display the note? She was afraid she wouldn't get it back together. Is it difficult?"

"Not at all. But you do have to pay attention to the creases."

"I can see that." Lilly gives a thoughtful nod. "I guess it would be hard to reproduce as well. It's not like those rectangular, laser-cut pop-up cards. I love those, too. Yours probably took forever to make."

"Maybe thirty minutes once I came up with the design."

Virginia's eyes ping-pong back and forth between us. Lilly talks like we're old friends. Which we're not. This is our first conversation, and the first time I've seen her up close. She's beautiful. Rocky calls her "hot," and I've heard others describe her as drop-dead gorgeous. They're not exaggerating. She has full brown lips, curly hair, and perfect skin. Lilly's brothers are handsome, but they don't compare.

We talk about art and origami for another minute or so until Virginia cuts in with, "Speaking of Mr. Cooper. Congratulations on becoming the new editor-in-chief of the *Gazette*."

Lilly offers us what looks like a guileless smile. "It's temporary, but thanks. I have to reapply after Christmas. Do you guys want to-go boxes?" She motions to our plates. "You can reheat these in the microwave. Forty-five seconds at eighty percent. Stir, and do it again if it's still not warm enough. It'll be just as good tomorrow."

"Sure," I say, trying not to squirm. I know what's coming next.

Virginia shifts away from Lilly, putting another inch or so of space between them as I hold my breath in preparation for the less happy portion of our conversation.

"So, you and Marisol," she says.

"What about her?" Lilly's body language gives nothing away.

"Oh, come on, Lilly. Cut the crap. We know you posted the Insta pic of me and Marisol in the stairwell."

Lilly's eyes round, and her jaw drops. "Oh, shit. Wait, hold up. That was you?"

"You know it was. You stood right behind me behind the door. When I left, you pushed her down the stairs."

"What? No. You're wrong! I found the photo on the camera. I never went into the stairwell. The memory card was missing when I checked it out. I didn't know until I came back later."

"Later from the stairwell."

"From the parking lot where I went to get some B-roll."

"B-roll?" I cut in because I'm unfamiliar with the term.

She turns her panicked gaze on me. "Background video for Zach's movie. Footage you add for atmosphere and scene transitions. Filler."

"Then what?"

"Well, like I said, when I got back to the lab, I discovered the SD card was missing. It's not unusual for kids to leave cards in computers. It happens all the time. And you can't always tell when you're taking pictures because what you're really looking at is the internal memory. Believe me, I was pissed. I borrowed a USB cable from Mr. Ivy and tried to download my stuff. None of it was there. But I did find the stairwell photo. It was like a sample stuck in the camera's internal memory."

"How's that even possible?" Virginia asks. "For pictures to get stuck without a card? Yours weren't."

"I know. I asked Mr. Ivy. He said it's pretty rare, but it can happen. Afterward, he went around and disabled the internal memory buffer on all the cameras so it wouldn't happen again."

"You showed the photo of me and Marisol to Mr. Ivy?" Virginia asks.

"God, no. Of course not." Lilly curls her upper lip.

Virginia leans in, invading her space and pulling out her phone with the picture of Lilly's signature she took this afternoon. "You don't need to look so fake-upset, Lilly. See right here? Surely, you haven't forgotten that you wrote your name, date, and the time you checked the camera out on the sign-out sheet. Isn't that your signature right there?" I gaze at Virginia in admiration because I have to admit Lilly intimidates me.

Kemen comes out of the kitchen, looks pointedly at Lilly, and then gestures to his watch. "We got customers waiting, Lil. Can you wrap this up?"

"Go away. I'll be finished in a minute!" she practically screams at him. Her eyes flare as she stares at Virginia's phone. "No." She shakes her head. "That can't be right. It was after four when I went outside to shoot. That says three. But it's not my writing. Someone else wrote that."

Virginia and I exchange a glance, and I'm wondering if she's thinking the same thing I am. That if Lilly's telling the truth, someone else did indeed use camera eleven before her. Someone else took the picture of Virginia and Marisol, shoved Marisol down the stairs, then removed the card as incriminating evidence and put the camera back on the cart. My head is spinning, but it sort of makes sense in its own weird way.

"What if we say we don't believe you?" Virginia says, leaning back and sliding her phone in a pocket of her coat.

"Then I'd say I'm fucked." All of Lilly's bravado has vanished. Her pretty brown eyes fill as if she's about to cry. She sits for a second, tapping French-tip nails on the table. "Look, you don't know what it's like after school in the video lab. It's nuts. Nobody pays any attention to people or cameras going out and coming back. That's what the sign-out sheet is for." She pauses and taps her nails again. "How about this. What if Mr. Ivy backs me up? He knows what I time I left the lab, and he knows the SD card was gone. He can also tell you who had the camera out before me. It'll be on the clipboard."

Virginia and I look at each other again. "What do you think?" she asks me.

I shake my head. "There is no other sign-out sheet. Your name is the first one on the list."

"That's because the previous page was full. But Mr. Ivy keeps them. Look, let's go to the lab tomorrow, all of us. I promise he'll back me up."

"Fine," I say, receiving a subtle nod from Virginia from across the table. "But one more question. Why did you post the picture on Instagram? Even if you didn't know it was Virginia in the photo, you had to know you'd be getting the other person in the picture in trouble, too."

"Because…god, this is going to sound so stupid—"

Virginia huffs a furious breath. "You thought you'd caught Marisol smoking a joint. Isn't that it?"

"Yeah."

"It sounds stupid because it is stupid. Marisol was holding a pencil."

"Well, yeah, I realized that later."

"And did you also post all that shit about weed from other handles just to ruin her reputation?" Lilly's non-reply is answer enough. "Get out." Virginia scoffs.

"What?" She looks at Virginia, startled.

"Get out. You're blocking me in."

"But…are you going to the cops?"

"Not yet. You're going to meet us at the video lab first thing in the morning. Then, we'll decide. In the meantime, anything else you got on Instagram, you take down tonight. You hear me?"

"Yeah."

"Say it."

"Fine. Whatever. Everything on the Gram, I'll take it down tonight."

CHAPTER FORTY-FOUR

VIRGINIA

Wednesday, December 18, 9:15 p.m.

Katie and I kiss and say good night, but we don't talk much about Lilly in the parking lot. There's so much to think about.

Mom, Dad, and Reggie are in the living room watching a documentary about video game design when I get home. Dad looks bored, and Mom's got her eyes closed. Computers are Reggie's thing. He's crouched on his knees in front of the coffee table with his gaze glued to the screen. "Markus Persson is worth about a gazillion dollars," he's telling them. "See, first you get an idea like for a game—"

"That sounds great, Reg. Just let me check in with Virginia. I'll be right back." Dad clomps into the kitchen and splashes water in his face. Reggie continues talking even though I'm almost positive Mom is asleep.

I stick my Sefina's leftovers in the refrigerator. "You're learning about Mojang Studios?"

"I'll have you know Minecraft is owned by Microsoft now. But yeah, more than I ever wanted to know." Dad yawns. "Don't tell Reggie that I find it tedious. He's trying to talk us into sending him to a spring break coding camp."

"Will you?"

"Probably. We'll make him work for it, of course. I just wish the process wasn't so painful for me." Dad grimaces at the image of a bald man with a beard on our big-screen TV.

Making us "work" for what we want is my parents' way of making us prove we'll stick to things and not be frivolous with their money. When Pete turned sixteen, he begged Mom and Dad for float plane flying lessons. Dad got him a summer job with a company at Lake Hood offering bear viewing tours. Pete worked his tail off. Flying lessons are expensive. A single lesson can cost a couple of hundred dollars, and certification runs into the thousands. But the lessons are probably why Pete joined the Air Force.

"How was dinner?" Dad dabs his damp face with a kitchen towel and peers into the fridge.

"Good. I brought home leftovers. Help yourself."

"Thanks. Don't mind if I do."

"Is Pete still here?"

"He's in his room. I'm taking him back to the base in the morning."

I leave my father to divvy up the rest of the sausages and gravy into a late-night snack for him and Mom and Reggie and head down the back hall to my brother's old bedroom. A couple of years ago when my parents remodeled the kitchen, Dad turned the room into a home office for his accounting business. He left two twin beds for when my grandparents visit from Florida. Pete's sprawled out on one of them, an open laptop on his belly. "Where's Camila?" I say.

"She went home to spend time with her parents before heading back to school."

"She's not staying through Christmas?"

"She said she had stuff to do." Disappointment rings through his voice.

"Maybe when she first heard about Marisol's um, accident, she left school in a hurry and now she has to get back to tie up a few loose ends." I drop to the other bed.

"You mean like feeding her cat."

"She has a cat?"

"No." Pete shuts the laptop and twines his long, thin fingers over the top of it. His duffel bag is packed and resting on the floor just inside the door. His crutches lean against the wall beside it. Pete used to be messy, often leaving boots, bike helmets, skateboards, jackets, even snow shoes all over the house. The Air Force has taught him to be neat.

"Why don't you just go ahead and say what you came in here for?" He stares at the ceiling.

"I'm sorry?"

"No, you're not. You want me to ask Camila if Marisol kicked dogs or beheaded cats. Sorry she couldn't find a joint; I'm sure you were counting on it for something."

"Pete. Did my asking about weed cause you and Camila to have an argument?" I'm not sure why he's so angry.

He sighs, running his fingers through his short brown hair. "Not really. Although I'm not saying it made things easier. She had a long talk about Marisol with her parents this afternoon. I don't think any of them wanted to admit their little girl had problems, but you can imagine how difficult it's been for them. First thinking her death was an accident, and then learning that someone deliberately hurt her."

That's my fault partly, too. If I hadn't started asking questions. If Lilly hadn't posted the photo. If Sonya hadn't made the posters blaming David. If I had just admitted up front that it was me, not David, in the picture. When I yelled at Lilly, I was also yelling at myself. Actions have consequences, Mom always says.

Pete grits his teeth and pushes himself to a sitting position. "Have you figured out who killed her?"

"I'm getting there." I tell him about Lilly and the photograph, our plan for in the morning.

"I went to school with one of her brothers," he says when I finish. "Nice guy. Clumsy as all get-out on a snowboard, but, man, could that guy play football. I don't think any of the Kahale kids really like working at Sefina's but they do it because

it makes their parents happy. For them, it's all about family."
Pete pauses, bends his right knee with a grunt, then straightens
it. "Damn." He groans.

"Are you returning to active duty tomorrow?"

"Desk work. I still have a couple of weeks of physical therapy,
but if I stay around here much longer I'll go crazy."

Poor you, I think. "I get it. Mom waiting on you hand and
foot, that's got to be torture."

"Exactly." He chuckles. When he bends his knee a second
time, it releases an audible creak. "Is it possible Lilly's signature
on the check out sheet is forged?"

"Not really. She admits taking out the camera. But she says
someone faked the time she signed it out."

"Mm. Then I don't know what to tell you. Hey, you never
did say exactly what you and Marisol said to each other in the
stairwell."

"How do you know about that?"

"Mom told me."

I lay back on the bed and drag a pillow under my head. "No
secrets in this household."

"Of course not. So spill."

"Well, it wasn't all that exciting. A day or so earlier, I
happened to walk by the journalism room, and she and Fatima
were sitting on the floor in the hall with one of those large
notepads, you know like the kind you see propped up on an
easel."

"Fatima?"

"Fatima Mann, a senior. She's co-captain of the varsity
volleyball team with Marisol."

"And also in journalism?"

"Yep. She's a senior reporter, but she doesn't do much more
than report game scores and take pictures for the paper as far
as I know. Anyway, they were talking about personal issues high
school students face."

"And you know this how?"

"Because I heard them. And it was written on the notepad,
titled 'Future Article Ideas.' They had a few items on the list

already. Incest. Eating disorders. Gender slash sexual identity. Cross-dressing."

Pete bends and flexes his knee again. "Go on."

"Okay, so Marisol looked up just as I was passing and tapped the notepad, saying, 'You know who we should talk to about bisexuality? Katie McRanes.' It was like she was waiting for me to come by, just so she could say it. Fatima glanced away uncomfortably and I said, 'Don't you dare.'"

"Oh. Interesting. They used to be neighbors, right?"

"Right. And for whatever reason, Marisol couldn't stand Katie, and she hated the fact we were together."

"Probably jealous."

"I sincerely doubt that. I knew she was trying to get to me, so I resisted punching her in the throat and called her a petty bitch or some such, and continued on my way."

"Until you caught her alone a couple of days later and pushed her down the stairs."

"Funny guy. I brought it up, that's all. And we may have exchanged a few heated words." *Extremely heated.*

He nods. "How are things between you and Katie now? Better, I hope?"

"A lot." I grin, thinking about our kiss in the parking lot. After Katie left Anchorage and a couple of years went by, I thought I would get over her, too. I didn't. Maybe we are too young to make this last forever, but we'd be idiots if we didn't at least try. Then I think of Rocky. "She's with a guy, the one whose sister disappeared."

"Right. Sonya Dare. I heard about her on the news. I guess everybody has stopped thinking she's with her mother. Did you know sixteen thousand people have gone missing in the Alaska Triangle since 1988?" The triangle runs between Anchorage, Juneau, and Utqiagvik, ten thousand miles of impossible terrain.

"She may be dead," I say grimly. "And here I am, making time with Katie when Rocky and his family are worried sick about her."

"Come on, Virginia. You can't blame yourself for that. You're barely seventeen. Rocky will move on. You're not responsible for what goes on between them."

It's nice of him to say it, but my mind immediately goes to wondering if Katie's truly going to leave him. Could I give her up again without a fight? Yes, I realize, because above all else I want her to be happy.

Pete pulls his good knee up to his chest and lets loose a giant fart, which I normally wouldn't mind, except being who he is, he invites me to move in closer and smell it.

"You're disgusting! I'm leaving."

"And going where?" he says, with a shit-eating grin on his face.

"I've got a day full of finals tomorrow. I need to study."

"All right then," he calls after me. "Good luck."

* * *

I study for a while, and then go to bed. I can't sleep. Random thoughts cycle through my brain. David's locker drenched in dog shit. Lilly smearing virtual shit online. Marisol's list of story ideas. Sonya and Rocky. The way Rocky smelled. A phone found in Valley of the Moon Park, all texts and history gone. The next morning when I get up, my weary thoughts slot into place.

I think I know what happened.

CHAPTER FORTY-FIVE

KATIE

Thursday, December 19, 7:15 a.m.

Rocky and I finally talked last night on the phone, and I felt like I was getting to know a different person. A guy who loves hockey but is always worried he won't live up to his coach and teammates' expectations. A guy who genuinely cares about his little sister, even if he doesn't understand her. I told him about spending time with Virginia, and how I feel about her. He sounded kind of sad, but said he got it and hoped we could still be friends. It was kinder than I deserved, given how little thought I've spared for him the last few days.

Mrs. Pugh intercepts me the minute I get inside the school building. "I want to talk to you about your final, Katie. You're on the bubble." It stops me cold. I can barely contain my shock.

"I'm failing?" My voice trembles. Granted, I didn't do that well on my last test, but I've turned in all my assignments. Did I spend too much time studying for my other subjects when I should have focused on English? It will be my last final this afternoon, and I was kind of hoping to skate through it. All these tests in a row are exhausting, and I probably haven't given any of them as much attention as I should have with everything else going on.

"I'm sorry. I didn't mean to alarm you. You're not failing," Mrs. Pugh says, her usual unhappy expression softening. "Your grade is teetering between a B and a C, and I thought you might appreciate an opportunity to bump it up. Doing well today will make all the difference. I recently heard about your father's situation and how you got a little behind at school because of it. I think I can help if you'd like to come by at lunch and study with me."

"Oh, well, thanks," I say, relieved. "I may just take you up on that."

"Good. Feel free to bring your lunch. I've got a couple of other students coming in, so we'll all sit down and go over a few key elements from the test together. See you then."

She returns to the door, readying to waylay her next "bubble" student.

It's nice of her to give up her own lunchtime, but it also sets my teeth on edge. How exactly do teachers find out about my father's *situation*? I can't imagine my mother coming to school to discuss it with them, and surely Mrs. Foster knows how to keep a confidence. Between Mom's recovery and my father's trial, I lost almost an entire semester of school. You'd think by now I'd be caught up, but I'm still struggling. In ninth grade, two teachers wrote on my report card that I had a bad attitude. At least Mrs. Pugh doesn't assume I'm a criminal like my father.

I race upstairs to the video lab, taking the steps two at a time. As I pass the girls' restroom, Lilly Kahale comes out and falls into step beside me. "Hey," she says, fastening the buttons at her cuffs and sticking her right hand in the front pocket of her jeans. "I hope you don't think I was shitting you last night about your art project. It's cool. I mean it."

I don't answer because yeah, it does occur to me she's flattering me, thinking I'll persuade Virginia that we should go easy on her. We reach the end of the hall where Virginia is sitting on the floor outside the video room. My heart leaps and I get warm all over, imagining running my hands down her bare skin.

Virginia's got a funny look on her face. But she gives me a smile, and then bobs her head at the room behind her. "Mr. Ivy's back, but he won't let me in."

"Let me try." Lilly presses her forehead to the glass, then knocks and waves to get his attention. "Open the door," she shouts, jabbing a finger in the direction of the door.

"Can I kiss you?" Virginia whispers in my ear. "Later?"

"That's gonna be a definite yes." I give her hand a squeeze.

"I'm busy." Ivy's muffled voice comes back. He's on his feet, typing at the keyboard on his desk. His oversized, black framed glasses are pushed up his forehead, past his receding hairline.

Lilly raises her voice and bangs the flat of her hand hard against the glass. "Open up, old man. Now!"

His forehead wrinkles in irritation, but he straightens his spine and takes his time coming over. He opens the door all of three inches. "Lillian, go away," he grumbles. "I've been out sick the last two days, and I've got students coming in in just a few minutes. Whatever you want will have to wait."

Lilly heaves a sigh. "It's Lilly, not Lillian. And you know it, Ivy. It's not my fault you've been playing hooky."

He presses his lips together, nearly swallowing his moustache. The underside of his nose is red and crusty, and his voice sounds congested. "Go away."

"Not until you tell these two"—she gestures at me and Virginia—"that the camera I returned last Tuesday afternoon was missing its SD card."

"Fine," he croaks, then covers his mouth to sneeze. "The camera you returned was missing its SD card."

"And I left to take pictures at four o'clock, not three."

"How would I know that?"

"Because that varsity basketball player came in after practice and asked if he could borrow a camera. I came into the green room to tell you."

"I don't lend cameras to students who aren't in film club," Ivy growls.

"Right. That's exactly what you said. And I took a camera out after that. Now show us the sign-out sheet."

"For the love of…I don't have time for this," he snaps. "Wait here." He stomps back between the computer tables to the plastic cart. Lilly follows him. And after a second, we follow her.

"Is he always this irritable?" I whisper.

"This is his good mood." She tosses her reply over her shoulder, apparently not caring if he hears her.

At the back of the room, he grabs the clipboard from the top of the nearest cabinet and thrusts it at her, making a show of looking at his wristwatch, and then glaring at her.

"I didn't write this," she says, pointing to the check out time, three o'clock.

"I did. You forgot to record your time. How often have I said—"

"You're impossible," she interrupts. "See?" She looks back at us. "Now show us the sheet before it. I know you keep them."

But this time, Ivy isn't budging. "Lilly. Dear child. How can I possibly make it any clearer to you that I'm busy? That I have a class starting in five minutes? I don't have time to look for it right now. If it's that important to you, come back after school."

"At lunch," Virginia pipes in, her gaze roving back and forth at the standoff. "Can you have it for us by lunch?"

Oh, no, I think, I'm supposed to study with Mrs. Pugh. Well, crap. To hell with that. "Please?" I add. "We appreciate you have a lot to do—"

"You're not in film club!"

Oh my god, where have I heard that before? "I know, bu—"

"Oh, for pity sakes! I give up." He throws his hands up as if we've just asked for something outrageous, like a bootleg copy of the next Marvel movie. "Just come back at lunch."

At last. Virginia and I both thank him and scurry out before he can change his mind. "Movie people are weird," we say almost in unison when we reach the hall.

"Not all of us," says Lilly with another one of her theatrical sighs. "Are we done here? I've got to get to math."

Virginia gives her a hard look. "You're not done. Meet us here at lunch."

"Why?"

"In case he still refuses."

"He won't."

"Just do it, Lilly!"

Lilly obviously wants to argue, but there's something in Virginia's tone that makes her decide to back down. She agrees. With a snarl, of course, and stomps off.

I turn back to Virginia. "You know something, don't you?"

"I think I do. The question is, will it be enough to take to the police?" Her expression is closed-off. "Meet me here at lunch?"

I nod, wishing I knew what she's thinking. The bell rings. "You bet. I love you." It comes off a little clumsy.

She must recognize it. "You, too."

* * *

One thing at a time, I tell myself, attempting to concentrate on my first two finals. I have math and science this morning. Communications and English with Mrs. Pugh this afternoon.

Amy Meeks is seated at our high-top when I get to chemistry. "Gum?" she whispers, holding a pack of sugar-free spearmint under the table while the teacher hands out tests.

"I'd rather have a beer," I joke, accepting a piece and unwrapping it.

She opens her mouth to smile, and I realize she's gotten her braces off, making her even cuter than she was before. "Beer, what a great idea. I wish you'd told me sooner."

"Next time," I say.

"Next time." She winks. I don't mean it, but I think she does.

The minutes tick by, and a thought unrelated to the periodic table starts tickling my brain. How did Sonya's cell phone wind up in Valley of the Moon Park if she didn't go there to meet her mother?

When the bell rings, I jump up and hand in my test, barely managing a "You, too," when Amy wishes me a merry Christmas.

Mrs. Pugh is standing by her door when I rush past her. "Katie? Are you getting your lunch?"

"I can't stay, Mrs. Pugh. I'm sorry," I say over my shoulder, barely slowing down.

"Just for a few minutes?"

"No. I'm sorry."

Virginia and I meet in the front hall and hurry up the stairs. Lilly comes up the film club stairwell, and we converge at the door of the video lab. Lilly must have reached the conclusion that this is serious business because she doesn't say anything annoying or obnoxious when Mr. Ivy hands her a thin sheaf of papers, curled around the edges and stapled in the upper left corner. We peer over her shoulder at the list. At the name at the bottom of the last sheet.

Zach Pratt.

"Lilly." Virginia hands it back with a grim look on her face. "Where was Zach Sunday morning?"

"Sunday? I don't..." Her eyes go dark. "Damn. Probably right here, editing his movie."

CHAPTER FORTY-SIX

VIRGINIA

Thursday, December 19, 1:25 p.m.

Finals. I've got five more minutes of this one, and then I take my last one of the semester. Katie and I plan to go to the police directly after school. But will Hess and Dietrich listen when we have no solid evidence? We can only speculate that Zach and Sonya ran into each other here at school Sunday morning. She caught him doing something, maybe hiding evidence after killing Marisol, and he kidnapped or killed her. I can imagine the condescending look on Hess's whiskered face when he asks me, "Tell me, Miss Eaton. Why would Mr. Pratt wish to harm Marisol Cowsill?"

For that, you'd almost have to have known Marisol to understand how badly she could get under your skin. How she could piss you off until you stopped caring that she died because you're that intent on ruining her reputation. I get Lilly's anger. Am I'm betting Zach felt it, too, when Marisol told him she wanted to do a feature on what it's like to be bulimic. I confirmed it with Fatima Mann this morning when I arrived:

eating disorders, the second item written on the easel notepad. I'd started thinking about it after getting a whiff of Rocky's body odor yesterday, which led me to consider Zach's awful breath and rotting teeth and the weight he'd lost since freshman year—all classic signs of purging. To have someone call attention to it must have been as humiliating as getting kicked out of journalism, your favorite class, for breaking a computer, or being asked to talk about your abusive father having sex with your twin sister. Fatima was obviously unhappy with all of it, but she's a go-along kind of person. The sort who was perfect to work with Marisol because she'd let her run all over her. She said so herself this morning.

My hands fidget, and I keep staring at the clock. I assume Katie's finished with her final too, because her texts start buzzing in one right after another.

Zach found Sonya's phone.

Valley of the Moon Park.

It was dark. How could he have possibly seen it? The police must know that.

And why would Sonya clear her texts and browsing history? I add to myself. I never do that. And how was there any battery left if it had been lying in the snow overnight? But is it proof?

He has dogs, did you know that?

She must have gotten that from Rocky. The dog shit in David's locker, and the anonymous tip we put it there to discredit us and drive the other suspect, David, away so David couldn't piece it together himself.

Maybe she isn't dead.

When the bell rings, I text back. *Meet me at the totem pole.*

Matty's standing by the front door, eyeing the parking lot as I push the door open. "Thinking of making a run for it?" I say, knowing he's done little to prepare for his exams. I'm not sure he ever worked on his civics notecards.

He shrugs. "There's always makeups."

True. I hope Mrs. Hicks will cut me slack since I'm about to miss my presentation. "How do you feel about skipping your last final?"

A small grin plays across his face. "I could be persuaded. Should I grab my coat?"

"You may need it." When we get outside, the ground is icy from a brief melt that's refreezing as the sun is past its peak.

"Got it." Katie rushes out to join us.

"Careful." I catch her elbow as she starts to pinwheel. "My car or yours?"

"Yours. You have four-wheel drive, don't you?"

I wish.

"I do," Matty says, doing his best not to appear too curious. He points to his dad's dark green Explorer in the first spot off the circle drive. His parents won the premier parking place at last year's school auction. Matty unlocks the doors, grabs a wig and a pair of heels from the passenger seat and tosses them in the rear. "Got what?" he says to Katie as I climb in next to him. Katie takes the back seat. I wish she was up front with us.

She looks at me. "Zach Pratt's home address. I got it from the student directory in the front office. We're running an errand."

"For him?"

"Not exactly."

"But he knows we're going to his house?"

"Mm." Katie and I exchange a glance as Matty's carefree expression turns to vague concern.

"He's pretty private, you know. Never invites us film club stars to his house. His parents are out of town, and they don't like company."

"That's why we're going now. He won't be there." Zach won't miss his last final, I'm sure of it. He's always said his father would tan his hide if he brought home anything less than straight As. Katie tries to get the seatbelt hooked. She fumbles for a second, and then clicks it into place.

"Here's what going on," I continue. "Zach took the photo of me and Marisol in the stairwell. They argued over something else, and he shoved her. Sonya figured it out. He's got her at his place."

"Probably," Katie amends.

"Hopefully," I say. This is the plan we just came up with on the phone a minute ago. Operation: Rescue Sonya Dare.

Matty eases the Explorer to a stop sign. His fingers dance across the steering wheel. I'm half expecting him to call an end to this. Instead, he says, "Zach's been acting strange. Well, stranger than usual. Finding Sonya's phone and barely taking credit for it? It isn't like him. He must have checked the video lab cameras a hundred times on Saturday. He kept saying he thought one was missing."

"Go straight for the next few blocks and turn right on Wooten. Shit." Katie bangs her phone against the back of my seat. "My GPS stopped working. No cell service. Never mind. It's not far from my old house. I think I know the way."

We drive for twenty minutes in anxious silence, then at Katie's direction, we pull to the side of the road. There's brush, bushes, trash, trees, a snowy ravine on one side. A six-foot cinderblock wall on the other with an iron gate and a metal KEEP OUT sign swinging from a bar. A heavy rusted padlock holds it together. Tall weeds poke through the snow in front of the wall.

Katie leans forward from the back and gazes out my window. "I've walked by this place a few times. My father used to say it belonged to a bunch of neo-Nazis."

Matty screws his nose up in a *Eww*, and I don't comment on her father calling someone else a neo-Nazi. Like he has room to talk. My dad used to talk about the racist homophobic shit he liked to spew at their wildlife meetings.

"Now what?" says Matty.

"We look for Sonya." Katie climbs out of the back seat.

"And no harm, no foul if we don't find her? We get the hell out of here and never say a word to Zach?" Matty unbuckles his seatbelt, still looking reluctant.

"Sure," I say, if that's what he needs to believe to get him through this. I follow Katie, stepping carefully through crunchy snow to the gate. Obviously with the lock, we can't drive up to the house, but it's fairly easy to squeeze around the metal posts leaning in from broken concrete studs. Matty joins us a second later.

Someone has made an attempt to clear the gravel driveway, but has done little with the large icy patches in random tire ruts.

A couple of old John Deere tractors and a faded truck sit off to one side. A huge Confederate flag pinned over the attached garage greets us.

"Way to make me feel welcome." Matty fans his fingers at his chin. "No wonder the Pratts don't like company," he mutters.

"I wonder where the dogs are?" Katie glances back and forth across a wide expanse of lawn bordered by sickly-looking trees as we move closer to a sprawling single-story with bars covering heavily-draped windows and a crumbling front step that's come away from the main structure.

"Dogs?" Matty practically shrieks.

My heart pounds, but I sound a lot cooler than he does when I say, "They're probably chained up."

I'm wrong. A huge gray pit bull with a jaw that could swallow my whole head lopes around the side of the house. Katie and I race for the front door. Matty turns back and runs for the gate, climbing the decorative iron leaves until he's a foot off the ground and can't go any higher. Fortunately for him, the dog sees us. The hair on its back bristles, and it puts on speed, braking in front of us and woofing like crazy as we cower on the step. It stops and sniffs.

"Good dog. You're a good little guy, aren't you?" Katie murmurs in a shaking voice.

Little guy? You mean compared to a moose? The dog must weigh sixty pounds. I'd tease her if I wasn't about to pee my pants. Drool hangs from its jowls, and it holds its front legs stiff as if ready to attack, but it doesn't come any closer. The woof gives way to a back-throat growl.

Slowly, Matty climbs down off the gate and squeezes around the post to the safe side of the wall. "Um, do you want me to throw a rock at it or something?" he asks in a high-pitched voice.

"No!" we both say at once.

Katie starts to put her hand out, but I snatch it back. "Are you serious?"

"I think it's hungry."

"And you want to feed it your hands?" She's probably right, though. I can see the poor dog's ribcage under a dozen scars crisscrossing its back. "How about this," I call to Matty. "You throw a rock over there"—I point toward a broken-down greenish shed twenty yards away—"and we'll make a run for it?"

Matty glances around the ground and comes up with a broken brick. "Ready?"

"Wait!" I try the front door. Locked. Katie gives me a cock-eyed look. The dog inches closer, its growl growing like a snow blower about to burst to life. "Now," I tell Matty.

"Hey, Cujo. How about a nice beef steak?" Matty tosses the brick with everything he's got. He pitched for North's JV baseball team freshman year, but his aim is off. It hits the gate and lands maybe ten feet away. Cujo goes for it.

"New plan. Find a window or another door!" Katie shouts. We take off around the side of the house, slipping on empty cans, sacks of trash, broken bottles, and random piles of dog shit. This time we get lucky. There's a back door hanging loose from its hinges. The screen door in front of it is just a frame that easily come off. I slam the wood door with a shoulder. It creaks, but doesn't give. Katie puts her shoulder to it and we both push, stumbling and falling with it as it teeters and crashes inside the house.

The dog's angry barking gets louder, and another hound, even bigger, comes running out of the trees.

"Oh, shit," I yelp. We're inside, but now we need to pick up the door and block the opening with it. Whatever room we've fallen into is so dark I can barely see my hand in front of my face as we squat and try to lift the weathered, paint-chipped door. Katie trips on something and I go down on top of her.

"Ouch! You're crushing my leg," she cries.

"Sorry!" We're all twisted up together, lying on the floor.

The dogs lunge toward the house. In half a second we'll be dog meat.

CHAPTER FORTY-SEVEN

VIRGINIA

Thursday, December 19, 2:00 p.m.

We're not. Cujo and his buddy drop to their haunches, thump their tails and stare at us expectantly. Is there an invisible fence?

Katie draws a ragged breath. "Virginia. No offense. You're on top of my foot."

"Oops." Carefully, with one eye on the dogs, I untangle myself from the heap, rise, and hold out a hand to help Katie up. "Are you okay?"

"Yeah, I think so. Listen, I didn't mean to yell..."

It's the very least of our worries. I pat her wrist. "I know. Do you think it's dinnertime?" I dip my chin at our four-legged friends who are close enough to pet.

"I'm guessing they've been trained not to come inside the house. My god, look how thin they are. And those scars." It's too dark to see her grimace but I can hear it in her voice.

My hand searches the wall for a light switch. Katie steps around the fallen door and moves gingerly to the room's interior.

It's a kitchen, I see, as my eyes adjust. She finds a window shade above the sink and shoves it up, revealing what looks like the inside of a hunting cabin. It's sparse and unkempt. Dirty dishes fill the sink. A splotch looking an awful lot like dried blood decorates the laminated countertop. A yellow Formica table with three plastic chairs occupies a corner near an old wood stove. Surely, this isn't the Pratts' main house.

"Zach lives here?" I say.

"Look." Katie points. I follow her gaze to a refrigerator and a heavy metal chain and padlock looped through the scratched-up silver handle. "Zach's parents don't want him to eat while they're away."

It sure seems like it. We step into another room. I toggle the switch on a table lamp, illuminating a living room with a big-screen TV and a dusty, sagging couch. An empty fireplace adorned with sooty river rock takes up one wall. A braided rug of a brownish color covers a speckled, vinyl floor, and a recliner with the footrest out is partially hidden with an old blue afghan. Another Confederate flag fills most of the wall opposite the fireplace. The rest of the room is cast in shadows with gray ghost-like shapes flickering over once-white walls. Perfect for Zach's horror films, I think. Is this where he gets his inspiration?

I can see my breath condensing. The furnace must be off. I haven't forgotten why we're there, but I can't help thinking, *poor Zach*. How can anyone live like this?

Matty's faint voice calls from outside, "Virginia? Katie? Are you guys all right? I really need you to answer me. I'm not sure what I'm supposed to do."

Katie tries the front door, twisting the handle and shaking it, then glances at her phone. "It's dead-bolted. Do you have service?"

I retrieve my phone from a pocket in my coat. "I don't. Matty, do you have cell service?"

"Just a sec. A little. No wait, it's gone."

A dead zone. Well, isn't that just peachy. Anchorage isn't like parts north where coverage is practically nonexistent, but there are still a number of areas where service is often spotty. I go to the front window and raise the musty shade. The dust bunnies make me sneeze. "Bless you," Katie says automatically, terror humming in her voice. The hairs on the back of my neck are standing on end. We need to find Sonya and get out of here.

Faded sunlight shimmers through the window, distorted by a couple of Y-shaped cracks snaking from the bottom of the glass. Seeing Matty on the far side of the gate, I rap my knuckles on the window and wave, all too aware that I can smell Zach in the house. It's an old odor, like cigarette smoke in upholstered furniture that never fully goes away. *Be calm, Virginia. He's not here.* "We're inside the house, but we're sort of trapped," I call out, glancing around.

"Speak up!"

"I said we're trapped! The dogs are blocking our exit at the rear of the house."

"Oh, I see you." He cups a hand to his forehead and waves back. "What do you want me to do?"

Katie steps up next to me. "Get help?"

"Get help!" I shout. "Head back to Klatt, or anywhere you can get a signal, and call the police. My parents, too. Let them know we're here."

"Are you sure? You do realize this is private property."

I want to strangle him. "Seriously? It's a little late for that. Go. Hurry!" I glimpse the time on my home screen. Shit, school will be out in forty minutes. There's no reason for Zach to hang around the building once finals are over. He'll be home before we know it.

Matty hesitates, then vanishes behind the concrete wall. I hear a car engine start and the crunching sound of gravel exploding, then dwindling away.

Katie wraps a trembling arm around my waist. "Now we wait."

I hug her back, and then look into her eyes for the kind of strength I hope she has. "Or?"

Her chin quivers as she slowly nods. "Or we make good use of our time and look for Sonya."

CHAPTER FORTY-EIGHT

KATIE

Thursday, December 19, 2:30 p.m.

Zach's house gives me the creeps. Once my father won a drawing permit for the Delta Bison Hunt and insisted Mom and I go with him. We walked for hours in thigh-deep, freezing snow and ended up in a tiny wood shack with bones and a partial decomposed bison carcass just outside the door. There was no furniture except for a bench and a couple of plastic buckets probably left by the last hunter who used it. I wanted to go home, but Dad called me a pansy and wouldn't leave until he made a kill. It was right after that my mother gave up red meat. We met another hunter that afternoon and walked with him for a while, my father and him chatting about how much fun it would be to shoot wolves with automatic assault rifles from helicopters.

This place takes me right back to the day Dad dressed his kill outside the shack. There's a rifle over the fireplace mantle, a crossbow in a corner, and boning knives laid out in a row on the hearth. I can see the remains of a ptarmigan hanging from a tree outside the window, too high for the dogs to reach it. Moose paddles lay tangled in a pile on the side of the shed. My heart feels tight in my throat, but I can't just stand here and wait for someone to rescue us. And without reasonable cause to get a search warrant, the police won't be able to look for Sonya.

Virginia and I make our way through a series of offices, bedrooms, and bathrooms. We peer in closets, behind moldy shower curtains, in cabinets that aren't large enough to hold a body.

Two bedrooms look surprisingly neat. One must belong to Zach's parents, the other to Zach. Virginia moves cautiously around the smaller room, lifting and folding back a lumpy camo bedspread, which reveals nothing except fairly clean sheets. The wastebasket is filled with candy and granola bar wrappers interspersed with empty dried-beef packages, the kind usually fed to dogs. That gives me pause. I open a dresser drawer and score a handful of long, thin bully sticks among neatly rolled-up socks.

"For Cujo and friend," I tell her as she lifts a brow, holding a knuckle under her nose to mitigate odors of stale stomach acid and bile left behind by Zach.

We glance at a dozen academic trophies lining a bookshelf, an assortment of textbooks on the shelf below them, and an expensive laptop on the dresser that we don't bother with because it's probably password-protected. The closet has hangers of neatly pressed clothes, polished dress shoes, and several pairs of hiking boots, heels out, lined up in a perfect row. The cabinet over the bathroom sink contains toothpaste, a well-used toothbrush, three nearly empty bottles of laxatives, the stub of a marijuana joint, mouthwash, air freshener, and aspirin. More crumpled fast food wrappers litter the wicker wastebasket. The toilet bowl is stained with dried brown chunks, clear evidence of Zach's purging.

"I don't get it," Virginia says over her shoulder as we head for the last bedroom. "The Zach who lives in this house and the one who goes to North aren't the same person. The one at North has swagger."

"And this one is a neat freak, well, except for his bathroom. Even his jeans are pressed."

We've been calling out Sonya's name every few seconds. "Wait." Virginia motions me to stop. I follow her as she returns to Zach's room, kneels quickly beside his bed and lifts the green and brown bedspread to look underneath it.

"Good thought," I say, although there's no fifteen-year-old girl's body stuffed under the bed. Just a bong and more food wrappers. Virginia puts it all back without comment.

In the larger bedroom, the only clues we get about Zach's parents are another very neat closet and a grandma-like doily on an antique dresser holding a worn copy of the Old Testament and a braided riding crop. "Spare the rod and spoil the child?" Virginia murmurs with a quick glance at my face. "Zach said his father would tan his hide if he didn't get straight As."

I shake my head. "We're done now, right? No Sonya here." I'm praying she'll say yes.

"There's still the garage. Maybe we can get out that way."

"Right." The house is designed like a rabbit warren, likely remodeled many years ago with additional rooms added on. We travel back through the labyrinth of halls and pause by a crawl space door next to the garage. "We can skip this one, if you like," Virginia says carefully.

Oh, hell. It's exactly what I want to do. But what better place to stash a body? Cold sweat tickles my armpits. "Damn it. Let's just do it." I give her a little shove.

"Sonya?" we both call out.

Virginia crouches and twists the handle, opening the door with a creak. She peers inside. "Oh!" she squeals, falling back on her butt. "You don't want to see that!"

My heart hammers my chest. "What is it?"

"Bones. But not like human bones. Like, maybe one of their dogs."

Shit! Who buries a dog in a crawl space? Of course I have to look. It's just an old skeleton off to the left in a pile of rubble. But I think I might throw up. Virginia gets up and we hang on to each other, our bodies pressed together.

She kicks the door shut with the side of her foot. "I was going to scream and scare you until I saw what it really was," she murmurs.

"Are you kidding?" I say, scoffing. "I'd slap the shit out of you."

She nuzzles my neck. "I wanted to break the tension. I'm sorry."

So not funny. But at least she didn't do it. I kiss her and say, "You're horrible. Let's get out of here."

We open the back door to the garage.

CHAPTER FORTY-NINE

VIRGINIA

Thursday, December 19, 3:00 p.m.

The garage is the most pristine part of the complex, with four bays, one of those commercial epoxy floors, and what looks like freshly painted plaster on the walls and ceiling. Three of the bays are empty. The fourth houses a silver Dodge Charger, circa 1970. Pete would be so jealous. An orange snow blower and parts of a ride-on lawnmower sit off to one side by a white freezer chest. Practically everybody in Alaska has freezers to store fish and game they catch throughout the summer. Not everyone keeps them padlocked.

Katie presses the garage door opener next to the step and the first bay door rolls up almost soundlessly. The two pit bulls stand side by side in the driveway, waiting for us.

"Hello, boys. Would you like a treat?" She tosses one of the bully sticks she found in Zach's dresser over their heads, and they both glance over their shoulders uncomprehendingly as it disappears in a snow trough.

"Careful. I'm really fond of your hands," I say as she steps out and sets another stick a foot and a half in front of them.

"Thanks," she mutters, lifting her chin in frustration. "They must respond to some sort of trigger." She sets another dried treat beside the first one. "Go." They wag their tails. "Please?" Nothing. "Release?" Still nothing.

At least they're not snapping at her throat.

I don't dare peek at my phone, but the sun is fading so we're almost out of time. School will be out shortly. Zach will be home any minute. And then what? Where are the cops? Where are Matty and my parents?

The Pratt property is huge with lots of trees and underbrush and several rundown outbuildings. If Sonya is here, she's likely in one of them. Or maybe she's buried in a snow mound. The ground's too frozen to dig in. What if she isn't here at all? Is there any chance we're wrong about Zach?

"Please," Katie pleads with the dogs. "You handsome fellas are obviously hungry. How about Virginia's mom makes you some nice hot soup?" I almost laugh. I've always loved her sense of humor. "Come on. Click-click or whatever. You've got to eat something." Cujo leans in toward the stick. "Eat?" she tries again.

It's the magic word. The dogs dive for the long, hard chews. They can probably finish them in a single bite, but they take them in their front paws and deftly gnaw the ends. "Katie, you're amazing!" I say.

"Right. Let's go." She steps cautiously around them as if making for the gate. It's the smart thing to do.

"She's here!" I blurt. The sound of my heart beating fill my ears like I'm about to ski right off a cliff.

"What?" Katie glances back.

"She's here. Sonya's here. I know it. You were right. You said it. If we leave now, we'll never find her. Let's take ten more minutes just to check these outbuildings. Or, if you'd rather not, I'll do it. Just don't leave me. You can wait outside the gate." My fingers clench inside my coat pockets.

I can read the fear in Katie's eyes, the way the whites stand out. She trembles all over, but manages, "I'm not leaving you,

Virginia. Five minutes, not a second more. Let's go." A tear slides down her cheek—that's how scared she is. I'm about to say never mind, but she starts determinedly toward the shed Matty threw the rock at. "Come on," she shouts. "Let's go!"

With one last look at the slobbering dogs, I speed-walk to catch up with her. We call out Sonya's name and try the door. It's full of tools and old machinery. We race to the next one, stumbling over rocks and hidden tree roots. A car motor sounds in the distance. It fades away a moment later.

Nobody should have this kind of property. It's cult-like, acres of cruelty hidden away from middle-class developments.

"Sonya? Sonya? Sonya?" we keep calling.

A bald eagle answers with a piercing cry. Moose pause to listen. Brown bears hide behind thick-needled trees watching us. Smaller critters scamper through the underbrush. The wind whistles through the empty branches of white-barked birch trees. Our footfalls crunch through icy snow.

"Sonya? Sonya? Sonya?"

We come across a shed of snow tires. A red-flaked, cast-iron pipe wrench rests in the corner. Another car goes by.

"It's over. Time to head back to reality," I pant. "I'm sorry." Sorry for scaring her, I mean. Sorry for risking our lives when we have no proof that a fifteen-year-old girl is out here.

"One more." Katie points to a far-off cinder block enclosure a hundred yards or so from the main house.

"Sonya? Sonya? Son—"

A muffled cry reaches my ears. "Did you hear that?"

"Hush," says Katie. "Listen!"

"I'm here! Please, somebody help me!"

"Sonya! Oh, god." We fall all over ourselves to get to the outbuilding. "We're here. We're coming!" we both shout.

The wood door is padlocked. I grab a rock and pound it over and over, scraping my knuckles over nasty splinters. Catching one in my palm that stings like a son-of-a-bitch.

"We're going to get you out. Just hang on," Katie yells over all the noise I'm making.

"Don't leave me. Zach…he's going to kill me," a young voice whimpers.

"We won't. Are you okay? The police are on their way. We're going to get you out," Katie sings in a soft tone, reminding me of the soothing sounds my mother makes when I'm sick.

I smash my hand against the padlock with the rock, and the lock breaks open. We push inside and see a girl chained by the neck to the wall. She's wearing a spiked-dog collar just like Cujo's. Her coat's half off her shoulders. Her face is dirty. Her kinky hair escapes a side braid.

"My name is Sonya Dare," she gulps, tripping over words that spill out both sides of her mouth. "Zach Pratt kidnapped me. He forced me into his car. His trunk. I think my arm is broken."

"It's me, Katie. Remember me? We're going to help you," Katie coos, dropping to her knees beside the girl. She gently touches Sonya's face and runs a hand around the collar. "There's a small combo lock. A foot or so of chain. It's bolted to the wall."

"Can you yank it free?" I clutch my screaming fingers to my chest. My eyes take in empty water bottles. Candy wrappers. A white sand bucket. Sonya's soiled, damp pants. The trash scattered across the filthy wood floor.

"I'll try." Katie takes hold of the chain and props her feet against the wall.

"No! I already tried that!" Sonya blubbers. "It won't work! Zach. He's crazy. He pushed that senior down the stairs. He told me. They argued about an article she planned to write. I found him crying in the stairwell when I went to school to put up posters Sunday morning. He said he didn't mean to hurt her. But after that, he wouldn't let me leave. Will you tell David I'm sorry for blaming him?"

"Of course." Katie pats her shoulder.

"You can tell him yourself." I'm trying to sound as calm as Katie. The sound of a breaking branch touches my ears, followed by hushed footfalls. The almost silent shush of snow. Somebody's rapidly approaching.

Katie jerks her head up at the open doorway. "Virginia, we've got to get out of here."

"No. Please don't leave me," Sonya sobs.

"Katie!" I gaze in shock as Katie bolts out the door. I'm tempted to go with her. We can escape. There's still time. We'll find the police and come back to free Sonya. Zach can't kill her now that the cops are on their way. My mom will talk him down. She's really good at it.

"Don't leave me," Sonya whimpers, and I know then that I can't.

All forward motion leaves my body, and I shift my weight to stand in front of her.

A silhouette blocks the doorway as Zach Pratt, holding a loaded crossbow, fills my sight. "Motherfuck, Virginia. You broke into my house!" His black pupils go back and forth between us.

"Zach, wait! Please," I beg, my voice raw with fear.

Tears fill his eyes. "For what? For my dad to come home and find out what I've done? This won't make him proud. Shit. Shit. Shit. 'Zach,' he'll say. 'You're such a disappointment. You're unteachable, like a dog.' Do you know what the bible says?"

"About what?"

"Eating."

"Oh." I'm having trouble following his line of thought. "Something about eating only for nourishment, I'd guess." I cradle my useless fingers, hoping the police will get here before Zach kills us.

He shakes his head. "Proverbs. Isaiah. 'Put a knife to your throat if you're given to appetite.' Doesn't matter anyway. I'm a failure in his eyes, always have been. Marisol. Damn. She really got to me."

"Why did you take the picture of her and me?" I ask, thinking to stall him.

"It was supposed to be a joke. Christ, the way you two went at it was hilarious. I'd been in the stairwell since school let out and saw the whole thing. She really hated you, you know."

"She hated everyone," I say. It almost feels like he's trying to put this on me.

"Yeah." He shrugs, deflated. "I guess you're right. She planned to do an article about my my illness just to humiliate me. How did you figure it out?"

"I saw her list. Eating disorders was on it. And then I started thinking about the phone in Valley of the Moon Park. The battery. The cleared texts and history. You found it, Zach."

"Oh." He stares at me and nods. "I had to, you know. I had to make them think Sonya was with her mother. They used to meet there so it seemed the ideal place, especially when Mr. Dare suggested searching there. I didn't know who she might have talked to, so I cleared everything I could think of. So stupid. Guess my father's right about me. I never wanted to hurt either one of them. It just happened."

I'm pretty sure kidnapping doesn't just happen. Neither does slamming a phone across the room or shooting your wife in the face. I force a smile. "Well, see, that's good then. It means you don't have to do anything except let us go."

"It's too late for that," he mutters. "Everyone will know."

"They don't have to. We won't tell," I plead. "Let us go, Zach. Both of us. I promise I'll never say a word."

Sonya has other ideas. "Fuck. You're kidding, right? You're pathetic!" She stares at him and spits. Fire burns in her eyes, and I wonder if she's seriously ill, maybe even dying. She's been here for days, chained to a wall and freezing, eating candy and shitting in a bucket, likely believing she'll never get away.

Zach snaps his head up. "Stupid bitch," he shouts. "You ruined everything!"

"No," I say. *No. No. No. Stay calm.* "Listen to me, Zach. All you have to do is unchain her and walk away. She means nothing to you. Get back in your car and go somewhere. Get away from your father. That's what I'd do. Leave North, and start over if you like. I know pushing Marisol had to be an accident. But this...come on. It's not too late." My throat is dry, and I'm running out of ways to stall this guy I've known since grade school, but never really knew.

If my fingers worked, I'd knock the crossbow out of his hands. Frantically, I search my brain for something else. Some words that will reach him. A reminder of how well he does in school? His movie success? His friendship with Rocky, the brother of the girl lying chained by the neck on the floor? Sonya crams herself against the wall as my ears tune in to the wail of a distant siren.

Zach clearly hears it too. "Time's up." He lifts an elbow to cock a finger around the crossbow trigger.

I squeeze my eyes shut—just as something, I'm not sure what, flies through the door and knocks him off balance. Zach falls to his knees with a heavy bang. A quarrel zings past my face and bounces off the concrete wall behind me. A second too late I duck, but it's okay because it lands harmlessly on the floor.

Katie straddles Zach's back, her legs wrapped around his waist as if she's riding a bucking horse and hanging on for dear life. One arm holds his neck, the other hand clutches the red-flaked pipe wrench, the one from the other outbuilding. She hammers his neck and shoulders with it.

"Get off!" he screams. "Get the hell off!" He drops to his belly on the floor.

Still shaking, I pick up the arrow and press the tip to his throat. Katie pins a knee into his back. "Take one breath and I'll drive this through your larynx," I hiss. I mean it. I want to. I want to stab him in the heart.

Zach has always been the smartest guy in our class. He holds his breath as long as he can, and then exhales shallowly. "I'm done," he says quietly. "I'm through."

"Oh my god, Virginia. I almost got you killed," Katie weeps, still holding him down with everything she's got.

And I was afraid you'd left me. I'm shaken and in a lot of pain, but I have the sense not to say it out loud. "Sonya, are you okay?"

"I—I." She stares, open-mouthed, at the wicked metal bolt just unleashed.

"Can you go to the front gate and show the cops where we are?" I say to Katie.

She rises and reaches over to stroke Sonya's arm. "I'll be right back. I promise."

Sonya draws a ragged breath. "I'll wait for you here."

CHAPTER FIFTY

KATIE

Friday, December 20, 8:30 a.m.

"Your injury is a lot like mine was. I'll teach you origami," I whisper, gesturing to Virginia's hand swaddled in a wrist wrap and resting in her lap.

She offers me a wink. "I'd be happy to try it, but I'm telling you up front I'm not artistic. Tell me about your card instead."

Mrs. Foster gives us a stern look. She's standing off to one side of the stage, bobbing her head enthusiastically as Dan Daily, at the podium, extols the virtues of good high school programs like our award-winning journalism program. Standing next to him, Lilly fights back a yawn. She doesn't show it, but I know for a fact that she's thrilled to be recognized as senior editor in Marisol's place. Especially after we promised not to say anything about her Insta posts to the cops. There's no point really because there's plenty of evidence against Zach without it. Sonya has given details of his confession and spoken at length about her capture to the police. We figure Lilly is just another one of Marisol's victims.

Virginia and I are sitting on the stage, the celebrated students who freed Sonya. NBC sent a six-member camera crew along with Mr. Daily. And with two of our local television stations in attendance, the jazz band, Mrs. Foster, and Mr. Cooper up here, it's pretty crowded.

The awards assembly was canceled at the last minute when Mrs. Foster received word that Daily would be arriving early this morning. I don't mind that Miss Langdon will have to give me my award later. Mom, Denise, and Josh sit with the entire Eaton clan in the front row of North's main auditorium, and that's enough.

Late yesterday, Zach Pratt was taken into police custody. Sonya was freed and rushed to the hospital. Her parents came at once, her dad doing his best to conceal his fraught emotions from the media swarming the place. I waited until the EMTs were loading Sonya into the ambulance before approaching Rocky.

"You did it, Katie. You found her," he said awkwardly, then he wrapped his arms around me. I hugged him back, noticing that he wasn't calling me "Babe" anymore. I'm glad we had our talk the night before, and I do think we can be friends eventually. He's a good guy. Just not the right person for me.

When I returned to the fire truck, a woman with a buzz cut was working very hard to convince Virginia to get her hand x-rayed.

"Can't I do it tomorrow? I'm ready to go home," Virginia mumbled in a whiny voice that almost made me laugh. She's so stubborn.

Her parents intervened and insisted.

We spent four hours at Alaska Regional Hospital where Virginia was told she was lucky that no bones in her hand were broken. Two fingers were dislocated, the other three bruised. They sent her home with the wrist wrap and an ice pack. She's supposed to call to arrange physical therapy next week once the swelling goes down. When Mom and Denise joined us in the hospital's lobby we told the story again how we found Sonya locked up in the shed. I mentioned the dogs because I knew my mother would want to call animal control right away. The poor things were so thin and hungry. They needed to be fed.

The audience applauds when Daily hands Mr. Cooper a certificate. Camera bulbs flash like a disco ball as Mrs. Foster moves to stand beside him. She, Lilly, and Daily cheese it up, all trying to hold onto the certificate at the same time. "And now I'd like to formally recognize two hero students who just yesterday evening rescued a young woman who might have died without their intervention." Daily extends an arm out to us.

We stand, inching around the trumpet player, Don Lucky, to make our way to the podium. Mrs. Pugh doesn't think I'm a hero. But at least she's letting me make up my final this afternoon. Same with Mrs. Hicks and Virginia's civics presentation.

"It's a fascinating story for those of you who haven't heard it." Which is probably nobody, I think to myself. "I'm going to let you tell the story yourselves." Daily gives us his trademark wide-mouth smile.

Virginia looks at me, and I give her a *you tell it* nod because if I know her, she stayed up most of the night thinking about it, worrying about how we both might have been shot dead with Zach's crossbow. Virginia feels sorry for him after hearing all that awful shit about his father's abuse, but I think at some point you have to stop blaming others and be your own person.

"Um, well, it was a group effort. Matty, Tally, Yoon-hi, will you join us? Come on, you each played a part," Virginia begins.

It's so like her not to want to hog all the credit. I bump her gently with an elbow and give her my best *I love you* smile.

Tally looks like she'd rather crawl under her seat, but she slowly stands. Yoon-hi rises gracefully, and Matty shoots to his feet, takes a bow, and sashays up the steps. He looks so proud and happy I almost expect him to invite the entire audience to Misconceptions for his next performance.

Virginia shares a shortened version of the story, leaving out how we broke into the Pratt house and discovered dog bones in the crawl space while searching for Sonya.

"Marvelous." Daily nods when she's done. "I bet plenty of newspaper stories will be written about that." He winks broadly at Lilly. "Now, I wish I could stay and visit with you wonderful people, but I need to get back to New York—"

"Wait!" My art teacher Miss Langdon comes rushing out of the wings. "I'm sorry to interrupt, but we were going to have an awards ceremony this morning, and I want to make sure Katie receives this." She holds a tiny clay statue she must have made herself in one hand, my origami card in the other.

My cheeks heat. Mom and Denise are leaning forward in their chairs. I suspect they put her up to this.

"Go ahead. Open it, and show Mr. Daily," Miss Langdon prompts.

I take a deep breath and pull the feather tabs on the head. My little bird of paradise unfolds flat just as I designed it, and I can't help beaming with pride.

"Well, isn't that pretty." Daily leans over, and then reads the card. I can sense the NBC cameras zooming in. "Oh." He awkwardly coughs. "Well, thank you."

I laugh because it reads: "I love you." I'm done hiding who I am. I take Virginia's uninjured hand, hold it up high, and say, "It's for her."

EPILOGUE

VIRGINIA

Six weeks later.

Mrs. Hicks told me Zach would have earned her award for the Causes of the Civil War presentation, but under the circumstances she'd decided to give it to me instead. I almost didn't take it. But then I thought: Why not? And vowed I'd start trying harder in school. It came with a fifteen-dollar gift card to the Moose's Tooth, which I used it to take my gorgeous girlfriend, Katie, out to dinner.

Zach is awaiting trial for manslaughter and first-degree kidnapping. Mom says he'll probably be tried in youth court and eventually plead to lesser charges. It may be months before anything substantial happens. My friends and I spent a lot of time talking about where his parents were while he was killing Marisol and holding Sonya captive in his shed. Katie and Yoon-hi decided they were dead, their bodies hidden in the rear of the crawl space behind the dog bones. Matty, Tally, and I speculated that they were staying away to punish him for eating too much candy. Turns out, they were at a month-long Confederates for Christ conference in Honolulu. Katie's right, I can't help feeling sorry for the guy.

Sonya came back to school a couple of weeks ago. I didn't really expect her to come over to our lunch table and thank us, but she did and even apologized to Katie for being rude when Katie used to stop by her house to visit Rocky. She also told us she's reconnected with Ahna who goes to a private school now. She said they FaceTime every day.

David hasn't come back to school, but Mom says Children's Services is trying to locate him with the hopes of placing him in the foster home with Ahna.

The Pratts decided they had enough on their hands arranging Zach's defense and readily gave up Cujo and his buddy to Katie's mother. Her apartment is too small, so George and Abe, as we call them now, currently reside in our backyard. Katie meets with a dog trainer three times a week to teach them manners. They're almost ready to come live inside with us. Dad and Pete built them an insulated doghouse in the meantime.

Camila's taking a semester off to help her parents cope with their younger daughter's death. She and Pete are still seeing one another. I don't know how Camila manages to put up with my jackass brother, but she does.

* * *

"Girl detectives," I mutter, staring at my computer screen one afternoon after school.

"What's that?" Katie's sitting across from me at the kitchen island with a plate of my mother's "homemade" brownies between us.

"It's Lilly's new article in the *Gazette*, the one about us finding out what happened to Marisol. I knew she'd write it eventually. She calls us 'amateur girl detectives.'"

Katie frowns. "I get the amateur part. But why not 'high school detectives,' or just 'detectives?'"

"My thought exactly."

Katie sets her sketchpad aside. On the top page is a portrait of me. I have to admit it's flattering. "That reminds me," she says casually. "A girl in my art class had her phone stolen the other day in the restroom. She left it in a stall, walked out, then remembered it. When she returned thirty seconds later, it was gone. There were five other girls in there at the time. They all say they never saw it."

"And she wants you to figure out who took it?"

"Us." Katie reaches over and squeezes my hand, which is now completely healed.

I grin back at her. "Does she know their names?"

"She gave me a list. Time for another investigation board, you think?"

I swipe brownie crumbs away from around my laptop and open a new Word doc. "Let's start one now."

Author's Notes

In 2005, long before the 2015 Equality of Marriage Act legalized marriage in all fifty states, the Alaska Civil Liberties Union and nine gay couples filed suit against the state of Alaska, winning equal protection for same-sex couples with regards to health insurance and various other rights accorded opposite-sex couples. This was of great benefit to me, moving to Alaska with my partner (now wife) and not having a job. In 2008, the U.S. economy was entering crisis mode due to lack of confidence in banks and mortgage lenders. And yet Alaskan prices were sky high. In remote areas, known as the bush (or villages), a loaf of bread could easily cost six dollars, a gallon of milk ten dollars, and that was only if you could get fresh food at all. In Anchorage, the big city, the situation wasn't quite so bad. Nevertheless, I feared I would spend my days at the downtown bus station with all the other unemployed, down-on-their-luck individuals who spilled out onto the streets in the not-so-pretty part of town. Luckily, I bluffed my way into a position teaching technology at one of the local middle schools. (Okay, I did have a license and nineteen years of teaching experience in the lower forty-eight, but not teaching technology!) This eventually led to opportunities I'd never dared dream of.

I traveled to Nome, meeting teachers who lived on school property in winter weather so brutal they strung a rope between their dormitories and the school, fifty feet away, so they could "feel" their way to work each day. I visited Seward, Homer, Fairbanks (in -48 degree weather), Girdwood, Cordova, Wasilla, Palmer, Denali, Talkeetna, Katmai National Preserve, and Valdez, to name a few places. I don't pretend to know all things Alaska, but I do have an appreciation for the place I called home for several years. In the winter of 2012, Anchorage broke the 1954–1955 snowfall record with accumulations in the Upper Hillside reaching 225 inches. A popular photo from the *Anchorage Daily News* showed a moose on top of a roof after a homeowner inadvertently left a snow ramp after shoveling. Fearing our roof would collapse as others had, we hired someone to shovel it, and then couldn't see out of our picture windows due to the snow mounds from the roof blocking them for weeks.

Living in Alaska, even suburban Anchorage, is not for the faint of heart. Getting used to nearly twenty-four hours of sunlight in the summer is almost as hard as living through the winter darkness. In the summer I couldn't sleep without blackout shades. In the winter, I'd go to school in the dark and watch the sun come up around 10:30 a.m. When I returned home at four, I'd walk the dogs in the pitch-black park at the end of our block. The park where I frequently came across moose such as the one Virginia and Katie encounter in the story.

As a teacher, I had the opportunity to take a number of criminal justice classes that helped me understand the mindset of both adult and juvenile offenders. The idea with juveniles, I believe, is to help us keep them on the right path. (Notice I didn't say "scare them straight.") And as a reader, I've always been fond of mysteries. Although the story itself comes purely from my imagination, many of the details come from my own experiences in Alaska. The strange compound I write about at the end of the story actually exists and was located mere blocks from my home.

Alaska is not known for liberal values. Despite over a hundred languages spoken in the Anchorage School District, prejudice is an issue, especially with regards to Alaska Natives. Many arrive in town from less populated areas without the skills and understanding of city life. And although everyone who has lived in Alaska at least a year receives PFDs (Permanent Fund Dividends from Alaskan oil), a few non-Natives are openly envious of the casino and Alaska Native Corporation funds some tribes receive. David Teal and Sonya Dare are composites of Native students I have known.

No story is created in a vacuum. To that extent, I'd like to thank my wife, Cheryl, for her love and unwavering support. My wonderful beta reader, Maggie Couper, for her enthusiasm and encouragement. My writers group: Lindy, Jordan, and Shelley (keep writing, friends!) My colleague Nick who led me down the thorny path of teaching technology, and Chris, the real tech guy, for his endless patience with my impatience. Thank you, Lori, for your insights into trophy hunting, Tina for thinking like me, and Janelle for brokering the peace among the four of us. And to Mrs. Mary Jane Fulton, my high school English teacher who made reading and writing fun. You believed in me, and I'm still grateful.

Also a huge thanks to Bella Books for publishing my novel, and to my amazing editor, Kay Grey, with her keen eye for details and invaluable assistance smoothing out rough edges of my story.

If you like this one, I hope you'll check out Virginia's and Katie's next adventures in *Is She Lying?* due out from Bella Books next year.

Lastly, I'd like to acknowledge my own Katie M. I still miss you.

Bella Books, Inc.

Women. Books. Even Better Together.

P.O. Box 10543
Tallahassee, FL 32302

Phone: 800-729-4992
www.bellabooks.com